THE PULL OF THE MOON
Darlene Graham

D0172489

HARLEQUIN®

TORONTO • NEW YORK • LONDON
AMSTERDAM • PARIS • SYDNEY • HAMBURG
STOCKHOLM • ATHENS • TOKYO • MILAN • MADRID
PRAGUE • WARSAW • BUDAPEST • AUCKLAND

If you purchased this book without a cover you should be aware that this book is stolen property. It was reported as "unsold and destroyed" to the publisher, and neither the author nor the publisher has received any payment for this "stripped book."

ISBN 0-373-70838-6

THE PULL OF THE MOON

Copyright © 1999 by Darlene Gardenhire.

All rights reserved. Except for use in any review, the reproduction or utilization of this work in whole or in part in any form by any electronic, mechanical or other means, now known or hereafter invented, including xerography, photocopying and recording, or in any information storage or retrieval system, is forbidden without the written permission of the publisher, Harlequin Enterprises Limited, 225 Duncan Mill Road, Don Mills, Ontario, Canada M3B 3K9.

All characters in this book have no existence outside the imagination of the author and have no relation whatsoever to anyone bearing the same name or names. They are not even distantly inspired by any individual known or unknown to the author, and all incidents are pure invention.

This edition published by arrangement with Harlequin Books S.A.

® and TM are trademarks of the publisher. Trademarks indicated with ® are registered in the United States Patent and Trademark Office, the Canadian Trade Marks Office and in other countries.

Look us up on-line at: http://www.romance.net

Printed in U.S.A.

"Fathers are important."

Matt spoke simply. "And I think my baby deserves a good one."

Olivia's smile softened. "I agree, Mr. Creed. But I'm afraid that with my daughter, there is little either of us can do to change her mind."

Matt leaned forward on the couch. "Oh, there's plenty I can do," he said. "I can take her to court and sue for joint custody."

Olivia answered quickly. "Nasty legal proceedings will solve nothing. Besides, you have no claim to the baby. Danni would have to name you as the father for you to have any legal standing."

There was silence for a few seconds, then Matt spoke. "Your daughter didn't tell you?"

Olivia looked confused.

"Mrs. Goodlove, your daughter and I are married."

* * * * *

"THE PULL OF THE MOON is a tender, memorable story of a remarkable man and a dedicated woman, who, through loving each other, heal the wounds upon their souls. It is a page-turning, feel-good book from beginning to end."
—Sharon Sala, award-winning author of *Reunion*

Dear Reader,

I worked as a labor and delivery nurse for many years and always wanted to write a story about a dedicated, funny, savvy, but lonely obstetrician who yearns for a love of her own. Dr. Danni Goodlove began forming in my mind all those years ago.

But it wasn't until I met the firefighters/rescuers after the bombing of the Alfred P. Murrah building in Oklahoma City (I was privileged to work as a volunteer at the site during the rescue effort) that I found the hero who would be Danni's match.

I hope my portrayal of Matthew Creed does justice to the tireless and truly heroic men and women who gave their all during that terrible time. To my own son Damon, a television reporter who was one of the first to arrive at the scene, and to everyone who suffered in the wake of that heinous crime, I hope that the references in this book provide only consolation and validation.

Though deeply emotional issues are woven into this story, it is a joyous account. Because it shows one woman's journey as she chooses change and growth, finds true love and receives the family of her dreams.

I enjoy hearing from my readers. You can write to me at: P.O. Box 720224, Norman, Oklahoma 73070.

Darlene Graham

Books by Darlene Graham

HARLEQUIN SUPERROMANCE

812—IT HAPPENED IN TEXAS

Don't miss any of our special offers. Write to us at the following address for information on our newest releases.

Harlequin Reader Service
U.S.: 3010 Walden Ave., P.O. Box 1325, Buffalo, NY 14269
Canadian: P.O. Box 609, Fort Erie, Ont. L2A 5X3

To Ray and Tonie Lueb.
Thank you for answering God's call
to become loving parents.

CHAPTER ONE

THE FULL MOON WAS THE trouble, and everybody knew it.

As Dr. Danielle Goodlove shoved her long, thick hair under a disposable cap and began the routine surgical scrub, she thought how ironic it was that all the simpering romantics out there in TV- and movie-land considered the moon a symbol of romance.

Romance. Ha!

In obstetrics everybody knew that all hell broke loose when Old Man Moon turned his fat face on the unsuspecting earth. Why did stuff like this—an emergency C-section with a life in the balance—always seem to happen when the moon was full?

Correction: two lives.

She nudged the knee handle to cut the water off, raised her dripping hands, and headed toward delivery room one.

A woman's scream from within caused Danni to break into a trot. She knocked the heavy door open with her bottom and yelled: "Fetal heart rate?"

A nurse turned up the volume on a state-of-the-art monitor and called back, "Sixties!" as the ominously slow beeps filled the otherwise-silent room.

Another nurse rushed forward to dry Danni's hands with a sterile towel while a third nurse came at her with a surgical gown mittened over fists. The circulating nurse filled Danni in on the case, her words fast and low. "It's a bad deal. The whole family was in the fire. Couple of toddlers. Mom's water ruptured at the scene—"

"When?" Danni interrupted.

The nurse glanced at the large clock on the tiled wall.

"Just before midnight—about thirty minutes ago. We've got a prolapsed cord and fetal distress."

"I hear it," Danni said. The beeps got slower.

The nurse with the towel finished the drying and dodged aside so the other could thrust the gown onto Danni's outstretched arms. The circulator continued to talk rapidly as she reached up and pushed Danni's glasses firmly onto the bridge of her nose.

"Mom ran into the trailer when they realized the toddlers were missing. A fireman pulled her back out, then went in for the kids himself. The dad's drunk, started the fire with a cigarette. The cops have him. She's about thirty-four weeks. No prenatal care. You're flying blind."

Danni nodded while she jammed her hands into the sterile gloves held open before her. Then she stepped up to the surgery table.

The patient was no longer screaming. She now lay gravely silent with eyes closed, her skin pale and smudged beneath pathetically singed eyebrows and hair. She cracked her eyes open as Danni adjusted the paper drapes. When she saw Danni she tried to talk through the anesthesia mask, then reached sooty fingers from under the drape and grabbed for Danni's arm. The circulator caught the woman's hand before she could contaminate Danni's sterile gown.

"Don't worry," Danni said and leaned over to look directly in the patient's eyes as they grew heavy with the anesthetic. "We'll get your baby out in time."

She opened her gloved palm for the scalpel and peered over her mask at the anesthetist. He adjusted the nitrous oxide and nodded.

"Let's go." Danni flipped the knife into position and cut.

Dr. Danni Goodlove prided herself on her head-spinning, machinelike speed in emergencies. The C-section team at Tulsa's Holy Cross Hospital—one of the best in the city—had scrambled to meet her exacting standard: six minutes from decision, to incision, to squalling baby.

In this business, sometimes you had to hurt the patient in order to help them. Sometimes they cried out. Danni might have let that affect her work, but she didn't. While still in her teens she had learned to ignore her emotions and focus on her goal. She'd acquired that skill the hard way—in a tragedy she didn't like to think about—but on a night like this she was grateful for it.

Because on a night like this—when the moon was full—Danni couldn't help thinking of Lisa.

On a night like this, Lisa and her baby had died. But tonight's baby was lifted out, free of the strangling cord, squirming under the Ohio warmer a mere ninety seconds after Danni's first swift, sure cut.

Danni hadn't even broken a sweat, but the rest of the team released a collectively held breath when they heard the first weak cries from the corner where a pediatric team labored over the tiny patient. Danni tried to ignore the palpable relief all around her. She never allowed herself to get emotional during a delivery, but tonight she was feeling the tiniest twinge of—*something*—as the infant's crying picked up steam.

Then the bang of the operating-room door startled them all.

A perky young ward clerk, breathless from her sprint down the hall, held a paper mask to her face, her eyes huge above it. "Dr. Danni!" she huffed. "Dr. Stone's having a *fit* down in the E.R. He said to close this case fast and get down there stat. A ton of OB's have flooded in."

"The *moon*," a nurse behind Danni moaned.

The girl spread a palm over her chest as if to calm herself, then noticed the baby. "That baby made it?"

One of the pediatric nurses called out, "He's perfect!" above the infant's wailing.

"You know," the transfixed young woman said, nodding at the unconscious mother, "that fireman that got injured saving her?"

The team, busy with their tasks, didn't acknowledge the question.

"Well," she announced with an air of importance, "Cooper said he looks *just like* Tom Selleck."

Danni gave the girl a cutting glance over her mask, then said, "Go tell Stone to cool his jets. I'll be there in a couple of minutes."

ONCE SHE GOT DOWN to the E.R., Danni took a second to look in the exam room where two toddler-size bodies lay side by side on two gurneys. The bustling E.R. teams obstructed her view, but she knew it was bad. The teams were too controlled, too quiet. It was the deafening silence of hopelessness. What would she tell the mother?

A commotion behind her caused her to turn.

Some nurses and an orderly had stopped the gurney they'd been pushing and struggled with the huge man on it. He was wearing a bloodstained T-shirt, and a fresh dressing and ice packs swaddled one arm. His turnout pants and fire boots told Danni he must be the fireman the ward clerk had been talking about upstairs. He was fighting to sit up and pushed the burly orderly back with one hand while he jerked the oxygen mask off his face with the other.

That ward clerk was wrong, Danni thought as she rushed forward to help. *This guy doesn't look anything like Tom Selleck.* And right now his face was so contorted with anger, his eyes were so wild with delirium, you couldn't even call him handsome.

"Let me see them!" he yelled as he shoved the nurses' hands away. "Dammit! I have to see if they're okay!"

One of his fireman buddies, a black man in full regalia except for the helmet, ran up alongside the gurney and got into the act. "Matt, you need that oxygen," he said as he forced the mask over the patient's face and fought to get his mighty shoulders back down on the gurney.

"What's he had?" Danni yelled across to a nurse, and as soon as she heard the answer added, "Get me some Ativan." The other nurse had gone off, anticipating the order, and a full syringe was instantly in Danni's hand.

"You hold him," Danni ordered the black fireman.

The patient fought like a bull, still ranting about the toddlers, while Danni shot the sedative into a vein.

When the patient finally moaned into semiconsciousness, the black man released his hold and turned to Danni. "It's not Matt's fault. This is old stuff—" The big man suddenly seemed choked up. "He worked the bombing. Saving these babies tonight kind of brought it all back."

The bombing. In Oklahoma they simply called it that—the bombing.

Danni nodded and felt her eyes mist when she turned to look at the man on the gurney as the nurses rolled him away, and saw the top of his dark head as he tossed it miserably from side to side.

The bombing—after all this time, so many still suffered from its aftershocks. Like that poor man.

"Matt's usually a really nice guy," the black

man said from behind her. "Are you gonna take care of his arm?" he added anxiously.

Danni turned and looked up at him. This one *was* a handsome man, even though he looked thoroughly exhausted. "No. I'm an obstetrician, but one of the E.R. docs—"

Before she could finish, a harried-looking nurse rushed up and said, "Dr. Goodlove, *please*," while she hauled Danni by the sleeve of her lab coat into an open area where the sight of five mounded tummies on five beds made Danni groan.

"All in active labor." The nurse held out a stack of intake charts. "Stone says they're all yours."

"Gee. Could the Old Man be testing me again?" Danni took the charts.

"Again? When did he stop?" The nurse plunked a Doppler device and a bottle of blue gel on top of the charts. "Don't worry, we finally located Dr. Bryant. Claimed his pager wasn't working."

Danni made a sarcastic face. "Oh, goody. Bryant." Bryant, if anything, was a bigger pain than Stone. As the chief of staff, Kenneth Stone, at least, was supremely confident and above petty one-upsmanship. Bryant was not. Only a hair older than Danni, he was fiercely competitive.

Moments later, when Roger Bryant came blasting through the E.R. doors like a Viking god to the rescue, Danni studiously ignored him and let the triage nurse give him report.

Another hour flew by while Bryant and Danni got the OB patients examined and admitted.

"I'll go up and cover Labor and Delivery now,"

Bryant said and ran a hand through his fine, sandy-blond hair, then pointed at Danni as he backed toward the elevator, beating an obvious retreat from the E.R. chaos. "You'd better take a break, sister. You look terrible."

"Oh, my gosh!" Danni framed her cheeks with her palms. "Imagine that! I look *terrible!*" She addressed this remark to Carol Hollis, her best friend and a top-notch scrub nurse, who'd appeared on her left.

"Gee," Carol deadpanned, then raised her voice as the elevator doors slid closed over Bryant's sour expression. "Could *four deliveries* and *two C-sections* have anything to do with it?"

Carol straightened, tossed her salt-and-pepper curls toward the elevator and muttered, "Prick." She turned to Danni. "But unfortunately, the prick can't handle what's developing upstairs."

"What's that?"

"Another C-section."

"When?"

"Maybe an hour. That's why I came down to find you."

Danni held up a palm. "Okay. But first I *gotta* eat something or I'll pass out."

But just as Danni and Carol plopped down in the break area, a nurse poked her head in the door and pleaded, "Dr. Goodlove, before you go back to OB could you possibly see the fireman?"

Danni gulped milk from a carton, then rubbed the back of her neck, not comprehending something this nurse obviously thought she should. "The fireman?"

"Yeah. The guy who pulled the twins out of the trailer. He's been waiting for over an hour. Somebody needs to check his lungs again and he has a nasty wound that needs stitches." The nurse shrugged apologetically while she held out a disposable suture tray. "We're swamped. In fact, we're so crowded we had to put the poor man in the supply room. Could you?"

"I'll help," Carol offered. "Bryant can survive a little while without you."

Danni sighed. Would this night never end? "Okay." She stood, tilted the milk carton up and drained it. "Let's go."

CHAPTER TWO

THE SUPPLY ROOM WAS cramped, even without the gurney, even without the over-six-feet of massive male snoring under the buzzing fluorescent light.

He was all alone, out cold, taking straight oxygen from a mask attached to a tank. He reeked of smoke and sweat, a few plastic cups littered the floor around him—at least they'd given him some water—and a thin blanket covered him to his chin. The dressing and cold compresses on the injured arm were pink-tinged with blood now, and the IV dripping into his other arm was almost empty.

Shameful, Danni thought. *This is how we treat our heroes?* She slipped the chart from under a corner of the gurney mattress and read.

Matthew Creed, age thirty-six. In addition to the Ativan, they'd given him a wallop of Demerol in the IV. There were third-degree burns on the same arm that had been gashed—by glass, the triage nurse had written.

As with every firefighter who plunged into a raging fire, the guy's lungs were the big worry. But so far, everything—electrolytes, blood gases—looked okay. And his color was within normal limits.

Assessing his face at rest, Danni decided that he

was handsome. His eyelids, though puffy—she made a note of the edema—were framed by thick dark brows and a line of lush black lashes any cover model would envy. Beneath the mask his square jaw was darkly shadowed with new-grown stubble.

His black hair, probably cut in a short, professional style, was now plastered straight up above a red crease where his helmet band had fit tightly. There was no apparent head trauma. She scribbled another note.

She handed the chart to Carol, peeled back the blanket to check the rest of him. He continued to snore into the oxygen mask.

"Holy cow," Carol muttered, and Danni shot her a censuring frown.

But Carol persisted. "Man!" she mumbled as she turned to prepare the suture tray. "I feel like I need a hit of that oxygen myself."

Though Danni disapproved of Carol's attitude, she could see her point. The patient had been stripped to the waist and he *was* big. Bronze. Amazingly fit. "Is there a weight recorded on the chart?" Danni asked. He was probably a lot heavier than he looked. She wanted to be sure he'd gotten enough pain medication.

"Two hundred fifteen," Carol read.

Danni nodded as she scanned his frame, looking for further damage, signs, symptoms.

He had huge muscular arms, massive hands, and a trail of black body hair that swirled neatly down taut abdominals. When she woke him up she'd have to make sure everything under his turnout pants and fire boots was okay.

She gently raised the edge of the dressing on his arm and called his name. "Mr. Creed?"

There was no response.

"Matthew?" As she reached for a pulse on the uninjured arm, a rolled-up, faded-red bandanna, knotted around his wrist, got in the way. She muttered something to Carol about why the EMTs hadn't cut the thing off before they started the IV, then added, "Gimme your bandage scissors," as she hooked a finger under the kerchief.

Without warning, the patient's other hand snapped up and seized Danni's wrist.

"Leave it alone," he growled in a deep bass voice that sounded hoarse and dry. The oxygen mask fogged with his breath, but nothing else about him moved. His grip on Danni's wrist, though, was like an iron band. His fingers felt hot, and Danni made a mental note to recheck his temp and then briefly wondered if it was her fatigue, her hunger, or *what,* that was making her suddenly weak.

"Mr. Creed," she said as she peeled his fingers from her flesh. "I need to get this thing off so I can evaluate you properly." She pulled on the bandanna, but he jerked his arm out of her reach. For an injured man, his reflexes were certainly quick.

He raised his head, opened bright-blue eyes and frowned at her. "I said, it stays where it is."

Something about his gaze made Danni swallow. "Of course," she answered softly.

His eyes slid closed, and he laid his head back,

groaning in that deep voice that made Danni's heart beat faster. Then he lowered his chin and looked down his long frame toward the door of the tiny room. "Where am I?"

"You're in the emergency room at Holy Cross Hospital."

"Oh, yeah? You a nurse?"

"No. I'm Dr. Dann...Dr. Goodlove. I gave you a sedative earlier."

"You did?"

"Yes, I did. Right now I'm going to stitch up that laceration you have there."

He glanced at his arm, then groaned, "Have at it," in his wonderful voice, and laid his good arm across his eyes.

Carol gently rearranged the IV to accommodate his position.

"Did those kids make it?" he asked.

Danni felt her heart constrict because, even through the mask, she could see his wide, handsome mouth tighten and pull down at the corners, betraying the emotion he was holding back.

She had to swallow before she spoke. "Yes," she said, although she feared that by now they had not. "And the mother's upstairs in maternity. She's fine."

"She's pregnant?" He moved the arm and stared, unbelieving, into Danni's eyes.

"Not anymore. I delivered her preemie by C-section."

"Damn," he said quietly and closed his eyes.

"The baby's okay. Let's tend to you, now."

Danni forced herself to sound calm, professional. She leaned over him and placed a stethoscope on his chest, moving it periodically as she listened. "Lungs sound clear," she said to Carol.

She moved the stethoscope to crucial points over his heart and concentrated. The beat was regular, but rapid. Stress maybe.

She glanced into his face. He was watching her like— Well, she didn't know like what. It was eerie, looking into those steady blue eyes while listening to his strong heartbeat.

She finished, pulled the stethoscope from her ears, and straightened. "Okay. Let's fix your arm."

Danni rolled a stool up beside the gurney, and while the patient watched them with drugged-sleepy detachment, Carol treated the burns and Danni checked the gash for foreign bodies, then started carefully stitching it up.

As Danni worked, she waited for his reaction to the painful things she was doing to him. He never once flinched. But every time she glanced into his blue eyes, she wished she hadn't. They sent a quiver through her, threatening to dissolve her professional armor.

The little supply room began to feel tighter than a tomb. Every time he moved—to raise a knee or fill that massive chest with a deep breath—Danni thought she might drop her hemostat.

It didn't help matters that Carol was acting strangely. She kept passing supplies in unnecessary anticipation; kept calling Danni "Doctor" in reverent tones; kept muttering in medical jargon as if this were brain surgery.

"You are being stitched up by the best of the best," Carol reassured the drowsy fireman, and Danni wanted to smack her. It was obvious what Carol was doing; she had noted the absence of a wedding band on his finger. Everybody was always trying to fix Danni up with men—but trying to impress a patient? Good grief.

"That so?" The firefighter turned his head and winked at Danni.

"Oh, yes." Carol seemed encouraged. "Dr. Goodlove—we all call her Dr. Danni—will stitch you up so fine, that scar will be almost invisible."

Danni frowned daggers at her friend, but the patient seemed to be enjoying himself. He grinned sleepily behind his oxygen mask. "Darn. I was hoping for a big old scar to show the boys at the station."

"Well, sorry, you won't get a scar from this dedicated doctor." Carol just couldn't seem to shut it up. "She prides herself on her handiwork."

Danni put her head down and worked doggedly, praying Carol would be struck mute.

"She's been at this awhile?" he asked through the mask. "She looks so young."

Danni could feel him staring at her blushing cheeks and slipping glasses. *Don't mind me, folks,* she thought. *I'm just stitching up this gaping wound, here.*

"About ten years," Carol assured him. "It's her whole life."

"Nurse Hollis!" Danni snapped. "I think the patient needs another drink of water."

Carol had the good grace to turn red, then she spun on her crepe soles and left the tiny room.

Suddenly the patient seemed, to Danni, too alert. She'd been more comfortable with him drugged.

As she cleaned up the exterior of the closed wound, and applied a sterile dressing, he continued to watch her like a— Well, now she knew what it was like—it was the way an interested man watched a pretty woman, only Danni hadn't ever thought of herself as pretty.

She finished the bandaging with a thick dressing. She was applying enough cling wrap to seal a mummy when he cleared his throat, reached up, pulled the oxygen mask down, and said, "Thanks for leaving the kerchief alone."

When she looked into his solemn eyes, Danni realized the kerchief had some special meaning, but he cleared his throat and quickly looked away. "And thanks for stitching me up."

"No problem." She continued to tape the dressing. "Just don't make a habit of this."

After a heartbeat he said, "If I do, would you be my doctor?"

Danni stopped her taping and looked back up into those blue eyes. This time the interest and flirtation there was unmistakable. And with the oxygen mask gone, she could see his mouth clearly. Beautifully formed lips. Firm. Utterly male. Curving into a lopsided, teasing grin.

Danni finished her taping with tense fingers and burning cheeks.

He, on the other hand, seemed perfectly relaxed. He raised his good arm and propped it under his head, revealing a massive, muscled armpit with the densest growth of black axillary hair Danni had ever seen.

She had a photo-flash memory of another time when she and Carol had been dragged down to the E.R. to help stitch up the aftermath of a big gang fight. One of the teenage victims had B.O. so bad that Carol had clamped wads of alcohol-soaked gauze over his armpits, claiming it was standard procedure.

Suddenly Danni was overcome by the worst attack of inappropriate laughter ever visited on a human being.

She tried to stifle it, and bent her head down below the gurney as if looking for something she'd dropped. Her shoulders shook and she thought she'd choke, but the silliest thoughts kept coming, all incredibly hilarious. She wondered fleetingly if there was a leaking nitrous-oxide tank in here somewhere. Even that horrifying idea couldn't sober her.

"You okay down there?" She heard his deep voice above her.

She tried to say yes, but that was a horrible mistake that opened the door to a new eruption of giggles. She was forced to sit up in order to breathe, and pushed with weak feet to roll the stool away from the table, away from him and his serious blue eyes, so she could regain her composure.

But she ended up leaning against the supply shelves, snickering and gasping and finally holding her middle and waving her hand, pointing at him, the way people do when they are helpless to explain their stupid behavior.

"What's so funny?" His face was as solemn as a judge's.

Nothing! Danni thought. *Nothing at all. That's the problem!* But she continued to titter helplessly. Then she wondered—and this thought only made *more* giggles come—if she looked like some kind of deranged woman, masquerading as a doctor.

He raised himself up on his good elbow, and stared with an expression so alarmed and serious that every time Danni glanced at him to try to explain that she was reacting to exhaustion, she broke up all over again. She laughed so hard, tears rolled down her cheeks.

Carol came in bearing a cup of water, which Danni snatched and gulped. Finally the urge to laugh subsided.

With a frown at Danni, Carol helped the patient sit up. He tested his injured arm, then flexed his amazing muscles as if they were sore. He glanced at Danni and smiled when he caught her watching him over the rim of the cup.

Firemen and cops, Danni thought. *All as cocky as the devil.*

Carol started helping him into the hospital gown she'd brought for him.

Danni finished drinking the water, let out a huge sigh, then pulled off her paper hat, and lifted her thick mane of hair away from her neck, fanning herself. "I'm really sorry," she said to the patient. She dug a latex tourniquet out of the pocket of her scrubs and tied her hair into a crude ponytail at her nape. "That was an attack of inappropriate laughter, precipitated by fatigue." She tossed the cup into a trash container. "We'll get you some more water."

"That's okay. I'm not thirsty. And I understand fatigue," he said, but his expression was skeptical as his eyes took in the haphazard ponytail.

He probably thinks I'm totally nuts, Danni thought.

Apparently so did Carol, judging from the scowl she gave Danni as she tied the gown strings at the patient's back.

Danni took another deep breath and stood. "I'm shipping you upstairs for overnight observation, okay?"

She took his mended arm in her hands, examined the fingers gently, checking the circulation one last time. She knew her cheeks were red, but she managed to keep her voice steady. "This looks fine so far. Tell me again, exactly how'd you cut it?"

"Squeezing through the broken patio door." He raised one eyebrow, then studied his boots. "Kicked it out when I couldn't follow the attack hose back. The crew thought I was going the other way."

"I see," Danni said, although she didn't, exactly.

She assumed he was telling her that something went wrong during the rescue. Her fingers trembled on his large ones for a moment, imagining the inferno, imagining him curling his body around the two babies, imagining such bravery. "And everything under your turnout pants…" Danni hesitated and reframed the question. "Uh, you're sure your feet and legs are okay?"

"Yeah, everything feels fine." He smiled at her with gorgeous, perfect white teeth and she noticed that he did, in fact, have deep dimples like Tom Selleck's. But there was something else familiar about him. Danni couldn't put her finger on it.

"Well, then—" she snatched up the chart, pushed her glasses up on her nose, clicked her pen "—all we need to do is add some strong antibiotics to your IV. Is your pain medicine still working okay?"

"Yeah. Thanks again for stitching me up, Doctor. Especially considering that you're exhausted and all, I really appreciate it." He spoke in a controlled monotone, but the look in his eyes was so sincere, so warm that Danni thought she'd melt.

"No problem." She resumed writing on the chart.

He turned to Carol. "Nurse, will they be taking me upstairs in a wheelchair?"

"I expect so," she answered.

"Well, then, would it be too much trouble to wheel me by to see the twins on the way?"

Danni turned her head, studied his handsome profile. He'd endured over twenty stitches, had enough drugs in him to knock out a horse, and had to be tired enough to die, but all the man could think about were those twins. Matthew Creed was an amazing man.

UPSTAIRS IN LABOR AND Delivery, Dr. Stone was pacing like a wiry little fox sniffing for prey.

"Sorry to disturb your *nap*, Dr. Goodlove," he said as soon as Danni and Carol stepped off the elevator.

"She wasn't taking a nap—" Carol, who could make two of Stone, jumped in to defend her boss "—she was stitching up a patient."

Stone's nostrils flared, his tufted reddish-gray eyebrows puckered, and his pointy little teeth flashed briefly as if he might bite Carol. But then he turned to Danni, and peered up over his glasses at her. "Dr. Bryant told me you had gone to sleep."

Danni folded her arms across her chest and turned a composed smile on Stone. "Now, why would I want to sleep through all this fun?"

Stone didn't even bother to smile at the quip. "We have several more drop-ins in active labor. I'll take them. Your C-section is waiting in Delivery One."

Danni didn't ask—although she'd love to have known—what the mighty Dr. Bryant was doing with his precious time.

"MAN! I HOPE THAT'S the last one," Carol mumbled through her mask after Danni had delivered another baby safely, verified the sponge count and started the routine stitching.

"Yep," Danni said while she tied off a stitch. "It's that damn moon, folks." She raised her voice. "Brings in the pregnant ladies like a truckload of pumpkins."

The weary team chuckled in agreement from behind their masks.

But Carol merely inflated hers with a sigh. Danni glanced into her friend's bloodshot eyes. "After this," she said in a low voice, "you're going home."

"And what about you, Doc? You going home?" Carol reached across for more suture, a flip of her wrist conveying that she'd stay as long as Danni did. After three years of working side by side, Danni and Carol read each other's movements like Morse code.

Danni said nothing. Only three years in private practice and already it was all getting to her. Carol's aggressive protectiveness. The full moon. Babies.

Babies.

Babies.

Danni's hands shook a little as she opened a palm for the subcuticular suture. Carol shot her a sharp, appraising look before she slapped the hemostat down on her glove.

Danni pursed her lips behind her mask. Damn Carol and the way she saw through everything, through everyone. Damn her with her big, brown, *understanding* eyes. Why were nurses always so ridiculously *kind* and *well-adjusted?*

Danni finished the suturing, stripped off her gloves and announced, "I'm taking a snore. Don't wake me until the next one's ears are out."

She heard Carol order someone else to dress the incision, and sensed her friend right on her heels as she hurried to the doctors' locker room.

The door hadn't even swung back before Carol banged it open again. Danni was just lowering herself into the recliner where the doctors slept fitfully while they monitored troubled cases in the wee hours.

"What is eating you?" Carol asked calmly as she reached up and took a blanket from the top of the lockers. "I mean, besides the fact that the whole month of August has been chaos, and now the moon is full to boot—" she shook the blanket out "—and it's three o'clock in the morning and you've done four deliveries and three emergency C-sections in the last twelve hours—" she spread the blanket out over Danni "—not to mention stitching up Mr. Universe downstairs."

Danni reached up, pulled off her surgical cap and tugged the tourniquet from her tangled hair.

"I mean, I've never seen you like this. What the hell was that laughing business?"

Danni winced, remembering how she'd acted in front of the firefighter. "Me?" she countered. "What was that stuff *you* were pulling?"

"Huh?" Carol's expression was all innocence.

"You know what I mean." Danni adopted a mimicking tone. "You are being stitched up by the best of the best."

"Hey. I was only trying to help. The guy was *cute*. And I think he liked you. *Somebody's* gotta help you meet men." She pulled her own cap off and ran her fingers through her thick, graying curls as she studied Danni's face. "What on God's green earth is eating you?"

"Nothing." Danni twitched around under the blanket for a second, then sighed. "Oh, all right, it's just that... Oh, I don't know." But she did know, and trying to hold it back gave rise to a spurt of sudden, surprising tears. *For heavens sake, don't bawl now,* she commanded herself. *Not with Stone coming back any second. He'll assume you can't handle the pressure.*

"You do know," Carol said flatly. She dragged a plastic chair up beside the recliner. "Out with it."

"No, I *don't* know, exactly. I mean, I've got everything I ever wanted. A thriving practice, a gorgeous house, my horse and my dogs..." *Then why the tears?* she wondered without Carol having to ask.

Carol extended a tissue. Danni dabbed her eyes and blew her nose. "I *never* cry," she said. "But tonight, it seems like every little thing brings tears to my eyes. I almost cried when I first saw that fireman in the E.R."

Carol shook her fingers as if they'd been burned. "Me too, honey."

"No! I mean when I found out he'd been a rescuer at the bombing."

Carol grew solemn. "He was?"

Danni nodded. "But all kinds of other things

have been getting to me, too. I'm just not myself. That inappropriate laughter..." Danni twisted the tissue. "It sounds weird, but I honestly think what's really bugging me is all this damned...*fecundity.*"

Carol's eyebrows shot up. *"Fecundity?"* she repeated.

"Yes, *fecundity,*" Danni sniffed. "I've got everything I ever dreamed of while I was struggling through med school and that hellish residency. The trouble is, I guess I didn't dream hard enough. The trouble is... " Danni's eyes filled with tears again as she stared at the acoustical tile ceiling. *What was the matter with her?*

But Carol Hollis was a trusted friend, and when Danni felt Carol's warm, plump palm close over her forearm, her defenses crumbled.

"Trouble is," she went on, "I've ended up with this manless, childless, *loveless* life for myself...." Danni threw an arm over her eyes. What she couldn't express aloud was the terrible fear that she would *always* be manless, childless, loveless, and the reason why.

"The trouble is," Carol said softly, "you're a human being. And a female human being to boot. And when you saw that hunk in the E.R. tonight, maybe he reminded you of what you're missing." She gave Danni's arm a squeeze, and Danni nodded but didn't lower her other arm. Admitting it was bad enough; she couldn't look into Carol's eyes at the same time. And she couldn't possibly tell her the rest of it, could she?

"And, let's see, you'll be thirty-three on your next birthday," Carol continued.

"Thirty-four," Danni corrected in a croaky whisper.

"Right. And at thirty-four, it's time for a reality check. Your biological clock is ticking away. You've seen this reaction often enough in patients. Why should you be any different?"

Danni gave a rueful laugh. "I always said I'd never have kids. Not after—"

"Not after what?" Carol prompted when Danni wouldn't continue.

But Danni couldn't go into that story now—not with patients out there needing her. "It's a long story. The point is, lately, my biological clock's been bonging louder than Big Ben!" She lowered her arm and looked at Carol, frustration with herself momentarily overcoming her pain. "But don't you think thirty-four's kind of *young* for that? I mean, rationally I *know*—"

"Rationality has very little to do with some things, hon. Maybe it's not so much biology as other factors. As you said, your practice is booming. You've proved yourself here at Holy Cross and now you're getting ready to take on a couple of partners. Looks like you've got it made, *career-wise*." Carol emphasized the last words.

Danni pulled the recliner upright. "You're right. I've been striving for so long, I haven't had time to think about my personal life. And suddenly, now that I've *succeeded*..."

"You want love, and a family, perhaps, along

with everything else.'' Carol shrugged her shoulders. ''Wanting to love and be loved is not exactly a crime.''

Danni felt a tiny bubble of hope rising. *Yeah. Love. Why shouldn't Dr. Danni have a family just like everybody else? Just like all her patients?* ''Yeah,'' she said aloud. ''Why shouldn't I have a baby of my own—''

''And a man, too?'' Carol suggested.

''Oh. Oh, yeah. And the man, too,'' Danni said vaguely. She had a sudden flashback to the fireman propping his head up on his muscular arm, only this time the image didn't make her laugh, and neither did the memory of his compelling blue eyes.

Carol gave her a dubious look. ''I don't understand you twenty-first-century women. When I was your age, babies were the by-product of the man, not the other way around.''

Danni grinned, feeling in control of herself again. ''When *you* were my age, you and George had already created a lot of by-products.''

Carol chuckled. ''Blame it on the moon, honey. But I wouldn't trade my four boys for anything.'' Then she patted Danni's arm. ''Listen, speaking of the moon, you'd better catch some sleep. A couple of the patients are already dilated to eight.''

''Right.'' Danni was relieved to close her eyes, because she was afraid that if they talked about men and babies anymore, the tears might start again. And she hated tears.

She'd convinced herself long ago that she could not afford to let tears begin. Not while she was at work. And long ago, she'd decided that she could never risk telling anyone about her sister's death—not if she wanted to remain calm and professional and take care of her patients.

As far back as medical school, Danni had learned not to even say Lisa's name out loud. That was why she hadn't told Carol the whole story just now. But then, who had she ever told? No one. She barely understood her feelings herself. That was the real problem.

No. The real problem was that Lisa had died.

And *that* would never change.

CHAPTER THREE

LATER, IN THE GRAY predawn hours, as she turned off Peoria Avenue onto her own street, Danni's mood had not improved. *The glamorous life of a doctor,* she thought ruefully as she struggled to keep her eyes open, grateful that she lived less than a mile from the hospital.

Precisely the reason she'd chosen this upscale, historic neighborhood in Tulsa's Woodward Park area.

She drove her BMW up the gentle incline of her driveway and wearily clicked the remote control. The garage door slid up with a flawless hum and Danni pulled into her immaculate, uncluttered garage, then punched the button again to seal out the world. Letting herself in through the utility room, she entered a completely dark, silent house.

Her silver weimaraners, Pearl and Smoky, rose like ghosts from their beds and brushed against her legs. "Well, hello," Danni crooned as she reached down and petted them. "How are my doggies?"

She pressed the intercom button on the security panel. "Jackie?" she called, and waited for her housekeeper to awaken and answer from upstairs. "Jackie?" No answer. Was it Jackie's night off?

She reached over to punch in the security code, then realized the alarm was off.

Dadgum that harebrained girl, she thought. How many times did she have to remind Jackie to turn on the security system when she went out? Danni hit another button and soft safety lights illuminated the stairwell, bathrooms and hallways of the entire 3,700-square-foot house. Last spring, Danni had hired the top builder in Tulsa to renovate this vintage house on a split lot, with impeccable attention to details like copper awnings, custom stonework, and real plaster walls with bullnose moldings. Underneath the gracious antique facade was every amenity of modern construction imaginable, from zoned heat and air to underground sprinklers. The house with everything, Danni sometimes thought, except people to share it with.

She took a sharp right into a central hall where a narrow oak stairway wound upward and a smaller hallway veered back toward the study and master suite. Arched doorways from this central hall led to the kitchen/great room, and the formal dining living areas. The dogs padded off in the direction of the kitchen.

Danni stood in the hallway, feeling like a laboratory mouse choosing between competing drives. The bathroom? The kitchen? The bed? She needed them all at once.

She trudged as far as the small guest bathroom next to her study, then washed her hands and splashed cool water on her face.

As she blotted dry she studied her reflection in

the mirror, and didn't like what she saw: sallow complexion, bloodshot eyes, limp hair. She gave her high cheekbones a pinch. Precious little color appeared, and her skin felt oily and coarse. She looked down at her bluntly trimmed nails and bleached, cracked cuticles. Well, scrubbing for surgery wasn't exactly a manicure. She backed away from the mirror, pulled off her wrinkled scrubs and dropped them in a heap at her feet.

Hopeless, she thought as she turned sideways and sucked in her tummy. That bulge was the result of too many fast-food meals on the run, those hips from too much horseback riding and not enough jogging, and these—she pushed her D cup breasts up a notch in the utilitarian support bra—what could she possibly do about *these?*

Disheartened, she cut through the study to the master suite where she threw on her trusty old pink chenille robe, then, pushing back the guilt by telling herself she deserved some comfort food, she headed for the fridge.

The kitchen/great room, a massive area with atrium doors flanking a huge stone fireplace, would have been dark except that, predictably, Jackie had not drawn the drapes. Moonlight streamed in through a bank of Colonial windows on the south wall, casting an eerie glow over the space. By daylight this was a stunning room with its pale taupe cabinetwork, oak flooring, and muted tapestry fabrics, but tonight it seemed as cold as a cave.

She hit the replay button on her answering machine as she rounded the granite-topped island in the kitchen, then padded to the double-sided refrigerator. She jerked the door open and stood in the blast of artificial light and cold air, surveying a staggering array of food. Jackie could cook—Danni would give her that.

Beep. "Danni, dear!" It was her mother's voice, sounding annoyingly cheerful at four in the morning. "Are you *never* to be found in your lovely home? Aunt Hetra and Aunt Dottie and I are going shopping at Utica Square tomorrow and I thought we'd drop by first so they could see how beautifully your house turned out. Would that be okay? By the way, Wesley Fuerborne's mother called me today, and guess what? Wesley is coming back to Tulsa! Isn't that nice?"

Danni rolled her eyes. Would her mother never give up? *Wesley Fuerborne.* Danni hadn't seen him since college. Their relationship had seemed to please all of Tulsa society—everybody but Danni. What was it about Wesley? Well, for one thing the sex had been terrible. Awkward and juvenile. Had that been her fault or his? Didn't matter. It certainly hadn't been good enough to offset Danni's irrational fear of becoming pregnant every time their relationship had gotten physical, despite the precautions she'd insisted on.

Her mother's voice was going on brightly. "Such a nice young man. He wants to see you while he's here, and I was thinking maybe you two could join me for the Tulsa Performing Arts Gala."

Pearl and Smoky had positioned themselves on their haunches at Danni's feet, staring expectantly upward. She tossed them each a chunk of cheese and said, "Go lie down!" in a stern voice that the dogs ignored.

"Call me soon, sweetheart. We'll drop by tomorrow." *Beep.*

Danni rolled her eyes again and focused on the food. She passed on the sensible tuna-and-pasta salad, and grabbed a grilled pork chop. She stood at the kitchen island and devoured it without benefit of silverware as she stared out at her moonlit backyard.

That moon.

Silent. Waiting. Calling.

How far the moon was from Earth, yet how intimately close it felt. How compelling. And how she hated the haunting sight of it.

Danni wasn't even aware of her movements as she wandered around the island and dropped onto the leather couch facing the southern windows. She keeled to her side and lay there, watching the moon float high over the trees.

She was so, so tired.

She wanted to sleep, not visit her old, sad memories; not think about all that she had seen tonight. "Sometimes I hate this job," she murmured to the moon, and closed her eyes, willing that last scene at the hospital—especially that one—away.

The things a doctor saw—birth and death and everything in between—were frequently heart-rending, but sometimes they actually marked your soul. That was the risk.

By three o'clock this morning, Labor and Delivery had slowed down enough for Danni to dash out to Postpartum to check on the burn victim. The patient was stable, Carol had called in the social worker and the chaplain to counsel and console, and there had been little else they could do. But Danni had wanted to make sure the woman's sedatives were working. As she'd approached the patient's door she'd heard her, quietly sobbing.

Danni turned to go back to the nurses' station to get more sedative when she heard the firefighter's deep voice. "I'll stay here as long as you need me."

Danni frowned and crept back to the doorjamb and looked in. He was standing by the mother's bed, holding her hand, with his back to Danni. He had put his fire pants back on under the hospital gown, and now wore paper hospital shoes.

"I'm so afraid," Danni heard the mother say.

"They're doing everything they can. You just have to be strong," his deep voice answered.

The mother broke into fresh sobs and Danni watched him bend forward and wrap his uninjured arm around her in a protective hug, causing the hospital gown to gape open, exposing his tanned back.

"Th-thank you for saving my babies!" the woman sobbed, and clung to his bare skin.

"I only wish I could have gotten them out sooner, ma'am." Danni heard a tightness in his voice. Was he crying? She turned to go, thinking she shouldn't eavesdrop, when something the mother said stopped her.

"Do you pray?" the woman asked.

For some reason Danni wanted to know. Did he?

He straightened and took the mother's hand again. "Yes, ma'am. I started praying about four years ago. It helps a lot."

"Would you pray for my babies?"

"Yes, ma'am." He got down on one knee, and still holding the mother's hand, began to pray so quietly, so reverently, that Danni had to strain to hear the words.

"Lord, we're coming to you now to ask you to help this mother and her babies. We ask only that—"

He stopped as if he had to consider what, exactly, to ask in these dire circumstances. Danni leaned forward.

"We ask that you take the babies into your care. We're turning them over to you, Lord. We trust in you and your will. Please give this mother the strength she needs... And give her peace. Amen."

Danni backed away from the door and went down the hall to get the sedatives, knowing that she could not match what this fireman had offered through his presence and his prayers.

Now, the memory of that scene caused tears to spring into Danni's eyes as she lay on her couch.

That poor, poor woman, Danni thought. She'd needed Matthew Creed's company and support tonight. Danni hoped there were people in the woman's life who would give her the strength she was going to need. We all need people, Danni thought, suddenly feeling more lonely than she ever had in her life.

She burrowed her cheek against the couch and allowed a single tear to slide onto the soft leather. "Why can't I find someone?" she whispered to the moon's mocking face. But the moon, so silent, had no answer.

Carol had guessed right, at least partially. Danni had been running scared for most of her life—running from what had happened to Lisa. Now that Danni had made it as a doctor, there was nowhere else to go, nothing else to distract her from the emptiness of her personal life; from that old, old pain that she thought she'd successfully sealed off so many years ago.

"Oh, sissy, I'm so scared," she whispered. Now—in her own home—she should be able to cry, if she wanted to; to sob and scream and break things, if she wanted to. But she'd trained herself for so long to hold her emotions in. She squeezed her eyes shut and, before long, sank into a bottomless sleep, where from deep recesses, disturbing dreams surfaced.

Not the usual dreams of Lisa, still alive.

These were feverish dreams. Dreams of a strong man, carrying her through flames, laying her under a cool moon, making fierce love to her, over and over. Dreams in which her longing and her pain and her loneliness at last melted away.

CHAPTER FOUR

THE SMELL OF HAM FRYING and the glaring intrusion of sunlight woke Danni. The pillow under her head and the woven throw tucked around her meant that Jackie was home, up to her usual ministrations.

Danni had originally hired nineteen-year-old Jackie Smith to work as a medical assistant, but had quickly noticed that Jackie had a habit of cleaning and straightening the office without being told. The hefty girl also regularly brought in wonderful homemade goodies for the staff to munch on. When Jackie had ended up needing a place to hide from her abusive, alcoholic man, Danni had asked if she'd like to move in with her in return for housekeeping duties.

Upstairs, a vacuum cleaner started, then abruptly stopped. Then came the sound of heavy footsteps galloping down the stairs, and Jackie's voice—"Shit!"—followed by the sound of a spatula frantically working to save the ham.

"Trying to do three things at once again?" Danni mumbled from the couch.

"Doc!" Jackie whirled around from her cooking. "You're awake!"

Danni sat up, looked over the back of the couch, and stretched. "Unfortunately. What time is it?"

"Eight o'clock."

Danni cut short a yawn. "Shoot! What have I got at the office?"

"Nothin'. It's Saturday."

"Saturday?" Had she lost an entire day in the full-moon craziness at the hospital? "Then, where were you last night?"

"My night class, remember?"

"Oh, yeah. How's that going?"

"Great! I love accounting. Doc, I just can't thank you enough for paying my tuition."

"You earn it." Danni waved a palm, dismissing her own generosity. What good was money if you couldn't have fun with it? Then she frowned. "But when I came in at four, you still weren't home."

Jackie looked sheepish. "After class I had a hot date. Hope that's okay. That's why I'm double-timing it today."

Jackie, a billowy size fourteen, always had dates coming out of her ears. Danni sighed, rose from the couch, pulled her robe up under her chin and padded into the kitchen. She poured herself a mug of coffee, swallowed a bit of her pride with the first gulp, and said, "Jackie, mind if I ask you a personal question?"

"Not at all—" Jackie was busy cracking eggs "—unless it's one o' them gynecological ones." Jackie cast her employer a knowing glance. "Don't worry about me. I'm careful." Her dark eyes twinkled mischievously.

"Oh, it's not *that* kind of personal. It's hmm, well…" Danni jammed her hands into the pockets of her robe as she felt her cheeks grow hot.

Jackie stopped whisking the omelet she'd poured. "Why, Doc, what's eating you?" She eyed her boss suspiciously.

Damn! The exact same question Carol had asked last night. Was it engraved on her forehead: Something is Eating Me! Danni screwed up her face. "Nothing is *eating* me," she protested. "I'm just sick and tired of working constantly, followed by lonely evenings in this big, empty house. How the heck do you do it?"

Jackie looked genuinely confused. "Do what?"

"Get all those dates, for crying out loud!"

"Ah," Jackie breathed and nodded, making her gigantic hoop earrings wobble. Then she pursed her thick brick-red lips and squinted at Danni. "Naw. You wouldn't listen even if I told you. You're above all that stuff!"

"Above all what stuff?"

"You know. Bein' a man-trap."

"A man-trap!" Danni's mouth quirked in a smile. Jackie was such a case.

"Told you." Jackie aimed her face back toward the stove and emptied the steaming omelet onto a plate, then held it under Danni's nose.

Danni took the plate and set it down on the granite counter with an irritated clunk. She planted her hands on her hips. "I'm serious. Tell me what you do to attract all those men who are constantly swirling around you. Just give it to me straight. I'm a doctor, after all.''

Jackie hesitated, still holding the omelet pan, and gave Danni a long, frowning assessment.

''You're a doctor, all right,'' she finally answered. ''Maybe that's why you think you're above the dating game. You know—too good to use a little perfume, a little color, a little pretty.'' She shook her shiny earrings for emphasis.

Danni's mouth popped open to speak, but Jackie was on a roll. ''You think a man should look at you and see your *brains* and your *character*. Well, listen, honey, a man don't want to screw Einstein— he's lookin' to screw a *woman*. A little advertising never hurt. A little something that says—'' Jackie arched a perfectly plucked eyebrow ''—'I am a female.' That straight enough for you?'' She turned, mercifully, to rinse the omelet pan in the sink.

Danni's mouth was still ajar. And she knew her cheeks were redder than the devil. But she had to do something. Even if it meant pumping a high-school dropout for information. Because the reality was, Jackie had men delivering roses *to this very house.*

''Are you telling me I'm unattractive?'' Danni looked down at herself.

Jackie turned from spraying the pan and in one squinty-eyed sweep took in the faded pink robe, the disheveled hair drooping from a center part in no discernible style, the skin devoid of makeup. ''Now, don't take this wrong—''

"Go on," Danni urged, looking into her coffee cup, then she took a long sip.

Now it was Jackie's turn to plant her hands on her hips. "I been working for you two years, and I'll tell you something, Doctor. You know a lot about human sexuality, as you call it, but not much about the human *male*."

"I..." Danni's mouth popped open, again to protest, but she clamped it shut. "I'm listening," she said softly.

"Okay. You're a smart lady, you tell me." Jackie turned to the sink and pulled on a pair of household gloves. "Say you're a man. What's more attractive? Those combat boots you wear, or my purple spike heels? Those industrial-strength bras and saggy cotton underpants—" she jerked her thumb toward the laundry room where she'd apparently washed a load this morning "—or my pretty little teddies? My Obsession—" she waved her wrist "—or your surgical soap? I ask you? Which?"

Purple spike heels? Teddies? Danni's mind rebelled. If she had to dress like a tramp to attract a man, forget it. First of all, she was too busty for a stringy, lacy *anything*. And what doctor in her right mind spent the day in *heels?* "You know perfectly well that I do not wear perfume because it nauseates some patients," she replied haughtily.

"That's fine for *work*—" Jackie plunged her hands into the sudsy water "—but what about the rest of your life? I have never even seen so much as a bottle o' toilet water around here. And you with money to *burn*. Girl, you can afford the best.''

Danni was thoughtful as she pushed her glasses up on her nose. ''Okay. I guess it wouldn't hurt to try a little perfume....''

''Yeah. And speakin' of money. Why're you so attached to those geeky glasses? I *know* you can afford contacts.''

Before Danni could answer that one, Jackie whirled around and lifted Danni's hair away from one ear with a soapy glove. ''You don't even have your ears pierced. It's like you're afraid of acting like a girl.'' Jackie stared at her for a moment, then turned back to the sink.

Danni sank down on the barstool. *Well. She'd asked for this, hadn't she?* ''You really think I should try those manipulative feminine tricks?'' she said to Jackie's broad back.

Without looking up from the dishes, Jackie nodded. ''I ain't talkin' to these pans, sister. And these things ain't tricks.''

''But I don't think I'd be comfortable.... I don't even know where to start.'' Danni threw up her hands. ''I don't have the slightest idea how to... how to be...sexy.''

Jackie shrugged. ''You asked me how I get dates. That's how.''

Danni shook her head. ''I'd probably make a fool of myself.''

Jackie looked up from the sink. Over her shoulder she gave Danni a thoughtful, sympathetic frown, then her best bad-girl grin. ''I know! What

you need is a sexy fairy godmother. And honey—''
she cocked her hip, planted one sudsy fist there
''—you lookin' at the sexiest.''

The doorbell chimed. Danni and Jackie glanced
at each other, puzzled. No one was expected. Then
Danni groaned and ran a hand through her messy
hair. "Oh, *no*. It's Mother and Aunt Hetra and Aunt
Dottie. I forgot they were going to drop by."

"I'll go and stall them with some coffee." Jackie
started to strip off her gloves.

"No, you finish your dishes. I'll let them in."
Danni tightened the belt of her robe and headed
down the hall, then called over her shoulder, "Actually, some coffee and rolls would be nice."

Hetra, Dottie and Olivia fluttered through the
door and into Danni's foyer like a flock of colorful
little birds. The three Bartlet sisters had grown up
among the privileged of Terwilleger Heights in the
shadow of the elegant Philbrook Museum of Art,
which had been dedicated when they were children.
The hours they had spent exploring the museum
with their mother, a docent, had imbued the sisters
with impeccable taste. Now all three were wealthy
widows in their late sixties, still active and produc-
tive in the community, still beautiful and stylish.

Unfortunately, Danni had not inherited the family
penchant for personal style, and as always, she felt
homely, drab and unkempt as she hugged her
mother and her aunts.

"Danni, dear!" Her mother pushed Danni's wild
hair back and kissed her on the cheek. "I hope we
didn't wake you. I'm afraid we're a bit early."

"It's okay, Mom. I was up, but I haven't pulled myself together yet." Danni straightened the collar of her robe and smiled at her aunts. "Rough day yesterday, and an even rougher night."

"Lots of ladies having their babies, dear?" her Aunt Hetra asked kindly.

Danni nodded. "That old full moon again."

"Well, as I always say, a good doctor certainly earns her money!" Aunt Dottie chimed in. "And you must be one very busy obstetrician! Look at this house!"

Olivia beamed. "Isn't it gorgeous?" The sisters walked ahead of Danni, fluttering and chattering, into the sunny living room.

Danni was pleased with their reaction to her remodeling job. At least she had inherited one aspect of the Bartlet sense of style—a flair for interior decorating.

The aunts noticed everything. They praised everything. Even Jackie's cinnamon rolls.

"Did you get my message about going to the gala with Wesley Fuerborne?" Olivia asked while she was stirring cream into her second cup of coffee.

"Uh…" Danni took a sip from her cup. "I don't know about that deal, Mom."

"What do you mean?"

"I mean, I, uh, don't have a formal dress."

"Well, who does this early in the season?" Aunt Dottie interjected. "That's why we're going over to Miss Jackson's this morning, to start looking— I have a wonderful idea! Why don't you come with

us, Danni? We can all help you select something stunning.''

Olivia and Hetra cooed their approval of this idea.

''Oh, something *blue*.''

''Yes, get it done early.''

Danni raised a palm in protest. ''I'm— Mom, I'm sorry.''

Just then, Jackie came into the room to collect the empty pastry tray.

''I can't go,'' Danni said and sent Jackie a conspiratorial glance. ''I'm already going shopping with Jackie.''

Jackie raised her pencil-thin eyebrows, only a fraction, but otherwise maintained her smiling silence as she loaded empty china dessert plates onto the tray.

''Shopping?'' Aunt Hetra asked as if something about the idea didn't ring true.

''Yes. We go shopping together once in a while. For...essentials.''

''Essentials,'' Jackie parroted smoothly, then bustled out of the room.

The ladies made their departure graciously, after Olivia had extracted a promise from Danni to decide about the gala ''soon.''

Before Olivia had even backed her Mercedes down Danni's driveway, Jackie pounced. ''You know what, Doc? You weren't lying. You *are* going shopping with me.''

DANNI APPRECIATED GOOD psychology when she saw it in action, and Jackie, it turned out, was the all-time master.

She started Danni out with a nonthreatening trip to the shoe department for some comfortable, classic, snipped-toe pumps, then she whisked her off to Better Sportswear to buy a silk pantsuit in a feminine shade of rose. Simple. Elegant.

Danni decided she was actually having fun.

At the perfume counter, Jackie sniffed and swooned like she was in heaven, but Danni developed a sinus headache. An astute saleswoman helped Danni choose a clean, understated scent that she loved, and that set her back $150.

"I will pierce my own ears," Danni protested when Jackie tugged her arm in the direction of the local ear-piercing emporium. "I am a *surgeon,* for crying out loud."

"Deal," Jackie said and steered her to a jewelry store where she coaxed her into buying a thousand-dollar pair of diamond studs.

"These will look great against your hair." Jackie held the open velvet jewelry box next to Danni's jaw while they were downing a quick lunch. Then her smile dissolved into an appraising frown. "Speaking of hair..." She continued.

"Oh, no, you don't!" Danni clutched the big braid curving over her shoulder. "I've been wearing my hair this way all of my life—"

"*Exactly.* About time for a change, don't you think? And I know somebody who could work *wonders* on you, girl."

Danni rolled her eyes, imagining that Jackie had

some friend of a friend who'd give her a big-hair job that would knock your eyes out, perhaps literally. "No," she replied in her best boss's voice. "That is final."

Jackie stuck out her full, crimson glossed lower lip. "Ah, now," she said, making a pinch between thumb and forefinger, "not even a tiny little trim?"

JACKIE'S FAVORITE SALON was called Tres, for three—hair, nails, and skin—and Danni had to admit it was pretty chic.

First, Jackie hauled her over to somebody named Loretta, a cousin's best friend, who gave Danni "the perfect French manicure," keeping the length compatible with Danni's professional duties. Not bad, Danni thought.

The facial they gave her while her nails dried wasn't bad, either, Danni reflected as she lay under the soothing mask.

And she decided she *definitely* liked the pedicure. Not for the way her toes sparkled with ruby tips when it was over, but for the way her beleaguered calf muscles had completely relaxed under the pedicurist's massaging hands.

Danni was beginning to wonder why she hadn't indulged herself this way before, and then it was time for the haircut. "I can't look!" she squeaked and covered her eyes as a "hair artist," whose name tag read Naomi, winked at Jackie and raised gold-plated scissors.

The "tiny little trim" turned out to be a heart-stopping transformation of hideous proportions.

Jackie and Naomi kept patting it and exclaiming "Gorgeous!" while Danni looked in the mirror and wondered, *What the hell have I done?* Her formerly long, wavy hair now mushroomed up from her widow's peak and cascaded into a thousand unruly layers that pricked at her cheeks and neck like tentacles. She looked like an extra on *Star Trek.*

"It's…it's *big hair,*" she stammered into the mirror.

"Uh-huh," Naomi intoned professionally. "Big is back. 'Course, even with the perm, I had to use a lot of volumizer."

AFTER BATTLING ALL WEEKEND to beat the mess on her head into submission, Danni showed up at her office Monday morning with two ridiculous little clips pulling her new bangs back from her forehead. She had seriously considered wearing a surgical cap for the next six months.

"What happened to your hair?" her staff asked in unison. The morning bustle of the office abruptly ceased, and they were all staring at her as if she'd walked in naked.

"Dr. Danni got a bad haircut," she snapped. "Now let's get to work."

But, as usual, Carol was on to her. Danni saw her eyeing the nails and the earrings. She poked her head into Danni's office after the last patient had gone. "George and the boys are at a ball game. Let's go eat. My treat."

As soon as Danni had taken a few bites of the comforting Mexican food, she confessed. "Jackie thought I needed fixing up. I let her drag me on a makeover spree.''

"So this is Jackie's handiwork.'' Carol brandished a tortilla chip to indicate Danni's hair.

"Yeah. Permed, highlighted, and—'' what had that woman called it? *"—volumized.''* Danni made a sour face and lifted a tassel of bangs that had escaped the clips. "Cute, huh?''

"Adorable. But the nails really aren't bad.''

"You should see my pedicure.''

"Pedicure?'' Carol stopped eating and gave Danni a skeptical look. "Why all this frou-frou grooming all of a sudden?''

Danni blushed, shoved in a mouthful of chili.

"It's the man thing, isn't it?'' Carol asked.

"The *man* thing? Now *you* sound like Jackie. She wants to turn me into some kind of mantrap. Besides, I told you it's not just a man, it's a family I want.''

Carol's eyes grew soft with understanding. "Oh? Well, I don't recommend it, but a family can be had without a man.'' She reached across the table, squeezed Danni's forearm and continued more quietly. "Come on. You're an obstetrician. Several unwanted babies a year slip through your hands.''

Danni bit her lip and considered that. As if she hadn't a thousand times before. She'd placed a few adoptable babies with single mothers. Those cases had filled her with joy. Why couldn't she just do the same thing for herself? She took a huge gulp of her iced tea. "Okay. I do want the man. I want a husband *and* a family. Okay?'' She looked down at the napkin in her lap. "I just... I just..." She smoothed the cloth. "The truth is, nobody ever asks me out." She was silent for a moment, then continued.

"Unfortunately, all the men I meet are soon-to-be fathers. And all the men I already know are either attached or they consider me a good buddy."

Carol could sympathize. She'd been in Danni's shoes herself, and her heart ached for the younger woman. All her own male friends from high school and church had known her as the studious overweight girl who would listen to their troubles—usually about other girls.

But then had come that glorious summer when she'd met George. The summer when she'd forgotten about her weight, forgotten about her social life, gone off to be a camp counselor, decided she'd spend the summer hiking with kids, being free and healthy. By the time she'd met George, she was tanned, firm, and vigorous. And because she'd thought she'd never see George again after camp ended, she had let herself relax around him. She'd flirted, been *silly,* and *fun,* and *feminine.*

Even now, she remembered the first time he'd asked her to dance at the camp social. Remembered how it had felt to dance with him, to be close to him, remembered his hand lightly resting on her hip when they'd ordered ice cream in town, remembered their first kiss. And that final stroll beside the lake when he'd proposed. It had all been so thrilling!

She looked Danni over now, with real compassion in her eyes. "Danni, have you ever considered that *maybe* you're sending the wrong signals?"

"Uh-oh." Danni started filling a fajita. "Signals. That sounds like what Jackie said. She said I needed *advertising.* Perfume and…*purple heels,* for crying out loud."

"Purple heels? Oh, for heaven's sake. What does that child know? I'm talking about healthy feminine signals, coming from real feminine confidence."

"I'm *confident,*" Danni defended as she bit off a corner of the fajita and chewed.

Carol stared at her. "I said *feminine* confidence."

Danni swallowed and looked miserable. "To tell you the truth, I don't have the slightest idea what you mean by that. I always assumed I could be myself and get a man. My mother always says there are plenty of fish in the sea."

"There *are,* honey. There *are.* And you should always be yourself, but when you go fishing…" Carol paused. "How do I say this? When you go fishing, you have to take some good bait."

"Okay," Danni said despite her misgivings—she hated the sound of the word *bait.* "What do you have in mind?"

What Carol had in mind almost caused Danni to choke on the mouthful of food she was chewing.

"I was thinking—" Carol smiled a slow, cunning—Danni thought maybe even a little fiendish— smile "—of putting you on a diet."

"A diet! You, of all people," Danni sputtered, "suggesting a diet. You're always saying weight's not an issue to a happy woman, how your husband loves you no matter what your weight is, how *long ago* you set aside those false notions about 'thin' equals 'attractive'—''

Carol held up a palm to halt her. ''We're not talking about *my* weight, here. And the diet isn't so you can attract a man. It's to make you feel good about yourself—healthier, happier. *That's* real feminine confidence. How about it? Just a little diet?''

BUT WHAT CAROL HAD in mind wasn't just ''a little diet.''

The next day after work she dragged Danni to Super Sports where she convinced her to buy enough exercise equipment to open her own gym.

''You have to commit,'' Carol said cheerfully while Danni wrote the astronomical check and arranged to have the stuff installed in the sunny southern bedroom upstairs.

The next day she persuaded Danni that they needed to take a long lunch, and told Jackie exactly what to cook for it while Carol and Danni were upstairs ''doing Danni's workout.''

''That woman's gonna *kill* you,'' Jackie complained a few days later while she rebelliously scooped homemade chocolate chip cookies onto a platter. ''One cup of steamed broccoli—'' she mimicked Carol's throaty voice ''—three ounces of broiled flounder, and ten—count 'em—*ten* green grapes.''

''I think it's already working,'' Danni said, but she nibbled on a cookie anyway.

Carol had a royal fit when she discovered the

cookies. She hauled them upstairs to "dispose" of them herself while she bossed Danni through her aerobics.

"You're tough!" Carol boomed around a mouthful of cookie. "You're pumped! You're buff! You're a lean, mean machine!" Carol took a big bite of cookie and Danni kicked higher, sharper. "You're sweating! Asking for more! You have the eye of the tiger! Grrrr—"

"Oh, shut the hell up!" Danni shouted, snatching a cookie and cramming it in her mouth.

After that, Carol decided she was setting a bad example as a coach, and Jackie decided if she was going have to cook diet food, she might as well eat it, too.

So, the three of them agreed to stretch and sweat and starve together.

Carol became a regular drill sergeant about the exercises, and Jackie got just plain vicious about the diet. Paper-thin tomato slices. Low-fat cream cheese spread in a transparent film. Sugar in any form banished.

Danni hated every minute of it.

But after a mere ten days of this torture, the results were definitely starting to show: Danni's skin was glowing, her green eyes were clear, and her slacks seemed looser. And she did feel healthier, happier.

And the fireman, of all people, was the first to notice.

CHAPTER FIVE

THE HEAD NURSE IN THE emergency room called upstairs herself.

"Have you seen Dr. Goodlove this morning?" she asked the young ward clerk, who hung up the phone, whirled her chair around and repeated the whole juicy conversation for the entire staff.

"That good-lookin' fireman—you know, the one that looks like Tom Selleck?—he's down in the E.R. to get his sutures removed, insisting that Dr. Goodlove do it herself. Says—get this—he likes her *laugh.*"

"Woooo!" the staff all crooned and turned to Danni, who stood at the chest-high desk, writing a note on a chart.

"I *never* laugh, and you all know it," she quipped without glancing up from her work.

But as soon as she finished examining a patient in labor, she hurried downstairs, telling herself she was agreeing to do this out of simple curiosity. Was the guy really as gorgeous as she'd remembered?

Oh my, yes. He really *was.*

He was waiting behind a curtain, sitting up on a gurney, shirtless, with his legs dangling in snug jeans and cowboy boots. Danni decided his chest was even more amazing than she'd remembered—well-defined pectorals tapering down into hard ridges of the intercostals, small dark nipples, that perfect pattern of hair, and so *tanned*—or was that his natural skin color?

Danni grabbed up the chart and spoke to him without looking up from the pages. "Mr. Creed, I trust everything healed nicely."

"You *are* Dr. Goodlove, aren't you?" he answered.

She glanced up at him and only then did she realize that he was staring at her somewhat incredulously.

"The same woman who stitched me up?" he asked.

"Yes." Danni frowned.

"You look so...so different."

"Well—" she smiled "—you were drugged the first time we met."

"No, really." He tilted his head, studying her, like a painter assessing a model. "You look really...different."

Danni felt a small surge of satisfaction. "Just a few pounds lighter."

She took his arm and examined the nearly-healed burns, the well-mended suture line. As she traced her fingers over his firm, smooth skin she wondered why she was feeling so self-conscious. He was only a man. But when she glanced up into those blue eyes, which were peering at her intently, she knew why. He was not just any man, he was the first man, ever, to actually cause her breathing to become un-steady.

He leaned forward and glanced down at her hips, and Danni felt her cheeks grow warm. "If you say so," he replied. "But there's something else. Hey!" He pointed with his free hand. "It's your hair, isn't it? It was a lot longer before, and—" he squinted "—it was...different."

"Yeah." Danni reached up and flipped one of the offending strands back. "It's *different*, all right. The haircut-of-the-month featured in *Beauty Doo*."

He laughed as she turned to unwrap the suture removal tray. "I take it you don't like it," he said.

Danni shrugged, slipped on her gloves. "Thank the Lord *I* don't have to look at it."

"Well, it's kind of pretty."

When she cast a disbelieving look over her shoulder, he protested, "Really." Then he gave her a teasing, dimpled grin. "But personally, I like my women more...natural."

Danni turned her blushing face back toward the tray and gathered up tweezers, suture-removal scissors, gauze. "Well, this is anything but natural. It takes a gallon of superglue and an Act of Congress to make it behave."

"So—" he tried to lean around to see her face "—this is not the real you. That's good. I liked the tourniquet better," he added, which made Danni smirk, remembering what a mess her hair had been when they'd met in the E.R.

She turned to him and reached up to snip the first suture. "Nope. This is certainly *not* the real me."

"That's good," he repeated—so quietly, so sincerely, that her hands stilled. Their eyes met.

They seemed suddenly to have run out of banter and fell into an awkward silence. Danni worked on his arm and, with a mixture of embarrassment, building excitement and hope, mulled over the fact that he actually remembered her makeshift ponytail holder.

His eyes traveled slowly from his biceps to her face while she worked. And just as she had on the night when they'd met, Danni tried to keep her mind firmly on what she was doing. But, with his eyes only inches from hers, watching every move she made, it was an effort. And this time instead of smoke, he smelled like English Leather. Had he slapped on the aftershave because of *her?*

When she'd finished removing all twenty-four sutures, she probed the area gently with her fingers to test the integrity of her work. He didn't even grimace.

"You've healed quite nicely," she said.

"Are you married?" he asked.

Danni, caught off guard, even a little shocked by his directness, managed not to show her reaction. "You know," she joked, "my mother warned me about firemen." She looked at him with wide-eyed mock seriousness.

"Oh yeah?" he challenged.

"Yeah. Always rushing into hot spots."

"Are you married?" he repeated. "Involved with someone? Yes or no?"

"N-n-no," she stammered, trapped by those eyes.

"Then could I call you sometime?"

"Call me? Well...I don't know...." Danni didn't know why in the world she was hesitating. "You'd probably just end up having me paged. I'm...I'm an awfully busy woman."

He hopped off the gurney. "Yeah, I guess you are," he said as he tugged a navy blue fireman's T-shirt over his head, then stretched it down over his massive chest. "Thanks for taking my stitches out."

With a sense of dismay, Danni realized she'd succeeded in putting him off. She wanted to kick herself. "You're welcome," she said lamely to his back while he jammed the tail of the T-shirt into the waistband of his jeans.

"Have a good day, Doctor." He turned to her and nodded. His mouth formed a tight line of disappointment as he picked up his ball cap.

"You, too." Danni turned her burning face to his chart, and before she could think of some way to recover the situation, he pushed the curtain aside and left the cubicle.

She stared down at his intake info. Why the heck didn't she give him her phone number like any normal woman would?

She noted *his* phone number, debating the ethics of copying it from the chart.

"Listen."

Danni whirled around at the sound of his voice.

He had come back behind the curtain, so quietly she hadn't heard him.

"You probably *are* really busy. Tell you what, let's do it this way." He held a business card out to her. "Why don't you call me if you feel like getting together sometime?"

Danni looked down at the card. It had the city seal of Tulsa in one corner and in the center it read: Matthew Creed, Firefighter. The address, fax, and phone number of his station were in the other corners. *Firemen carry business cards?* "Oh. I—I couldn't bother you at work," she stammered.

"No, you couldn't." He flipped the card over. "That's why I wrote this stuff on the back." His home phone number was written in a neat, bold hand. Below that, of all things, he'd written an e-mail address. *Firemen have e-mail?*

He smiled when she looked up with a tiny, puzzled frown. "The e-mail's for the truly shy." His smile softened. "Is that the problem? Are you 'truly shy'?"

"No!" Danni protested and took the card from him. *Shy* was definitely not a word she would use to describe herself, except that right now her cheeks were blazing and she couldn't come up with a single word to say.

"Well, then, you're not stuck-up, are you?" He grinned.

"No!" Danni protested again and found herself grinning back at him. This guy really was *cute.*

"Okay, then." He took a big breath that stretched the T-shirt across his chest. "Not shy. Not stuck-up. So call me.'' He winked and walked away.

No, I am not shy, Danni thought. *And I don't think I'm stuck-up. What I am,* she admitted as she watched his broad back and long legs, *is scared clean out of my wits.*

MATT FOUND THE ELEVATORS, punched the up button, and planted his feet in a wide stance as he waited for one to arrive. Two young female physical therapists were chatting and waiting for an elevator going down. One of them, a pretty, athletic-looking blonde, smiled and said, ''Hi,'' to Matt.

He responded with a polite ''Hi,'' then took a couple of long strides to the nearby window and pretended to look out.

Damn. He should have asked Dr. Goodlove about the twins' condition while he'd had the chance. She probably thought he was completely cold, not to have even mentioned them.

But the woman was so beautiful he couldn't seem to think straight around her. It had been a long time since he'd been this interested in a woman, and it scared the hell out of him. *A doctor.* Was he crazy?

Well, at least he'd given her his card and put the ball in her court. *This time* he was going to be sure. No more messing up his life. He was getting too old for that.

The elevator bell dinged and, as soon as the doors closed and he was alone, hurtling skyward to the pediatric burn unit, his thoughts focused on the twins.

Over the past ten days, while he'd been home on medical leave, he'd thought of little else. Had he saved their lives, he worried, only to leave them to a future of endless pain, surgeries, rehabilitation, scarring, misery? When he'd gone in to see the babies last week, the scene had been haunting.

After he'd changed into scrubs, a tall, wiry nurse had given him a brisk rundown on how to do a surgical scrub. When he'd finished that, she'd helped him don the sterile garb—gown, mask, hat, gloves, paper shoes—and he'd followed her into the pediatric intensive care unit. All this trouble, Matt thought as he hurried to keep up with the nurse whose paper gown billowed out at her sides like wings, because the mother had given her permission for him to be in the room. And what would he say to her? What good could he do?

The room seemed bathed in bright light and a torrent of perpetual whispering white noise—monitors and pumps beeping and clicking, the rhythmic whoosh of two respirators. A nurse was there— busy, busy. He focused on the mother first; he couldn't look directly at the loosely gauzed little mummies in the two crib-size beds. The mother's burns looked better than the last time he'd seen her—they had been mostly second degree—but otherwise she looked considerably worse. Exhausted. She got out of her rocking chair and hugged him, their sterile gowns rustling between them. Who was taking care of her other baby now, Matt wondered, the one born a few days ago?

Matt released her and, silently, she took his hand and led him to the beds. It seemed important to her that he look. He'd seen burn victims before—other firefighters, mostly. Victims who had healed eventually. Nothing like this.

The twins were swaddled from head to toe in the gauze—even their eyes were covered—and under that, Matt knew, were the pigskin grafts. They were flat on their backs with their small feet supported on footrests and their tiny arms strapped out to their sides, the pose of the crucified. The kneecap of one baby was exposed. Perfect skin with no damage. That was all Matt could see. Matt focused on that little kneecap, concentrated on it.

Finally he whispered, "How are they doing?" Because, what else could he say?

Instantly, one twin's heartbeat shot up—the out-of-control beeping was terrifying—and Matt understood why the mother hadn't spoken. The nurse busied herself adjusting an IV drip.

Suddenly the beds started humming, and Matt startled again, wondering if he'd set something else off, until one side of each mattress tilted up. Then he remembered—automatic pressure beds.

Another nurse came in. She'd obviously been on a cigarette break, and in this sterile room, to Matt the smell seemed as odious as a skunk. He didn't want anything contaminating the twins environment. She signaled for them to leave. Report time, he supposed.

Out in the waiting room, he had told the mother, before he'd left, to take things one day at a time. He needed to take his own advice, didn't he?

The elevator doors opened, facing the large chest-high counter that wrapped around the nurses' station. A man and woman, both wearing blue scrubs and all the other telltale paraphernalia of busy nurses, stood behind it, concentrating on a chart they had opened on the counter.

"I think we should call Dr. Miller and see what he thinks about staggering the dose," the man was saying.

The woman looked up at Matt and asked, "May we help you?"

"I'm here to check on the Taylor twins," Matt said quietly. "I wondered if I could look in on them."

The two nurses exchanged a sad, secretive glance that gave Matt a sinking feeling in the pit of his stomach.

"Who are you?" the male nurse asked kindly.

"I'm Matthew Creed, the firefighter who rescued them. I've been up here before. Their mother gave her permission for me to see them."

The female nurse was flipping through something below Matt's line of vision. "Yes, Mr. Creed—" she looked up "—your name is on the Kardex, but I'm afraid…" The nurses exchanged that look again and just then an older couple who looked like grandparents came out of a nearby room and started walking down the hall toward them.

"Let's step in here, okay?" the male nurse said, indicating a small cubicle off the nurses' station.

Matt followed the nurse inside. There was a large window in the wall, apparently soundproof, because when the nurse closed the door Matt could no longer hear the phone beeping or the voices of the grandparents as they stood earnestly talking to the female nurse.

"Have a seat, Mr. Creed," the nurse said as he lowered himself into an institutional plastic chair.

Matt took the other plastic chair, facing the window, and awkwardly arranged himself—arms folded across his chest, feet planted wide—for what he guessed was going to be a blow.

"Mr. Creed, the Taylor twins died an hour ago, within minutes of each other."

Matt leaned forward, propped his elbows on his knees, and hung his head. He honestly didn't even know what he felt most at that moment: relief for the babies or sadness for their mother.

God, sometimes he hated his job.

"The hospital media coordinator has asked us not to speak to anyone about it yet," the nurse continued. "She wants to control media access to the mother if she can. This case has generated a lot of local publicity, as you know. But I figured you, of all people, deserved to be told. I'm sorry."

"It's okay," Matt said, when it was anything but.

Burn-unit nurses and firefighters, sharing a common enemy, knew how to talk to each other. "The twins couldn't sustain any kind of fluid or electrolyte levels," the nurse explained. "They'd been in kidney failure for a week.'' Then he clamped his beefy hand on Matt's broad shoulder. ''We all do our best, but sometimes we lose.''

''I know.'' Matt had started to think about the babies, how little they'd felt when he'd lifted them out of their smoldering crib, how limp, and tears stung his eyes.

''Listen.'' He cleared his throat and stood. ''I really appreciate your telling me.'' He extended his hand to the nurse and they shook hands. ''I won't tell the other firefighters until your media person has had time to deal with it.''

''I appreciate that,'' the nurse said, opening the door.

A ward clerk and a couple of nurses gave Matt sympathetic smiles. Matt knew he looked stricken, knew his nose was as red as a cherry. It always turned red like that when he tried to suppress tears.

As he walked toward the elevators he realized that, just like after the bombing, he had no place to go except a lonely apartment, and no one to share this with. Later there would be Ty, of course, and the other guys. They'd understand the hollow sense of loss, the horrible ambivalence. But now, there was no—his mouth twisted in a derisive smile—''significant other.''

An irrational urge grabbed him as he stepped onto the elevator. He wanted, very badly, to push the button for the fourth floor—the OB ward—and find Danni Goodlove and tell her. She'd listen, he felt sure. There was something about her—something deep. She'd understand. But he could be wrong—hadn't he been *way* wrong before? They hardly knew each other, and she hadn't seemed too keen when he'd mentioned getting together for a date. If he showed up now, only minutes after he'd left the next step to her, with his red nose and these unshed tears threatening, wanting…what? Well, sympathy, obviously.

He pushed the ground-floor button. He had promised himself he'd never chase a woman again, no matter how attracted he was to her, and he was sticking to that.

As the elevator went down, he dug his keys out of his jeans pocket. On the way home he'd stop and get Mrs. Taylor a sympathy card.

CHAPTER SIX

CAROL STOPPED THE treadmill and leaned on the handlebars. "Excuse me, but isn't that the whole idea behind suffering the tortures of the damned, here? To attract some bona fide male attention?"

"I thought you said all this diet and exercise stuff was to boost my self-esteem, not so I could attract a man," Danni countered.

"Don't be cute. You know what I mean."

Danni stopped her stationary bike long enough to think. All right. She knew her response to Matthew Creed's interest was...weird. How to explain this to Carol? How a woman could want something so badly, yet be scared to death of it at the same time.

From the corner where she was lifting weights, Jackie inserted her two cents' worth. "If a man gives you his number, honey, he wants you to *use* it."

"I don't know." Danni's shoulders slumped and she wiped a trickle of sweat from her temple with her towel. "I just feel so...uncomfortable around him. Like I can't finish my sentences. Maybe it's just that we're so different. Maybe he's just not my type." Danni sighed and pressed the towel against her face, then mumbled, "Not that I know what my type is."

Carol and Jackie exchanged knowing glances.

"Listen, honey—" Carol started the treadmill again "—Matthew Creed is *any* woman's type. Maybe you're not used to the male species coming on to you like that. But keep this up—" she gestured for Danni to resume her pedaling "—and you'll get used to it. You'll have more male attention than—"

"A heifer in a bull pen!" Jackie cackled.

Danni lowered the towel and scowled at her. "A *heifer?*"

"Well, okay, a really *slim,* really healthy heifer," Jackie amended with a grin. Danni had to laugh.

But what Carol had predicted turned out to be true. Another two weeks on her diet, and even Dr. Bryant noticed Danni's new look—and commented on it.

She was leaning over the desk in the doctor's dictation area one morning, reaching for a chart, when he came up behind her, made a frame with his palms and said, "That is one stunning picture."

Danni straightened and skewered him with a frosty stare, but felt herself blushing anyway. No man had ever talked to her like that, and while part of her was irked, she was shocked to discover that a tiny part of her was flattered, too.

"Just a compliment." Bryant raised his hands in self-defense. "Too bad—" he backed up "—it's wasted on the Ice Queen."

Danni narrowed her eyes. Their equal positions,

and the resulting competition—sometimes friendly, sometimes not—had bred a certain familiarity, but this was too much.

He reached around her and picked up a chart, then shook his head. "Nothing to get your undies in a wad about, *Doctor*."

"The condition of my undergarments is none of your business, Doctor," she answered calmly. "And keep your opinions about my anatomy to yourself." She proceeded to jerk charts out of the cubicles.

"Well, pardon me for noticing," Bryant said in a low, confidential tone. "But what's all this exercise and diet about, if it's not to attract a man's attention?" He took a step toward her.

Danni swiveled a chair between them, then sat down, snatched up the handset, flipped open the chart, and started to dictate.

Bryant's attitude suddenly seemed genuinely conciliatory. "I meant no offense. Honest. You really do look terrific."

Danni didn't glance up from her chart. Out of the corner of her eye she saw Bryant give an exaggerated shrug. Then he walked around to the nurses' station and started kidding with the staff in a too-loud voice.

The incident niggled at Danni as she read the routine admission notes. Carol may have predicted that the new Danni would attract male attention, but somehow, the attention Bryant had given her wasn't exactly what Danni had had in mind. Was being ogled the price of being an attractive woman? The more she thought about Bryant's behavior, the madder she got. But, she had to admit, she liked herself slimmer; she certainly felt better. And she was going to stay on her program and not let unwanted attention from men like Bryant change her mind.

After that encounter, Danni added new fuel to her fitness campaign. She stepped up the exercise routine to wilder music. She and Carol started jogging after work three days a week, and Danni insisted on going out to the stables herself to groom her chocolate-brown sorrel, Quick, just to burn the calories.

In only six weeks, Danni's body had become amazingly fit. She would never be tiny—she had inherited her father's rawboned frame—but her figure was a shapely size ten and she had a new, attractive date wardrobe hanging in her closet.

But still no dates.

One rare Friday night when Dr. Stone had actually agreed to take calls for the entire weekend, Jackie came bouncing down the stairs dressed in a leopard-print jumpsuit. Danni was slouching around in her old pink chenille robe, sipping a second gin and tonic.

"Going on safari?" Danni smirked and swirled the ice in her glass as she followed Jackie down the long entryway hall.

"You could say that," Jackie called cheerfully over her shoulder. "You have to go out into the jungle to hunt." She stopped at the front-hall mirror to pat her elaborate cornrows and adjust her huge copper-and-ivory earrings, and when she caught sight of Danni's cynical expression reflected over her shoulder, she turned on her. "Listen. I go where the men are. Is that so wrong?"

Danni sipped her drink. "Carol claims a woman has to let the men come to her."

"Well, Carol's not dating in the nineties, is she? Let's be honest. The real trouble is, you think you're too much of a *lady* to go after men."

Danni stepped back and knocked her pesky bangs out of her eyes. "I do not! I mean, you're wrong."

Jackie gave her a skeptical once-over, then pointed at the highball glass. "What is that? Gin? That stuff's fattening, you know." She snatched the tumbler and sniffed.

"I put a lot of tonic in it—a lot," Danni said as Jackie whirled away and marched back to the kitchen.

Danni rounded the corner just as Jackie was rinsing the glass and plunking it in the dishwasher. "Looks to me like you've had enough 'tonic,'" she said as she closed the door.

"I won't argue with that." Danni went to the fridge and pulled out a bottle of spring water.

Jackie looked chagrined. "Sorry, Doc. I guess I still have a tendency to freak out about drinking, after Willie and all."

Danni waved a palm at her. "Forget it." She took a long draw on the water bottle. "That stuff *is* fattening. I'm just wallowing."

"Want me to fix you something to eat before I go?" Jackie offered kindly. "Or...or maybe you'd like to come with me and my friends? It's just us girls."

Danni cocked an eyebrow. Had she sunk to this? Being invited to tag along with a bunch of girls barely out of their teens because her housekeeper felt sorry for her?

"Thanks, Jackie." She smiled and took another swig of water. "It's sweet of you to ask. But I have a ton of reading to catch up on in there." She jerked her head toward her office. "In fact, you can take some extra time off this weekend if you like. Stone's on call until Sunday, and I can heat up my own diet dinners." She turned toward her brand-new upright freezer.

"Okay," Jackie said quietly from behind her.

A moment later the front door closed with a soft click, as if not to disturb a sick person.

Maybe she thinks I am sick, Danni thought as she pulled out a frozen diet entrée. After all, I can't even get a simple date on a Friday night. She tossed the dinner in the microwave.

"Lord. What's the matter with me?" she said aloud as she stared at the digital numbers ticking down, thinking that the years of her life seemed to be slipping away just as fast. "Get a grip," she mumbled. "Finding a mate is just another goal."

She thought of how she'd made her way through medical school and a tough residency on sheer will-power. When had she become the kind of woman to sit hunched over a TV dinner, feeling sorry for herself?

Time to take action, she told herself, pulling out

her telephone directory. She called every contact she thought might be able to help and told them in no uncertain terms that Danni Goodlove was in the market for a date—and not another perfect, boring, safe "Wesley Fuerborne" of her mother's choosing, either. Danni was ready for some excitement.

BY THE FOLLOWING afternoon, an old friend had come through—with an accountant who had "great potential." Danni's first ever blind date.

And the worst ever, she hoped.

Within five minutes she realized that "great potential" meant skinny as a stick and hopelessly compulsive. His tapered fingers perpetually smoothed back his hair, picked lint and straightened silverware—not just his own, but Danni's, too—until she wanted to snap those fingers in half.

The conversation over dinner reminded her of the times she'd attempted to start a fire in her father's enormous stone fireplace: Danni would keep stuffing in paper and striking more matches, but in the end she always produced only smoke. No heat.

The worst part was the way this guy behaved. He sniffed her. He pawed her. Once too often, he laughed nervously while his glittering gaze fixed directly on her bosom.

Danni felt as if *she* were the main course, and long before dessert arrived, she was ready to bolt for home.

She counterattacked subtly at first—leaving her silverware helter-skelter around her plate, dropping her napkin on the floor—but finally, on the way home, she messily unloaded the contents of her purse all over the front seat of his car, pretending that she couldn't find her house key. "My purse is *always* such a mess."

That should do the trick, she thought, but just to be on the safe side, she left a crumpled tissue on the floorboard.

"Good night," she told him succinctly at her front door, and after an excruciating moment of averting her lips from his and fumbling to get her key in the lock, she slipped into the sanctuary of her home, wishing never to leave again.

She retreated to the enormous master suite, ran a bubble bath and decided to soak away her misery. After she lowered herself into the steamy water, she thought again of that fireman in the emergency room, Matthew Creed.

She couldn't get him out of her mind. Why?

She smiled at her reflection in the mirrors that surrounded the tub. Gee. Could it be those yard-wide shoulders, those powerful legs, that movie-star face? But a hunk like that would never give a woman like her the time of day. Or would he? Hadn't he already?

Danni slowly rose, stood shin-deep in the water and surveyed her trim new form, covered with streams of bubbles. She ran a hand slowly over one hip, and down the side of one long, slick thigh. *Oh, no,* she thought. *There's not a thing wrong with me.* True, she'd successfully sublimated her normal urges for so many years that she hardly knew what to do with them.

Intellectually, as a physician, she knew her repressed love life was a direct result of Lisa's death. And surely it was no accident that she'd chosen to become an obstetrician.

But emotionally, it was all much harder to face. She could see her sister now, as clearly as if she were looking in the mirror and brushing her glorious hair, yammering to Danni in that engaging way she had. Everything was a joke to Lisa, and serious, studious Danni had loved her boisterous big sister for that. Lisa always got the boys—any boy she wanted, any time she wanted.

To keep from crying, Danni pressed her lips into a hard line. What difference did all of that make now? Lisa had died so long ago—twenty years ago this December.

But Danni knew her sister's untimely pregnancy and death still haunted her and prevented her from allowing herself to become emotionally involved. How many times had she had this argument with herself? Reasoned it all out? And how many times had her pain and her grief—her *fear*—won out? She looked directly into her own eyes, which reflected that old pain back at her from the mirror.

But love was what she really wanted, wasn't it? *A man* was what she wanted. A real man.

She wrapped herself in a thick white towel, brushed her hair for three vicious strokes, then slammed the brush down on the marble countertop and marched into the bedroom. She opened her bedside drawer where the pale gray business card was carefully tucked away, but she didn't really need it.

She'd memorized his home phone number the minute he'd handed it to her.

She snatched up the phone and before the clawing monster of fear could win yet another battle, she called Matthew Creed.

CHAPTER SEVEN

"HELLO?"

A *woman's* voice! Sounding husky. Tipsy, maybe. Or...

For a split second Danni wondered if—*hoped*—she'd punched in the number wrong.

"Uh, is Matthew Creed there, please?" she asked. Then she bit her lip, held her breath, and prayed she *had* gotten the wrong number.

There was no answer, merely a rustling sound like...sheets! And before she could hang up, his deep voice spoke: "Hello?"

Oh, good heavens! What had she done? She punched the disconnect button like some adolescent making a prank call. She tossed the phone on the bed and stared at it as if it were a live grenade.

Then it rang.

She jumped back and clutched the towel around her breasts.

It rang again.

She felt duty-bound, as a doctor, to answer. Even though Stone was on call, he might have a question about one of her private patients, and she'd turned her pager off. By the time the phone rang the third time, she'd mustered the courage to pick it up and answer evenly, "This is Dr. Goodlove."

"Oh…" It was his voice, sounding sleepy, too, and thick, liquored up, or— She didn't want to think about it. "So it was *you.*"

Danni felt her pulse skyrocket and her throat constrict.

"Caller ID," he answered her silence.

"Yes, uh… We got disconnected."

"Oh. Well, what can I do for you, Dr. Goodlove?"

Danni wanted very much to ask, *Is there a woman in bed with you?* But instead she croaked out, "I'm sorry to disturb you at home."

"That's okay," he said and she heard the rustle of sheets again. "I'm not doing anything important."

Surely a woman couldn't be anywhere in the vicinity if he was talking like that.

"So. What can I do for you?" he repeated.

In the second that she hesitated, Danni's overactive mind came up with all manner of lies: *Your wound culture came back positive. You need more antibiotics. I left a stitch in. We had an outbreak of Ebola the night you were in the E.R.* She opted for the truth. "I was wondering if we might get together for a drink sometime."

"I'd like that," he said in a low, seductive voice. "I'd like that a lot."

Oh, good heavens! What *was* she doing? She clutched the towel and the phone tighter and said, "Tomorrow night?"

"Sure. Where?"

Danni wasn't sure where. She didn't exactly ask men out for drinks every night. But she wanted to be in control, here. "Uh, let's see. Do you know where The Wild Fork is?" She bit her lip as soon as she'd said it. He was a fireman, for crying out loud. Probably hung out at Hooters after Oilers games. *The Wild Fork*—he'd love that. Trendy art and Ty Nant spring water. But it was close to her house; on her turf.

"'The Wild Fork'?" The sheets rustled again. "In Utica Square? Yeah. You wanna meet there?"

"Around seven?"

"Sure. What kind of hairdo should I look for this time?"

Danni smiled. He really *was* cute.

"Spiked. Bright green," she said. She wasn't exactly a dullard, either, she thought, congratulating herself for ending this ordeal with at least a smidgen of style.

DANNI HAD ALWAYS THOUGHT of The Wild Fork as a cozy place with great ambience and great food where a woman alone could eat a nice meal without feeling conspicuous. But tonight, as she sat waiting for Matt, seeing it as he might see it, the atmosphere struck her as snooty and trying a little too hard.

A series of molded Plexiglas female busts in neon colors graced the walls of the room where Danni had requested a table by the window. Had those hideous things always been there? She got up and moved to the chair that faced them, so that when he joined her he'd be looking the other way, toward the foyer, which she now noticed had wood-work painted in a most unnatural shade of magenta. The color had always looked festive, classy—even daring—to her before. Now it looked goofy and affected.

She glanced down into her lap and hoped the little black velvet dress was the right choice. What if he showed up in jeans? Then she checked out her reflection in the window, which was foggy and wa-ter streaked. The weather certainly wasn't cooper-ating. Rain and more rain. Cold, uninviting for an evening out. Maybe he wouldn't even show up.

Sometimes her new image was still a shock to her, even reflected in a watery window as it was now. Without her thick glasses she thought she looked wide-eyed; vulnerable, even. She tucked strands of the hated hairdo behind her ears. Jackie had fiddled with it at the last minute, then insisted she wear these oversize earrings. The hammered sil-ver glittered in the reflected light from the candle on the table. *"I like my women natural"*—his words came back to her. Well, tonight she liked herself done up. She turned away from her reflec-tion, took a quick sip of wine and tried to relax.

Before long the aroma of gourmet food made her mouth water. But when she glanced at an artfully arranged plate of lamb rib chops being served at a nearby table she worried that the fancy food might merely annoy him.

The only men in the place looked effeminate, except that two or three of them had given her—a woman in a sexy black dress, sitting alone over a glass of Merlot—inquisitive looks.

Danni had eaten alone plenty of times—no problem there. But she had never waited alone for a date. It was nerve-racking. She began to regret her decision to arrive early. That had seemed like the polite thing to do—after all, *she* had asked *him*—but now, as she waited, all manner of doubts assailed her. A mere twenty-four hours ago, asking the fireman on a date had seemed free and bold. Now, she couldn't imagine *what* had possessed her. She asked herself for the hundredth time, why *had* she done it?

But she only had time to worry for another second before she spotted him, striding across puddles as he rounded the corner to the treed courtyard outside the restaurant window. He was wearing a loose barn jacket and crisp chinos, and was carrying an umbrella. He looked magnificent.

That was why she had done it. *He* was why.

He slowed his gait long enough to admire a large brass sculpture of a young girl holding a bird—a move that surprised and pleased Danni. Then he noticed her, smiling at him through the window, and his face lit up in an answering smile that melted her heart. Maybe this wasn't going to be so bad after all.

It wasn't. Except that Matt made fiendish fun of the dainty food and at one point said "artsy-fartsy" loud enough to cause some nearby diners to turn their heads.

And later, he actually whistled when he stepped

into her foyer and looked around at her luxurious home. Danni couldn't help but admire his openness. And it was that candor—and his ability to make her laugh—that had kept her intrigued all through drinks, dinner, and their stroll under his umbrella around Utica Square. After only a couple of hours of getting acquainted, Danni had felt comfortable enough to invite him to her home for a late-night coffee.

Pearl and Smoky padded in from the utility room and immediately allowed Matthew to pet them, which counted as another plus. They weaved around most strange men in a suspicious figure-eight pattern and had actually snarled at the accountant.

"That's Pearl, and that's Smoky," Danni said as she moved around the room, turning on lamps.

He bent down on one knee and gave both animals a good rub. "You're good old doggies, I bet."

"Okay, go lie down!" Danni commanded the dogs, but they stuck by Matt, nuzzling him.

Disgusted, Danni marched over and collared them. "You'd think, for what I pay their trainer," she said as she struggled with the sleek canines, "that these dogs would learn to obey."

"They probably smell Miss Verbena."

"Miss Verbena?" Danni asked over her shoulder as she trotted the dogs off toward the utility room.

"She's my dog," he said, following her. "Hey, guess what?" He stood in the center of her unusual, multiangled hallway and spread his arms wide as a candid smile spread across his handsome features. "I *know* this place!"

"I beg your pardon?" Danni wanted to pinch herself. She'd been talking like that all night, like some starchy old-maid librarian. Even the two glasses of Merlot hadn't relaxed her. She imagined he was just about bored out of his mind with her, but she had to give him credit, he had remained unrelentingly cheerful.

"I've been in this house before."

"Really? When? I've only lived in it a few months."

"During the remodeling work. You changed the landscaping and the entrance so much that at first I didn't recognize the house, but I refinished these floors myself." He squatted with the grace of a jungle cat and stroked a shining plank of oak at his feet. "This color... I *love* this color. Medium walnut, right?"

Danni had to find her tongue to answer. She'd almost swallowed it, watching his movements— watching the way his jacket molded itself to his broad back, the way the muscles of his thighs stretched the chinos. "Yes, uh... Yes. Medium walnut. You worked on these floors?"

"Yeah. My best friend, Ty—he's a fireman, too—he and I run a floor-finishing business on the side." He stood and brushed his palms together, though Jackie kept the place as clean as a surgical suite. "Actually, we've branched out into all kinds of renovation work on our days off. Firemen have funny schedules, you know—big chunks of time off between shifts."

"Yes, I know. So, you finished the floors in my house?"

"Yeah. They said some rich doctor was remodeling the place. It never dawned on me the rich doctor would be a beautiful woman."

Danni blushed, then stammered: "Well…I must say…" *Here comes that uptight librarian again.* "I… You guys did a great job. Nearly perfect."

"Nearly?"

"Well, there *is* a spot with a few tiny ripples in the polyurethane, but I covered it with an area rug."

"Really? Ty wouldn't like that. He's a perfectionist. So am I." He splayed his large hand over his chest in sincerity. "Could I look at that bad spot?"

Danni blushed. "Well, it's…it's in the master bedroom."

"Oh." He pinkened a little himself. "I don't have to look at it tonight. But why don't you give us a call sometime and let us come over and fix it?"

Feeling uptight and prudish was not the way Danni wanted to feel with him. "We can go and look at it now," she said, smiling.

He whistled again when they entered Danni's twenty-five-by-eighteen-foot master suite with double doors at one end that opened into the huge, airy, master bath.

"Wow! You have certainly brought out the full potential of this space." Danni laughed with pleasure. He'd been surprising her with comments like that all evening.

"Look at this!" he exclaimed, and went straight to the giant-pillowed window seat that was hung with muted pastel tapestries held back by enormous gold tassels. "Can you actually close it off?"

Danni smiled and nodded. He'd homed in on her favorite spot. "Sometimes, on rainy weekends, I crawl in there with a cup of herbal tea, close the drapes, and watch the rain."

"Wow. I can imagine." His eyes traveled up the ceiling-high Palladian windows that bowed out around the seat. Rows and rows of small square panes rose to the ceiling. "Who gets to wash all these?"

"Why, my maid, of course." Danni immediately wished she hadn't said it exactly that way. After all, Jackie was more than a housekeeper, she was a friend. "Her name's Jackie," Danni added in a quieter, almost-apologetic, tone.

Matt turned from the window, frowning at her. He was incredibly good-looking, even when he frowned. Danni had never seen such a handsome man, and she wondered again: What was *she* doing with him? More to the point, what was she *going to do* with him?

"Of course. Your maid," he said, with what Danni thought was a note of sarcasm. His gaze swept the windows again. "These are thermal panes?"

"Yes. Double glazed."

"How do you open them?"

"Way up at the top." Danni pointed to the long levers that operated transoms eight feet up on the wall of glass. "It's a security measure. Makes it tough to break in."

"Or get out," he mumbled as he crossed the room and leaned into her enormous bathroom. "I don't suppose there's a back door, either?" His voice echoed off the Italian-tile floor and enormous glass-block window above the tub.

"From my bathroom?"

He turned and his frown relaxed into a smile. "Just thinking like a firefighter, ma'am. Let's see the bubbles, shall we?"

"Bubbles?" Danni said stupidly, thinking that he was talking about a bath or something.

"In the floor." He took two huge strides from the bathroom door toward the Persian rug. "Didn't you say the flawed area's under this rug?"

Together, they rolled the rug up enough for Danni to show him the rough area. Matt dropped to one knee, ran his hand over the surface, and said, "This would be no problem to fix. Just let us know when it would be convenient for you and someone'll get right over here and make this right."

"Will *you* personally come and do it?" Danni spoke almost breathlessly, because her heart was pounding. When he looked up, she added, "You know—like you wanted *me* to take your stitches out."

His fingertips still rested on the rough spot, but his eyes, full of some comprehension that made Danni tremble a little inside, slowly assessed her.

Maybe she shouldn't have said that. She knew so little about men.

Without taking his eyes off her, he rose, crossed to where she stood with her arms folded over her middle.

"Yeah, my stitches," he said softly. He reached down and took her by the wrists, raised her arms away from her body, and openly looked her up and down. Danni found his frank assessment both excruciating and thrilling. "I certainly had my reasons for wanting *you* to take them out." He lifted his eyes up to her face and held her gaze. "You know, you are a very pretty lady."

Danni blushed and tried to wriggle her wrists out of his grasp. But he held on to them and lowered her arms, sliding his hands down over the tops of hers. "I'm glad you called me last night. I was just sitting around talking to Miss Verbena." He captured her gaze again, this time with a look of mischievous challenge.

"That Miss Verbena must be quite a dog." Danni raised her brows innocently. "She sounded like a woman when she answered the phone."

He threw his head back and laughed, then brought her hands to his lips and kissed her knuckles enthusiastically. To her surprise, Danni found she could tolerate this sudden intimacy because he'd prepared her so well throughout the evening: touching her fingertips while they talked over wine, lightly holding her elbow as they left the restaurant, pulling her close as they strolled the sidewalks and shared his umbrella. His touch felt way different from the accountant's. Way different.

He continued to hold her hands captive, gently rubbing her knuckles. "Tell me something," he urged. "Have you ever asked a man out before? That is, if it's any of my business."

Danni shook her head, looked down. "No."

"I've never been asked out before, either. At least not directly."

"I wasn't sure what I was going to say when I called you. I'm still not sure what I'm supposed to do."

"You know what?" He drew her hands around to his back and planted them there, then wrapped his muscular arms around her, pulling her close. Danni felt small—smaller than she ever had in a man's arms—and more sexual. Completely, utterly sexual. For the first time in her entire life. "You don't *have* to do a thing—" his voice shifted to a low murmur as he brought his mouth down on hers "—not one thing."

CHAPTER EIGHT

THAT KISS, SO SOFT AND tender one instant, so firm and demanding the next, did amazing and terrible things to Danni. It filled her with a crazy wanting...and at the same time, an indefinable fear. She pushed at his chest, wrenched her mouth free. "Wait," she said, and put her hand over her breastbone, struggling for breath.

He immediately released her. "Sure." He took a step back and looked genuinely puzzled. "I'm sorry," he added. "I guess I misread your signals."

Danni, still struggling to breathe, could only utter, "Huh?" rather stupidly.

Just then, Jackie's voice interrupted, sounding mellow and otherworldly through the intercom speaker above the light switch. "Dr. Danni? I'm home."

They both jumped.

"That's my housekeeper," Danni explained. "We always check in like that when we come through the garage door, no matter what time it is. A safety rule."

"I see," he said.

"Obstetricians keep weird hours, too."

"Right," he added. He planted his hands on his

belt, pushing his jacket back, his stance wide, like a stallion looking for a way out of the corral.

Danni crossed over to the intercom and pressed the button. "Jackie?"

"Yes, ma'am?" came the answer.

"I'm entertaining a guest. Would you make us some of that nice vanilla hazelnut coffee and serve it in the living room, please?"

There was a too-long pause and then Jackie said, "Yes, ma'am," quickly and clicked off. Danni's cheeks flamed when she realized the display on the intercom would have indicated that she was speaking from the master bedroom; then she decided things were at a sad pass when you worried about what a loosey-goosey nineteen-year-old thought of you.

Matt was cool, Danni would give him that. He behaved as if her awkward reaction to the kiss had never happened. They adjourned to the living room and kept up a polite conversation until Jackie entered, bearing a lacquered tray laden with coffee and goodies. Danni eyed the chocolate pirouettes and small wedges of chess pie and wondered what other contraband Jackie had stashed away in the kitchen.

Jackie eyed Matt while she took her time laying out napkins and pouring coffee into delicate china cups. She raised her eyebrows at Danni as she left the room.

They sipped the coffee, and Matt helped himself to the pastries, then launched into a round of amusing stories about Miss Verbena, which were designed, Danni guessed, to relax her.

"Miss Verbena is my deceased aunt's spoiled-rotten toy poodle. I made the mistake of making a deathbed promise to Aunt Opal."

"A deathbed promise?" Danni was intrigued.

"Yeah. I promised to take care of Miss Verbena for the remainder of her natural life."

Danni grinned and sipped her coffee. "And I take it Miss Verbena's somewhat of a pain."

"She whines, she shivers, she pukes—sorry." He swallowed a mouthful of pie.

"Anyway, when I took her on, I assumed she was at death's door—Aunt Opal had had that poodle as long as I could remember—and I figured, what have I got to lose? I can make an old woman happy and that obnoxious dog can't last more than a year or two, tops."

"But..." Danni prompted, sensing that the end to this story had to be as cute as the guy telling it.

"But *my* Miss Verbena is actually the *second* Miss Verbena. It seems Aunt Opal's first poodle died while I was being distracted by a nasty divorce."

At the word "divorce," a red flag went up in Danni's mind. *Well, what do you expect?* she reasoned. The man was thirty-six years old. And divorce wasn't always a bad thing. But he'd said "nasty" hadn't he?

Then Danni blushed—wildly, uncontrollably—because a divorce, even a nasty one, seemed preferable to her own sparse history: one very luke-warm affair with Wesley Fuerborne.

"DON'T—*DO NOT*—CALL that man again," Carol admonished the next day when Danni related the whole evening to her: how he'd written his next week's schedule on the back of another of his business cards, how he'd accidentally left his silver pen on her coffee table, how he'd asked her to call him again as he'd left.

Danni was on her wooden deck, stretched out on a chaise longue under the shelter of her two-hundred-year-old red oak, one of the oldest and largest trees in the Woodward Park area, and her pride and joy.

She pressed the phone to her ear and felt a mild annoyance building. "Oh, for heaven's sake. It's practically the twenty-first century," she protested. "I can call anybody I want. I was thinking of taking his pen back to him. You know, getting a look at him in his territory."

"You'd go to his *house?*"

"Don't be dumb. I don't even know where he lives. But I do know where the fire station is, and he gave me his schedule."

"Okay, have it your way, but don't expect chasing a man to get the results you want," Carol countered. "The male mind may be enlightened, but the male body still has to perform the hunting ritual. When you reverse that order, you get his DNA all discombobulated. Scientific fact."

"I suppose you're going to recite *The Rules* or something to me now," Danni said sarcastically.

"I wouldn't know *The Rules* from the Koran, but you could at least be sensible enough to realize that men *do* love a challenge."

"Oh, Lord." Danni rolled her eyes heavenward and examined the patchwork of leaves and sunlight above her. Then she threw her long legs over the side of the lounge. "First, Jackie tells me to act like a hot-blooded man-trap, then you tell me to act like a cold-blooded manipulator. All I want is a nice man to share my life with, and maybe a couple of nice babies from that union. Is that so dang terrible?"

"No. It's perfectly normal. But you've got to let the men come to you. You shouldn't go around calling men you hardly know. Even a blind date would be better than that."

"Wanna bet?" Danni retorted meaningfully.

Carol gasped. "You tried a blind date?"

"Saturday night. Personality of a houseplant. Near-death breath."

"Lovely. Bet you didn't have any trouble resisting *him*— Oh! Did I mention that? How it's a good idea to always resist them on the first date?"

"Arrrg!" Danni groaned. She didn't want to admit to Carol that she had ended up resisting Matt, all right, but not because of any plan. She knew her reasons had nothing to do with gamesmanship. The fact that she'd pulled back even though she hadn't really wanted to was scary. Scarier than Jackie's red teddies and dangly earrings, scarier than Carol's cheesy self-help-book strategizing. Danni's own sexual resistance—something real that came from deep inside herself—was the scariest thing of all.

And even though Danni was aware that Matthew Creed's kiss and the fears it had stirred up had somehow left her feeling vulnerable and defensive, she could no more have stopped what happened next than she could have halted a meteor.

She and Dr. Stone had finished a tense hour and a half delivering premature triplets by emergency C-section, when he caught up with her in the doctors' lounge.

"You do magnificent work, Doctor," Stone said as he groaned and lowered his dwarfish frame into the recliner.

"Thank you," Danni replied without turning away from her locker.

Stone reached forward to unlace his surgery oxfords. "No. Thank *you*...for not disappointing me. I was the one who encouraged the board to recruit a female obstetrician. I thought it was about time we caught up with the rest of the country."

Danni bristled. Stone probably didn't even realize how condescending he was being, or did he? Danni's credentials were impeccable and she knew the board had been impressed with her from the start. Stone knew it, as well. She slammed her locker a little too loudly and turned to go to change her clothes in the bathroom, which was her habit, whether the lounge was occupied by others or not. Several times she had considered moving her locker to the nurses' lounge, but instinct had told her that with throwbacks like Stone, that move would reduce her status. For now, she had to tread a fine line, being the only female obstetrician at Holy Cross.

If she could hold out for six months longer, two of her close friends from medical school, Dr. Alice Clemmons and Dr. Cynthia Bornay would be joining her practice. The three of them planned to open their own birthing clinic, offering low-cost obstetrical care. *And then*—she smiled as she slipped into the rose-colored silk pantsuit—she might make less money, but she'd be free of Stone's goading.

Danni dropped a gold caduceus on an extra-long chain around her neck. Carol had ordered the unusual necklace from one of her professional catalogs and surprised Danni with it for her last birthday. It was flashy, but elegant. Danni smiled and adjusted the medical symbol. If this irked Stone, wait till he saw the little naked-baby earrings Jackie had bought her the other day.

When she came out of the bathroom, Stone had changed from his scrubs and was evidently waiting for her, sprawled out in the recliner again with his hands folded behind his head.

"I was thinking," he said, squinting at her. "Will you be going to the American College of Obstetrics and Gynecologists meeting later this month? Dr. Donnar from Johns Hopkins will be presenting his seminar on intrauterine fetal-assessment techniques."

Danni felt torn. She should go. To pass up the chance to learn the latest in intrauterine assessment would be unprofessional, but her practice was so hectic right now. She didn't have time for five days in the Caribbean.

Stone apparently misread her hesitation. "Dr. Goodlove, I hope you didn't misunderstand what I said a moment ago. I meant it as a compliment."

But to Danni, so often stung by what she perceived to be Stone's subtle brand of sexism, his tone had sounded more arrogant than apologetic.

She opened her locker while she gathered the courage to say what she'd been wanting to say for months. "Dr. Stone, I appreciate what you said earlier," she started calmly, "but I am not here to either disappoint or please you." She faced him, kept her expression composed. "I am here to practice medicine. Period."

Stone's jaw dropped and hung in disbelief for one second before he sprang up out of the recliner like a bulldog on the attack. "I have had it with your attitude." He jabbed a finger at her. "I'm trying to tell you what a fine doctor you are and you act as if I've insulted you! For your information, *everyone* has to prove themselves in the field of medicine. The trouble is you women are all so damned emotional!" He glared at her, his beady gray eyes radiating anger.

"And I suppose that this fit you're having right now isn't at all emotional."

Stone actually sputtered at that. For a second he looked as if he wanted to strangle her. Then he snatched his lab coat from the arm of the recliner.

Steven Bryant barged in the lounge door just as

Danni turned and slammed her locker for the second time.

"I thought I heard shouting," Bryant said. His eyebrows shot up at the sight of Danni in her silk pantsuit.

"I was just trying to compliment Dr. Goodlove on her surgical skills." Stone thrust his arms into his lab coat and jerked the lapels into place. Then he raked his hands through his sparse, faded-orange hair.

Danni felt her cheeks growing hot. Maybe she had overreacted. But Stone had been goading her for a long time. She'd have liked to clear the air with him, but the opportunity was lost, with Bryant standing there, smiling and seeming somehow pleased by the tension he sensed between the other two doctors.

"Sorry to interrupt," Bryant said.

"Excuse me," Stone said, and marched toward the door. Then he stopped abruptly and turned. "Dr. Bryant, are you attending the ACOG meeting?"

"Five days on the island of St. Martin? Are you kidding? Just try and stop me."

"Good." Stone jerked the door open. "One of us needs to represent Holy Cross." He stalked out.

Bryant turned to Danni. "Are *you* going to this year's conference?"

"I doubt it." Danni rolled her scrubs into a ball and rammed them into the hamper.

"Whoa. What'd Stone say to make you so mad?" He scanned Danni's figure. "You know, you do have trouble taking compliments."

Danni didn't respond. She headed for the door.

"Let's practice." Bryant blocked her path and persisted in a teasing tone, "That's a nice outfit."

Danni went around him.

"Seriously, now—" he grabbed her arm as she passed "—I can assess a woman's weight in one glance. You've lost quite a bit, haven't you?"

Danni reached for the handle, but Bryant flattened his palm against the door. He squinted and looked her up and down, as if seeing her for the first time. "You look great." He glanced at the caduceus that lay against her bosom.

Against her will, something inside Danni stirred. Anger, certainly, but also something...female. She hoped it didn't show on her face. She smiled, determined not to lose her cool with Bryant the way she had with Stone. "Carol told me your wife was asking about our diet the last time she dropped by the nurses' station."

The allusion to his wife was not lost on Bryant, but true to form, he was disparaging toward his spouse. "Liz on a diet? That'll be the day. I guess you heard we're separated."

Danni frowned. "I'm sorry to hear it."

"Are you as hungry as I am?" He leaned toward her in a way that made Danni nervous. "Why don't we run down and grab a bite to eat before afternoon rounds? That is, if we can find something on your famous diet in the cafeteria."

Danni was baffled. Instead of sabotaging her, suddenly he was asking her to lunch? That female feeling—a physical thing deep inside her—stirred again, responding to the frank interest in his eyes. Bryant *was* handsome, in a slick, spoiled-rich-boy sort of way.

"Jackie, my housekeeper, brings in my meals," she replied as she tried to go around him.

"Really?" He blocked her again and smiled a predatory smile, as if he was certain she would break down and eat lunch with him anyway. "How does she know when an emergency C-section has delayed your lunch by two hours?"

"I page her." Danni was telling the truth. Jackie now carried a pink pager, and even if she was out shopping or whatever, when she got the page she dropped everything to run a diet meal over to Danni and Carol. They'd agreed to stick with the diet rigidly. And they'd all three lost almost fifteen pounds each.

Bryant feigned a pout, then brightened. "Hey! I know. Have her bring lunch for two."

The man apparently had no boundaries. Danni practically knocked him out of the way as she tugged the door open.

"I don't think so," she retorted through clenched teeth and left.

"DR. BRYANT ASKED YOU TO lunch?" Carol was incredulous when Danni told her about the incident as they went through the warm-up stretches for their evening jog. "You mean as a colleague-type thing?"

"Not exactly." Danni elaborated on the story.

"Well, this just proves what I told you. Men like

to chase. You're always giving him the cold shoulder, and he can't stand it, so now he's asking you to lunch.''

"The trouble is, I don't know how to deal with him," Danni admitted. "As long as I was fat and dowdy he limited himself to delivering barbs about my professionalism. I could cope when he was just a jerk, but I don't know how to handle him now.''

"Well, just make it abundantly clear to him that you refuse to get involved with a married man.'' Carol, seeming satisfied with her conclusion, bent forward into a stretch.

"He's not exactly married. He and his wife are separated.'' Danni stood, looking down at Carol's springy hair.

Something in Danni's tone made Carol straighten. She planted her hands on her hips, eyed Danni suspiciously. "You aren't interested in *him*, are you?''

"Hell, no! He's a sleaze. It's just that when he looked at me a certain way...I felt so...''

"That's just chemistry, honey. Don't get confused. There's a lot more to falling in love than chemistry. Sometimes you can have great chemistry with somebody who's all wrong for you—you know—morally, socially, emotionally, intellectually, et cetera, et cetera.''

"I know that.'' Danni was thinking about Matt, not Bryant. "But how do you really know whether someone is right for you or not?''

"You don't—not all at once. That's why we have a custom called dating.''

"Dating—" Danni rolled her eyes "—is so much work."

"Everything worthwhile involves work. Now get back to your stretches."

Danni started her deep knee-bends, but after a moment she straightened and said thoughtfully, "You know what's sick?"

"What's sick?"

Danni stood there for a second before she answered, turning a little pink. "It was more than chemistry with Bryant. Deep down, part of me felt some kind of secret victory. I mean, Bryant's treated me like a cow for so long, I actually got some kind of perverse satisfaction out of having him notice that I'm attractive."

"That's natural. Don't be too hard on yourself." Carol sat on the grass and planted one foot against her inner thigh. "All you need is to find the right kind of man to give you the right kind of attention on a regular basis." She leaned forward to stretch her hamstrings.

"But how in the heck do I find him?" Danni interlaced her fingers and, palms up, pushed her arms above her head.

"Well, like I told you, I don't think it does much good to chase after men. They have to come to you."

"But what if they never do?"

"They will. Look how Bryant's suddenly acting. Think of it like sperm." Carol exhaled as she changed to a knee/calf stretch. "You let them swim to *you*. Then you just reject the bad ones. And always keep in mind that you only need *one*."

"Swimming to me, huh? Well, past experience has taught me that men aren't exactly fighting the tide to reach Danni Goodlove."

Carol stood, started jogging in place. "That was then, this is now, as the saying goes. Your job now is to make sure you're the best you can be. If you like yourself, you can be sure the right man will come along and like you just as much. Now let's go." She jogged off.

Right, Danni thought, as she trotted after Carol. *And then the prince will kiss me awake, and we will live happily ever after.*

CHAPTER NINE

DESPITE CAROL'S ADVICE, Danni had made up her mind to go to Matt's workplace. She had to see him. Somehow she felt that if she got another look at him—by the clear light of day, in his world— her confusion would disappear.

She got up at dawn, obsessed for thirty minutes about what to wear, finally settled on an elegant cream-colored turtleneck and glen-plaid slacks, and left for her office early. She knew he'd be at the station. She'd calculated exactly how much time to give herself—enough to talk to him for a little while, but not too much. If the encounter turned awkward, she'd need an excuse to make a quick exit.

It was cool but sunny. The giant old trees of Woodward Park were turning crimson and gold, and a touch of mist lingered in the hollows of the rolling hills as Danni drove to the fire station near Utica Square.

It was a quaint limestone two-story, built at about the same time as the surrounding neighborhood— in the 1930s, Danni supposed.

As she approached the building, Danni couldn't believe her eyes. A big yellow fire engine was parked in front and a half-dozen firemen in their navy blue uniforms were running around it, spraying each other with hoses like a bunch of teenagers at a car wash. When she pulled up, she heard their excited shouts through the BMW's closed windows.

She parked in the wide driveway, and the moment she opened her car door and got out, the crew froze. They stood like dripping statues, gawking at her. She could hear water splashing and high-pitched, fiendish male laughter coming from the other side of the engine.

"May I help you?" the nearest man asked.

The black firefighter from the emergency room was among them—he was staring at her as if she'd just beamed down from outer space—but she didn't see Matt anywhere.

"Yes," she said. "I was looking for Captain Creed."

Matt's head popped around the engine, soaking wet, grinning widely. "Danni!" he said. He came around and threw aside the running hose he'd been holding. "Wha—"

"Hey! You're the doctor," the black man said.

"Am I interrupting something important?" Danni asked Matt.

"Yeah!" a younger man called out. "Hose training!" The other men laughed.

"Okay, guys, finish up. The lady's here to see me." Matt swept his wet hair back with a palm. "Let's sit down over here." He pointed to a couple of old-fashioned metal lawn chairs painted with flames—cute, Danni thought—under the canopy of a huge old elm tree.

She walked ahead, anxious to put some distance between herself and the men, who resumed washing down the fire truck and joshing with each other. But now some were stealing glances at her.

"This doesn't happen often." Matt looked sheepish and ran his hands down his water-drenched trunk. His navy T-shirt and gabardine pants were plastered to every muscle. "We wash the trucks regularly. Sometimes the guys get carried away. Horsing around relieves the tension, the boredom. I like to keep my team's morale up. Here. Have a seat." He touched the back of one of the chairs.

When Danni sat down, the cold metal chilled the backs of her thighs right through her wool slacks. She shivered. "Aren't you cold?" she asked.

"Yeah. But firemen fight fires in the cold, and they get wet doing it. This toughens 'em up."

"What if there's a fire right now?"

"We go wet. Just a few pounds heavier. No big deal. Like I said, you get wet in a fire anyway. So. I'm glad you dropped by, even if you did catch us acting up." She noticed he hadn't sat down. She suddenly felt out of place.

She reached into her purse and withdrew the pen. "I wanted to return this. It looked kind of special." She held the pen out to him. "You left it on my coffee table."

He took the pen. "It is special. My ten-year-service pen. I figured I'd get it from you next time...." He shrugged. Her move.

Danni felt her pulse race. Why did this dating thing have to be so *hard?* "Well, I was afraid I'd lose it." What a dumb lie. She'd kept it right on her bedside table like a glowing jewel. Realizing her motives must be glaringly transparent, she stood. She could feel her cheeks heating up, despite the cool morning air. "I guess I'd better get to the office."

"If I wasn't soaking wet, I'd give you a quick tour of the station. It's interesting. We just installed a whole new weight-training room." He turned his head and looked over his shoulder at the building. Even soaking wet, he was incredibly handsome. "The fireplace inside is built like a miniature castle. It has little windows that light up. Promise you'll come back?"

She smiled. Matthew Creed seemed to make everything so easy.

Then he added, "Call me, okay?" and put the ball in her court again, where she absolutely did not want it.

"Well, I guess I'd better get back to the office." She bit her lip. *You said that already.*

He walked with her to her car and opened the door for her, seeming oblivious to the curious eyes of his men.

Danni drove away, significantly less sure of herself than she had been before. Had he really been glad to see her or was he merely being polite? He was, after all, a nice guy. Too nice to let a lady doctor know she was overstepping her bounds. Was there no help for it—this terrible uncertainty called "dating"?

BEFORE DANNI HAD EVEN DRIVEN out of Matt's line of vision, the hooting started, one of the younger guys, Bob Creighton, arching an eyebrow and hollering, *"Doctor?"* Which set off a chorus.

"Man! I could use a checkup."

"I'd play doctor with *her* any day."

"I think I'm havin' a *pain!*"

Matt felt his face going red.

"My God, boys!" Ty hollered, "Look at his face! The man's on fire!" Three of them turned their hoses on Matt at once.

And later on, during the afternoon doldrums, Ty slipped into Matt's office and said, "That's the first time I ever saw you blush. You looked like you had a second-degree burn out there. Why didn't you tell me you and the lady doctor had a thing going?" He settled into the vinyl-covered chair opposite the metal desk.

With his elbows propped on the desk, Matt was rolling the silver pen between his palms, thinking thoughts about time passing so fast, about the next ten years, about Danni Goodlove. "The lady doctor and I don't have a 'thing' going," he mumbled.

"Why not? That is one good-lookin' woman."

"We had one date. That's when I left this pen at her house. I wonder if she returned it to me at work, you know, to cut things off, to sort of say, 'Here's your stuff. Bye.'"

Ty was wolfing down a candy bar and stopped mid-chew. "Is this old Love-'em-and-leave-'em Creed talking?" He swallowed and raised an index finger. "One. The chick came here to see *you*. And two—" he put up a second finger "—she's a *doctor*—"

"That's the point," Matt interrupted.

Ty looked perplexed.

"I've had a little experience with women like her, remember?"

"So?"

"So, they're game players."

"Hey. *All* chicks are game players, man." Ty stuffed in the rest of the candy bar. He chewed thoughtfully for a second, then added, "And their number one game is called Matrimony." Ty emphasized every syllable of the word.

Matt tossed down the pen and raised both palms. "Not for me."

"Right. That's why it's a good thing she's a doctor. Don't you get it? A woman like that's independent, has her own money and all. She ever been married?"

"That hasn't come up, but I don't think so."

"Cool."

Now Matt looked perplexed.

"If she wanted to play Matrimony, she would have tied the knot by now, right?"

Matt shrugged.

"So enjoy the ride."

"It's not that simple. A woman like that— Remember how Carla was always trying to *improve* me?''

''So? You don't want a repeat of the Carla scene. Test this one. Take her on some bad dates. Show her what a beast you really are. And if she's still hangin' around, messin' with your *pen,* then—hey, man—you have got it made.''

But Matt had his doubts about ''having it made'' with a woman like Danni Goodlove. He had sworn to stick to his own kind after Carla. From day one, Carla had launched a not-so-subtle campaign to reform and remake him. She'd even called him a ''diamond in the rough'' a few times.

Well, then, maybe old Ty had a point. Maybe it would be a good idea to call Dr. Goodlove up for a couple of special ''dates,'' and test her mettle. Naw. He'd asked her to call him, and what had she said? *''I'd better get to the office.''*

THE FOLLOWING SATURDAY, Matt unwrapped a giant submarine sandwich as he slumped in his BarcaLounger, watching Kansas State smoke Colorado. But his mind wasn't really on the game, or the sandwich. His mind was on *her.* Where it had been for most of the week.

The entire week had gone by and he hadn't heard anything from her. So, he'd been right. He'd doubted he'd ever hear from the lady doctor again. And he'd be damned if he'd call her after the way she'd acted—as if he'd choked her instead of kissed her, and then rushing his pen back to him, as if she couldn't wait to get it off her hands.

If she hadn't wanted to be kissed, what the hell had she called him for? And what the hell had he apologized for? Women were such game players—especially classy women. Women like Carla, who spoke a certain way, moved a certain way, thought a certain way.

Women like his mom, the Tulsa society girl, married to the renegade Choctaw Indian. The fact that they were both high-school teachers had never quite closed the cultural gap between them.

But they'd always seemed happy enough, and, Matt thought, the best parents a guy could ask for. Still, being raised by a refined English teacher and a tough football coach sometimes made Matt feel like some sort of social half-breed. Especially when it came to women.

"Miss Verbena—" he quizzed the little dog as he slipped her a potato chip "—why can't I find a good woman like you? Somebody high maintenance who makes constant demands on me and whines and complains all the time. Oh, yeah, I forgot. Been there. Done that."

He scratched the little dog's ears as his thoughts went back to Carla. What had gone wrong? Sometimes he could dredge up a list a mile long, and sometimes he still wondered why they hadn't been able to make the marriage work. The part that really bothered him was wondering if the divorce was his fault.

He remembered her standing in the doorway as she was leaving him, running back to her rich daddy, telling him how the bombing was a whole year ago and to "just get over it." As if he could do that by a simple act of will.

If they'd had children, would things have been any different? A child of his own to stop him from obsessing about all the precious little ones that had been lost? What had that counselor called the rescuers? "The forgotten victims"?

He pinched the bridge of his nose and tossed the remains of the sandwich onto the coffee table. Maybe Carla had a point: Maybe he had taken the whole thing too personally. Other rescuers had moved on; had gone home and let their families comfort them.

He picked up the phone and punched in his parents' number. Maybe his dad would like to come over and watch the game. Their machine answered. His mother's voice. Refined. Proper. "We are so sorry to have missed your call. Please leave a message at the tone. Thank you."

"Mom, Dad, it's me. I was just hanging out and wondering what you guys were up to." Then he remembered—they were on vacation in New Mexico. "Uh, I just remembered about your trip. Hope you're having fun. Call me when you get back. Love you!"

Someone—the neighbors, no doubt—talking loudly in the apartment breezeway caused Miss Verbena to hop off Matt's lap and run to the front door, yapping furiously.

"Please, desist!" Matt hollered, hung up the phone, and turned up the volume of the game. But Miss Verbena ignored him completely.

"That's enough!" he shouted above the poodle's barking and punched the off button on the remote.

He bolted up out of the recliner and Miss Verbena darted off to the bedroom.

Matt sighed. It was a beautiful fall day, too good to waste in this stuffy apartment. He had to get out of here. Ty was free today. Maybe they could run over and fix the doctor's floor, as long as she wasn't there.

She had called Ty's business phone and left a message: "Make the arrangements with my housekeeper." Once again he wondered, what had gone wrong?

HE WAS GLAD they'd called ahead, glad that Danni would be out of the house. Because walking up to her front door made him nervous.

"Man! This place turned out *nice*. First-class," Ty muttered from behind him.

Yeah. First-class, Matt thought. *Like the woman who lives here.* Why couldn't he stick to women who didn't live in $300,000 houses? *Because you like things complicated, don't you, Creed?* he added sarcastically as he rang the doorbell.

The black girl answered the door. "Oh, I know you," she said as she waggled a long red fingernail at Matt, while her eyes kept shifting to Ty with coquettish interest. "You're the guy who was over here the other night." She looked up into Ty's eyes. "And who's your friend?"

Matt jerked a thumb at Ty. "This is Ty, my partner in the floor-finishing business." He nodded his head at Jackie. "This is Dr. Goodlove's house-keeper."

"Hel-lo." The woman extended her hand—which looked too perfectly manicured for a maid's—palm down as if she expected Ty to kiss it or something. "My name is Jackie."

Ty took her fingers lightly. "Jackie," he repeated in a voice that had a hint of too-cool in it. "Very nice to meet you."

Jackie batted her eyelashes, then said, "Follow me." She turned on her heel and started down the long entry hall, hips undulating saucily in tight-fitting jeans.

"Anywhere, baby," Ty muttered and Matt smirked.

"How'd you meet Dr. Danni?" Jackie said to Matt's back once he and Ty had bent to the task of rolling back the Persian rug.

"She stitched me up."

"Ooh. Lucky you. Dr. Danni's the best. Hey!" He heard her fingers snap. "You must be the *fireman*. The one who gave her your card."

He stopped rolling the rug and turned to look at her over his shoulder.

Jackie made big eyes at him. "I overheard her talking to one of her friends about you. After you came over here the other night. Oh, you've got her attention all right."

Now Ty turned and looked at her also, then he pulled one corner of his mouth back grudgingly at Matt, as if to say, *Very impressive.*

"Really?" Matt replied, and he suddenly wanted

to know exactly what Danni had said about him. It was ridiculous—the way he was obsessing about this woman. "What'd she say?"

"Oh, she heard from the nurses upstairs that you cried when those twins you rescued died. That really touched her heart. Uh-huh. It sure did."

Matt felt his neck turn red. He glanced at Ty, but Ty was suddenly extremely intent on rolling back the rug. Ty had gone to Oklahoma City, too. They all had.

"Jackie? That's your name, isn't it?" Matt said. "Could you, uh, would you open the windows and turn on the ceiling fan for us? There'll be a lot of fumes."

The corners of Ty's mouth were pulled way down now, for a different reason, Matt suspected. Would it ever leave them? This grief? This guilt?

The chime of the doorbell broke the strained silence.

Jackie went to answer it while Matt and Ty dragged the rug out of the way.

As they started the light sanding, Matt heard voices coming from the front of the house. First Jackie's in greeting, and then a man's, coming from the entry hall, and then quickly getting closer as footsteps tapped the hardwood flooring. "Danni's not here? That's okay. I'll just pick up the journal and go on. Whose Jeep is that out front?"

He heard Jackie's voice again. "A couple of guys who're refinishing the floor. I don't think she left anything for you, Dr. Bryant, but if it's important, I'll go in her study and look. What did you call it?''

''We just call it the green journal. That's okay. I'll get it. You wouldn't know which issue I need.'' The guy's voice was coming from the study off the master suite now. ''Here we go.'' Then suddenly he poked his head in the bedroom door. ''Hi,'' he said. ''So you guys are here to refinish Danni's floor. Great house, isn't it?'' He sauntered into the room, waved at the floor with the rolled-up magazine. ''Having to do a little remedial work, are you?''

Ty frowned at Matt, then nodded curtly at the intruder and kept sanding.

Jackie appeared in the doorway from the hall and tucked her arms under her bosom as if getting ready to watch a performance.

The guy wandered in, looking around Danni's bedroom, and for some reason Matt felt himself getting annoyed. He stood, gestured with his sandpaper. ''The surface just needs a little touch-up. Matt Creed.'' He stuck out his clean hand.

The guy shook Matt's hand. ''Dr. Roger Bryant. I'm Dr. Goodlove's…good friend.''

Matt frowned and swiped his nose with a knuckle lightly, then glanced at Ty, who kept on sanding steadily as if Dr. Bryant was not really worth much notice.

Bryant moved toward the door. ''Well, guess I'll let you boys get back to work.'' He aimed a finger at Matt like a six-shooter. ''Let's hope you get it right this time.''

Ty glanced up at Matt with a look that said, *What an ass!* Matt nodded in agreement.

"Tell Danni I'll call her later," Bryant said to Jackie as he squeezed past her and left the room, "to thank her for the article."

Matt, back down on one knee, turned his head and watched Bryant exiting down the hallway, his heels tapping energetically on the hardwood floor. Alligator tassel loafers. Who was this jerk, anyway? For some reason he didn't really seem like somebody who'd be Danni Goodlove's "good friend."

A WEEK LATER, DANNI had pulled another "full mooner" and she was so tired, she could barely focus as she groped for the ringing phone beside her bed. Her mind was so numb she didn't recognize his voice at first. "Matt Creed?" she said, as if he hadn't just repeated his name.

"Yeah. Hey, I didn't wake you up, did I?"

She sat up and squinted at the glowing green numbers on her alarm clock: 7:32 p.m. Bet he thinks I'm a loser, sound asleep at seven-thirty on a Friday night.

She quickly explained: "Actually, you did, but that's because I worked through the night, then ended up seeing two borderline patients in the office after hours today. I'm beat."

"Oh, gosh. Well, it's kind of a crazy idea for a date, anyway. Maybe you're too tired to go."

A date? Danni sat up among the pillows and ran a hand through her choppy bangs as it dawned on her that *he* was calling *her*. Maybe it was *happen-*

ing, just as Carol had said. Suddenly she was fully awake. "Too tired to go where?"

His answer was low, provocative. "To a real, live, *hot* bonfire."

SURELY THIS ISN'T HIS *idea of a date,* Danni thought as she was buffeted by a crowd of screaming Tulsa Central High students, jostling their way closer to an enormous pile of scrap wood topped by an effigy of a Tulsa Hale football player. She realized she was irritable from lack of sleep, but this was ridiculous. She hadn't even seen Matt since they arrived. Why had he dragged her here?

He'd come for her in his pickup, dressed in turnout pants, suspenders, a firefighter's T-shirt and boots. He'd driven her to the Central High practice field with country-and-western music blaring the whole time, refusing to offer a hint of explanation.

"Now you get to see me in action," he'd said as he reached behind the seat for his turnout coat and helmet. "Normally for this event, I ride in with my engine company—" he inclined his head toward a pumper truck parked beyond the bleachers and the crowd "—but tonight I'm meeting them here, because I wanted to bring you."

Danni thought about the look in his eyes when he'd said that. Captivating. Maybe it was just chemistry, the way Carol had said, but Danni liked these female feelings. She really did. And she had to admit, just watching him put on his gear in that parking lot had been...entertaining. Watching Matthew Creed do anything was entertaining.

But then he'd escorted her out onto the field crowded with excited teenagers, a marching band, a smattering of indulgently smiling parents and teachers—and not one soul she knew. "Wait here," he'd said. "Then meet me over there when this is over." He'd pointed toward some old wooden bleachers. Then he'd left her.

She stood around through several band tunes and some speeches by the principal and the student leaders, getting more weary and peeved with each passing second, wondering what the heck she was doing here when she could be at home, sleeping.

Then, with a clamor, the attention of the crowd shifted to the bonfire pile.

There was Matt, crawling up on the wood, with a pike pole in one hand and a gas can in the other.

He raised the pike pole high above his head, and for one split second Danni thought he looked like some kind of ancient warrior as he drove the pike into the dummy hanging from a frame above the wood. The girls squealed and clapped and the boys punched the air and roared, "Yeah!" in their deepest voices. Matt started dousing the wood with the contents of the gas can.

He was the star, and he was playing his role to hilt. He crawled down and emptied the last drips of the liquid at the foot of the pile, then he tossed the gas can and pike pole aside and snatched up a long torch made of rags and wood.

The crowd, silhouetted against the setting sun, seemed like one organism, focused totally on Matt, waiting expectantly for something.

Finally he lit his torch, and at the first sight of flame, the crowd roared again. He waved the fireball in slow circles above his head while the band accelerated its frenzied drumbeat. He did a rhythmic dance, jamming the torch toward the woodpile but not letting it ignite, teasing the yelling teenagers.

Watching his strong arms and legs, his broad back, the way he worked the crowd, Danni thought, *If he were mine, I'd be videotaping every second of this.*

If he were mine? Danni rubbed her arms and looked at the kids around her. Some of the football players had hoisted the cheerleaders onto their shoulders and the girls were clapping to the drum rhythm. Suddenly the whole thing seemed so... hedonistic. The beating of the drums in the chill fall air. The electrified, jumping, dancing crowd. And Matt—big, daring, wielding fire.

A boy near Danni cupped his hands around his mouth and yelled, "Light it, man!"

But Matt teased some more, standing back, shrugging his shoulders, cupping his hand at his ear as if he didn't understand what the kids wanted.

Finally the school principal, standing on a platform at the edge of the crowd, gave Matt a silent signal and Matt lowered his face shield. He rushed forward and plunged the torch into the kerosene-soaked wood. The crowd yelled deafeningly as the flames leaped out with a giant whoosh, and a column of black smoke twisted skyward.

The heat was instantly intense and the crowd

backed up. But Matt stood near the fire, seeming impervious to it. He raised his face shield and looked directly at Danni.

"That your husband, lady?" a gangly girl with a mouthful of braces asked from beside Danni.

"No," Danni replied. But as she watched Matt, circling the fire, kicking up dust as he booted stray embers back toward the center, she realized that some part of her was imagining what it would be like if the answer was yes.

"Too bad! He's a hunk!" The girl cupped her hands to her mouth and giggled as her friend pushed her away.

When things had died down, Matt signaled in the water truck that had been parked at the edge of the field, and he and two other firefighters doused the fire.

The principal walked over and shook their hands and then Matt signaled his buddies to take in the hose while he trotted over to Danni, who was waiting for him, alone on the bleachers.

"Well?" he said breathlessly as he took off his helmet. "How'd you like it?" He unhooked his turnout coat.

She'd liked it. Very much. Watching Matt light the fire, that is. But as for the rest of this so-called date… "It was certainly…*different*," she replied. "You really got the crowd worked up."

"I light the Central High bonfire every year. Keeps everything safe. I figure the kids deserve a show. I'm crazy about kids." He lowered himself to the bleacher in front of her and proceeded to pull off his boots. "I thought you might like to see what I do when I'm not saving lives."

He stood and popped his suspenders off his shoulders, unsnapped the turnout pants, and Danni felt herself turning red. Was he going to pull those things off? What was under them? Then she saw it—the kerchief he'd had on in the E.R. that first night they met, knotted around his wrist again.

He peeled the pants down and, much to her relief, uncovered a pair of snug Levi's. He jerked the turn-outs off, then pulled the fireboots back on. He bent down and picked up the rest of the gear and said, "Come on. I'll put this stuff back on the engine. I've got my other boots in the pickup."

She hooked a finger under the kerchief, halting him as he turned. "Tell me about this." She said it quietly, as a gentle request.

Matt suddenly seemed to grow dark and solemn, as he looked down at the kerchief. "It belonged to a friend." He cocked an eyebrow at her as if gauging her reaction. "I wear it every time I bunker up."

"Oh? Why?"

"For luck." Then his expression sobered again. "And so I don't forget."

"Don't forget what?" Her curiosity about this man was so strong she couldn't help pushing.

"Sparky."

"Sparky's the friend?"

"He was. He was the search-and-rescue dog we kept at the station. He, uh… He lived with me while

I trained him, back when I still had a house and a yard.''

"Oh?" She waited for him to say more, but he stared out over the field, as if lost in some distant memory. She thought about the fierce look in his eyes in the emergency room when he'd grabbed her wrist. Finally she said, quietly, carefully, "Does Sparky have something to do with the bombing?"

"The bombing?" He frowned down at her. "What do you know about the bombing?"

"That first night when you came into the emergency room. Your friend—"

"Ty."

"I guess. You were agitated, so I gave you a sedative— You really don't remember any of this?"

Matt shook his head, looking curious.

Danni went on: "Well, your friend told me you were one of the rescuers at the bombing."

Matt shrugged. "Yeah. So was Ty. So were a lot of people."

"And Sparky? Did he help you search for victims?"

Matt looked down at his big hands. "We used these little leather booties, but his feet still got cut up so bad in the rubble—he got an infection that wouldn't heal."

"And?" she prompted quietly.

He looked down into her searching eyes. His own were calm and sad. "And we had to put him to sleep."

Danni suddenly felt that she had stepped over a

line, and that her trespassing might cost her something—exactly what, she couldn't say. She looked away. "That's so sad. I'm sorry I brought it up," she said truthfully.

"It's okay. Some things you have to accept."

Danni knew that. And some things were impossible to accept. She knew that, too.

"You know what sticks with me?" he said. "What I've had nightmares about?" He was not looking at her. Instead he stared out over the abandoned football field at the pile of ashes where he had clowned around only an hour ago.

"What?" She could hardly breathe, waiting for his answer as he stared out over the field.

"How it would get so quiet."

Danni only nodded, not wanting to break his trance with words.

"When I dream about it, it's always so quiet like that. The rubble. The blood. Silent. Respectful. Like we all knew, even as we were working so hard, that there had to be people already dead, buried in there."

"I never thought of that, how awful the silence must have been," Danni whispered. And her eyes were rimmed with the tears that had been trying to come out ever since the night she'd met this man. What was it about Matthew Creed that did this to her?

To her everlasting shame, Danni had not been able to really cry after the bombing. During the horrible aftermath, she'd desperately wanted to cry—the way everybody around her had been crying—

but for some reason she hadn't been able to. Maybe that was when she'd first started to wonder if something was wrong with her, with her life, if she couldn't cry along with everybody else.

But now, suddenly, alone with Matt on a silent football field, she felt the unshed tears building.

"It's okay to cry about it," he said, as if reading her mind. "I still do sometimes."

Danni bit her lip, took a huge breath, closed her eyes, and the first tear rolled down. "Could you...hold me?" she asked.

"I could use a hug myself right about now," he said softly.

She stood and he took her hand and helped her climb down from the bleachers.

They faced each other for a moment before Danni opened her arms to him and he stepped toward her.

For Danni, there had never been a hug like this. He slowly wrapped his strong arms around her and rested his cheek against her hair, as he pulled her body against his.

She laid her face against the muscles of his chest and thought her own body would burst at the impact of full contact with him. She could hear his heart beating, feel his steady breathing. He was amazingly warm in contrast to the night air, and he smelled faintly of cedar, smoke and leather. He snuggled her tightly against him. He was relaxed, calm, yet radiating power and energy.

They stood like that for a long time while Danni felt something in her chest actually loosen and expand. She closed her eyes and wanted to stay like this—in this man's wonderful, wonderful arms—forever.

Then he kissed the top of her head, pressed his lips there, like a father kissing a precious child. "Thank you for asking about the kerchief," he said against her hair.

"You know what, Matthew Creed?" She tilted her head up and studied his face from below. "There's a lot more to you than a pretty face."

His mood shifted suddenly to easygoing again. "Yeah, I know. There's this great *body,* too." His arms tightened around her with a hint of masculine urge where there had only been comforting tenderness before.

Suddenly flustered, Danni laughed and wriggled out of his embrace.

He let her go and winked at her, then shifted the firefighter's gear onto his back and took her elbow with his free hand. "And speakin' of bodies, mine's starving."

THIS TIME, HE CHOSE THE place. Smoky, greasy, noisy. Packed with overweight folks in sweatshirts and well-worn jeans. Danni hated it.

"My kind of food," he said, and didn't even bother to look at the menu.

But Danni pored over it, looking for something, anything, among the chicken-fried steak and barbecued ribs that wouldn't completely wreck her diet.

The waitress came and said, "Hi, big fella," to

Matt as if she knew him. "What can I get you folks?"

"The usual." Matt smiled up at her.

"Side of pork ribs with the works," she said, wrote it on her pad, then turned her attention to Danni. "And for you, ma'am?"

Danni closed the menu. "Just a salad."

Matt and the waitress looked horrified, as if Danni had ordered a plate of worms.

"I'm on a diet," Danni explained.

Matt blew a raspberry sound with his lips. "You don't need a *diet,*" he said. He turned to the waitress. "Sally, bring the lady a Sampler Platter." The waitress nodded with a satisfied smile and waddled away.

Danni resented his audacity. "I know what I'm allowed to eat," she informed him in a low voice.

"Oh, you don't have to eat it." Matt winked. "Just do me the honor of looking at it."

Danni could have looked at it without weakening, but when she smelled it, she salivated. It turned out to be the most delicious food she'd ever tasted. She allowed herself one moment of guilt before she dived into the enormous platter of tender barbecued ribs, juicy smoked chicken breast, coleslaw and fries.

While Matt devoured his food, he kept his eyes on her. At one point he reached over with his napkin and gently dabbed some barbecue sauce from her chin.

"You can go back on your diet tomorrow," he

reassured her. "Sometimes, Doctor, you gotta live for yourself."

DANNI WONDERED WHOM, exactly, she was living for when she let her mother badger her into a date with Wesley Fuerborne the next day.

"Danni, sweetheart, you realize that the Tulsa Performing Arts Gala at the Gilcrease is coming up soon." Her mother had called her bright and early.

"And?" Danni only half listened as she leafed through a stack of routine discharge notes.

"And I still have two seats at my table. I'm the cochairman. Two empty chairs would not look nice. I was wondering if you and Wesley would help me out and come together. You have worked so hard on your diet and you will look stunning in an evening gown. And Wesley is such a sweet man. Wouldn't you enjoy seeing him again?"

In answer to Danni's silence, Olivia added in a soft, coaxing voice: "Dear, don't you think it's about time you allowed yourself the luxury of a decent social life? You know, you never even went to your own senior prom. Please? For me?"

Between the flattery and the begging, Danni found herself saying yes.

When Jackie heard that Danni was attending a black-tie fund-raiser at the Gilcrease Museum, she squealed. "A party at the Gilcrease! Your picture might even end up in the Sunday paper!"

She and Carol insisted on helping Danni shop for the dress, a gorgeous beaded silk faille sheath in a shade of royal blue that contrasted dramatically with Danni's rich brown hair.

When Danni saw herself all done up in the full-length mirror, she decided that maybe her mother had a point. Maybe she had cheated herself—never going to the prom, never allowing herself the kinds of glamour dates other women enjoyed.

And objectively, Danni had to admit that the date turned out to be a dream date. Wesley Fuerborne knew how to treat a woman. He sent flowers in the afternoon. He introduced her to all the Tulsa luminaries as if she were the queen herself. He waltzed her around the dance floor with perfect grace. He put his tux jacket over her bare shoulders on the way home.

A real dream date.

Except Wesley Fuerborne, bless his heart, wasn't Matthew Creed.

Matthew Creed, who rescued babies. Matthew Creed, who jutted his hips with wild abandon as he lit a bonfire. Matthew Creed, whose kiss she simply could not forget.

CHAPTER TEN

MATTHEW CREED, WHOSE IDEA of a date was not exactly dreamy.

"Hi," he said when Danni answered his page the following week, "Are you busy saving a life or anything?"

"Nope. Saved my quota for the day." Danni smiled into the receiver.

"Listen. I've got to go downtown to test a chute in about an hour. Why don't you come with me? I thought you might pick out another one of your fancy restaurants and we could go eat."

"Test a chute?" Danni asked.

"Yeah. Every so often, we go into the downtown office buildings and test the fire escapes. The guys had a problem in a newly remodeled office today and wanted me to go back and do a little teaching at closing time. The chutes are like big slides, circling around. We go down them to make sure they're all clear—no snags or anything. It's fun."

It didn't sound like fun to Danni. "How far down?" she asked.

"This one's twenty-three floors. How about it? Dinner at a fancy restaurant? I'd sure like to see you in that black dress again."

Danni felt a little skip of excitement. Then she thought, *Twenty-three stories!* Danni wanted to see this, but she didn't want to wreck her diet again. "Listen. I have a better idea. I want to see this chute stunt but I was going to try to get in a horseback ride before the sun went down. Why don't we do that instead of going out for dinner? I'll bring a picnic."

There was a long silence and she thought they'd lost their connection. "Matt? Are you there?"

"A horseback ride…like on a horse?" he asked.

Danni giggled. "No, on a giraffe."

But there was a long, unhappy sigh on the other end.

"Matt?"

"Okay. Horses it is."

MATT STOOD WAITING in front of the building, dressed in cowboy boots, jeans, a plain white T-shirt and a black bomber-style jacket unlike any Danni had ever seen. The snap front, ribbed waist and cuffs, and tan leather sleeves looked like any other varsity jacket. But what made this one unique was the small logo on the right chest—Tulsa Co. Fire Department—and the "Matthew Creed" embroidered on the left.

"Wow," Danni breathed in honest admiration. "That is one cool jacket."

"It's a Gall's Gear. Best there is. I had it specially made." He tipped his shoulder to show her the large fire-department logo in the shape of a Maltese cross embroidered across the back. "Come on, it's quittin' time downtown. The folks on the top floor are waiting.''

OFFICE PERSONNEL, clutching purses, briefcases, and take-home paperwork, were already gathering around to watch Matt.

Unlike when he'd performed for the teenagers, there was no showmanship in Matt's attitude tonight. Danni tagged along while he made a quick tour of the large architectural firm's offices. He stopped once and quietly pointed out to one of the partners that the boxes and mailing tubes cluttering one hallway had to go.

He went back to the fire-escape area and explained how the chute opened onto a landing at each floor, and only that area would be lit. The rest of the chute, he emphasized, was pitch-black. ''In a fire, hesitation can be deadly, but so can panic,'' he said. ''The idea is to get out calmly and quickly.''

He asked if anyone else wanted to ''take a ride'' down, and the little crowd of employees chuckled nervously.

He pushed on what looked like heavy paneling and then a small set of doors, which Danni hadn't even noticed before, popped open. A dimly lit hole gaped below a small landing. Danni could see the metal escape tube spiraling down. *Twenty-three stories!*

Matt stepped onto the narrow landing. ''Remember, feet first, keep your arms up over your head, and gravity does the work. If you get stuck or balled

up, straighten your legs out. Don't struggle, lie flat.
If anybody wants to practice, I'll be waiting at the
bottom.''

As he stripped off the bomber jacket, Danni saw
a young woman purse her lips and roll her eyes at
a co-worker. ''Sometimes there's a burr in the
metal,'' he explained quietly as he handed the
jacket to Danni. ''Guys have torn their uniforms.
Meet me downstairs.'' He winked at her, jumped
into the chute, and disappeared.

Murmuring and more nervous laughter rippled
through the crowd. A couple of the workers stepped
forward to peer down the way Matt had gone.

Danni looked, too, and shuddered. She clutched
Matt's jacket—the leather was still warm—and
breathed in his scent. Then she took the elevator
down.

AN HOUR LATER SHE wondered if he was the same
guy who had slid twenty-three stories down a spiraling black tube as if it were a playground slide.

Big, brawny Matt was as nervous and skittish
around horses as a little old lady. Though the bay
Danni had borrowed for him was a tame old pet,
Matt was acting as if the animal might eat him alive
any second.

Danni pulled Quick off the trail sooner than she
had planned, in order to give the poor man a break.
They dismounted and she told Matt to take the sad-
dlebags to a small red-rock clearing at the top of
the slope while she tied the horses—his and hers—
to some low cedars.

"You haven't done much horseback riding," Danni said a few minutes later as she spread the blanket and then knelt to lay out the simple picnic Jackie had prepared—baked turkey for her, fried chicken for Matt.

"Nope." He knelt beside her and started helping her with the food.

"You should have told me you don't enjoy riding," Danni said.

Matt sat back on his heels, studying her face. "I guess I thought I could pull it off. The truth is, I hate horses. I haven't been on one since I was twelve years old. That's when a big old rascal named Demon bit me on the behind."

Danni grinned up at him.

"It's not funny. It left a scar."

"Really?"

"Yes. It was very traumatic," Matt said forlornly as he leaned in closer to her. "And I desperately need the love of a good, understanding woman to help me get over it."

He leaned down, examined her lips in the same way he had on their first date. In contrast to the cool air in the cedar glen, his breath was hot, beckoning.

Then he kissed her—kissed her as thoroughly as he had the first time. While his mouth worked, he took her hand and massaged the inside of her palm with his strong thumb. The effect on Danni was overwhelming. It was as if he were caressing, awakening, some mysterious region inside her.

Finally he pulled back. Danni released a shaky

breath, looked into his eyes, and bit her lip, afraid of the passion flooding through her. Could he guess what she was feeling? Was he feeling this same amazing intensity?

He ran his thumb over her lower lip.

"So. Do you wanna see my scar?" he murmured as he regarded her lip.

Danni blushed and turned her face to the picnic pack. "Oh, look!" she said, evading him. "Jackie made pasta salad. I'm starving." She glanced at him.

Matt had settled back on his heels and was giving her a quiet appraising look. He shrugged and smiled. "Me, too. Let's eat."

She turned her burning face away again and pulled out the containers. She couldn't look at him now because while she realized that she wanted to see, to know, to feel everything about Matthew Creed, she had also realized a deeper, more sobering truth just now. Danni was absolutely terrified to take that awesome step.

CHAPTER ELEVEN

"I WAS WONDERING, DO YOU have a bathing suit?" Matt asked when he called her a few days later.

"A bathing suit?" *In November?*

"Yeah, a bathing suit. Wait. Let me start over. This is your weekend off, right?"

Danni's heart started to beat faster, the way it did every time he called her. "Uh, no, it's not, but I can get someone to cover for me," she said, struggling to control her breathing, hoping that didn't sound too eager.

"Well, listen. I have a couple of buddies who've organized a canoe trip down the Illinois River. I was wondering if you might want to come along."

A canoe trip? As opposed to spending the weekend curled up with back issues of *Contemporary OB/Gyn?* Gee, tough choice.

"When—" her voice cracked "—uh, when are you going?"

"Bright and early tomorrow morning. Could I come and get you at, say, seven?"

Carol's voice invaded Danni's head, solemnly intoning a "rule": *"Never accept a date at the last minute."* Yet it seemed that with this man, Danni was breaking every rule.

"Sounds great," she answered without hesitation. Screw the rules.

MATT SHOWED UP IN HER driveway with two other firemen and their dates at seven sharp the next day.

The morning light glinted golden off the doors of their freshly waxed sport-utility vehicles as the men got out. It promised to be one of those rare Oklahoma days in late autumn when a last drenching of Southwestern sun pushed the temperature back up into the seventies, sometimes even the eighties.

Matt introduced Ty. Danni recognized him as the man who'd restrained Matt in the emergency room. But she didn't want to bring attention to the fact that she was a doctor. "You did a beautiful job on my floors, Ty." She smiled as she shook his hand.

Ty smiled back. "Thanks. I really like what you did with your house, Dr. Goodlove."

"Everybody calls me Danni."

Ty's date, a delicate-looking young woman named Gloria, smiled shyly and nodded from the window of his Jeep.

The other man, Gil, was chunky and redheaded. The first thing Danni noticed about his girlfriend, Rena, was her tattoo: a tangle of snakes around her wrist.

When they got into his pickup, Matt produced a picnic basket, which looked so new that she expected to see a price tag dangling somewhere. "This time *I* brought the picnic," he said proudly.

He grinned and held the basket open for her approval.

Inside there was a brand-new tablecloth and matching napkins, a set of plastic tableware and cutlery in bright fuchsia, and enough French deli food to feed the masses. Also, wrapped in a blue Kold Pack from a fireman's first-aid kit, was a small bottle of Cabernet with an expensive-looking label. Danni smiled, touched by the trouble he'd gone to.

And she *loved* the way he looked. Today he was wearing baggy khaki shorts and a deep red golf shirt with a well-worn deck jacket thrown over it.

"You like?"

"I *love*." Danni was surprised by her own gushiness. Must have been the effect of that aftershave he was wearing.

Then a bulge at the side of his jacket moved!

Danni jumped. "What's that?" She pointed.

Matt raised his eyebrows while slowly lowering the jacket zipper. A shivering gray poodle poked her head out, lifted rheumy little eyes at Danni, then retreated like a turtle back into the folds of Matt's jacket.

"Miss Verbena?" Danni asked.

Matt nodded and put his finger to his lips. "She's rather shy," he whispered.

"Oh, I *see*," Danni whispered back, playing along, though she was somewhat surprised that he would bring a fragile lapdog on a canoe trip.

But an hour later, Danni understood his strategy. Miss Verbena, like a mischievous child or a dyspeptic duenna, was the perfect distraction as they made their way along the Illinois River, alone together in a canoe for the entire day. Except for a few silly remarks to the poodle, Matt was mostly quiet at first, paddling steadily, and Danni found she was grateful to have the dog as a diversion.

The river—all green and gold, thickly overgrown with old willows and massive cottonwoods that leaned out over the water—was so wide and smooth in places that trees and sky were reflected on the surface like shimmery upside-down paintings.

"This reminds me of *The English Dreamers*," Danni said.

"Huh?" Matt turned from his paddling.

"A collection of nineteenth-century paintings. The river reminds me of them," she explained.

"Oh, cool," was all he said, then went back to his rowing and his silence.

"Miss Verbena," Danni stage-whispered to the dog, "a refined lady like you would appreciate *The English Dreamers*."

"Naw." Matt turned and grinned. "She prefers the Impressionists."

She smiled at him and patted the dog. She did like his style.

When they got to a perfectly calm section of the river, and the watery ripple of his paddle slowly dipping in and out was the only sound, Matt said quietly, "Do you ever see Mary Taylor?"

"Who?" Danni, who had been lost in reverie, enjoying the shadowy beauty around them, couldn't recall anyone named Mary Taylor.

He turned so that she could see his profile, and

she was struck again by how handsome he was, even when he was frowning. "Your patient. The one whose twins died in the fire."

"Oh." Danni's mouth formed an embarrassed circle. She should have remembered that name. Obviously, *he* did. "Uh, no," she stammered. "I, uh… She never came back for her follow-up appointment."

He stopped paddling and faced her full on. His frown deepened. "She just didn't show up? After having a cesarean section?"

Danni shrugged. "It's not unusual for some patients to disappear once they're discharged from the hospital."

"You didn't have your office call to check on her?"

Danni's cheeks grew warm. "Actually, my nurse did call. We always call at least once. But when there's a disconnected number, what else can we do, other than report the case to Child Welfare?"

His frown dissolved, was replaced by an expression of contemplative sadness. He stared up at the trees across the water. "Man," was all he said. He turned and resumed paddling. Danni studied his strong shoulders, which looked tense now.

Again they fell silent until the sun grew warmer, and Matt removed his jacket. "Aren't you getting hot?" he asked.

"I'm fine," Danni lied. She wore only her bathing suit, a wide-strapped maillot, under her windbreaker and jogging pants, and she knew it was silly, but in front of this man who practically exuded sex, she felt self-conscious about exposing her generous bosom. *Don't be silly,* she thought, then quickly stripped the jacket off. She sat very still, with her shoulders slightly rounded.

Matt smiled pleasantly. "Now you look more comfortable," he said, never once glancing at her cleavage.

"What?" He bent toward Miss Verbena, who was lying with her muzzle on her paws near Danni's feet. "You say you are starving? Oh, *okay.* Then I suppose I shall be forced to find an appropriate place where we might picnic." He scanned the riverbanks ahead.

"Why do you always talk to her like that?" Danni asked, squinting up at him.

"You mean in those long, complicated—" he tilted his nose into the air and affected a British accent "—rawther *erudite* sentences?" He cocked an eyebrow at the little dog. "Miss Verbena does not care for sloppy speech. It irritates her. Ain't that right, Miss V.?"

Miss Verbena jumped to her feet and barked excitedly as if agreeing.

Danni gave him a sly grin. "And I bet you always call her Miss V. when it's time to eat."

"You are *such* a bright lady." He raised an oar to signal his friends in the other canoes to head to the bank for the picnic.

When they'd all come ashore, Gil, who'd obviously had one beer too many, *did* glance at Danni's cleavage. Rena obviously didn't appreciate that. "Gil, get your fat ass over here and help me unload this ice chest,'' she said, glaring at him from under her sun visor.

"Rena, girl, you talk so dadgum pretty,'' Matt joked, but Danni could tell he was embarrassed. She scooped up Miss Verbena and used the little poodle as a furry shield for her front as she and Matt walked past Gil and Rena toward a shady spot where Ty and his date were spreading a quilt.

Gil opened his ice chest and started popping beers. "How about a beer?'' he asked Danni, already twisting the cap off one for her.

"No, thanks,'' Danni replied. "I'm not much of a beer drinker.''

A heartbeat of uncomfortable silence stretched, then Gil shrugged and handed the beer to Rena. The girl with Ty smiled in a mincing, apologetic way at Danni.

"Hey!'' Matt interjected cheerily. "That's exactly why I brought this.'' He pulled the bottle of Cabernet from his picnic basket. He uncorked the wine and poured it into two tiny plastic wineglasses.

"Matt, buddy, who are you tryin' to impress?'' Gil said loudly.

"Miss Verbena.'' Matt winked and handed Danni one of the wineglasses.

Danni raised the glass in salute. And just then her pager went off.

Matt watched as she checked the pager clipped at her waistband, dug around in her tote for her cell phone, punched in a number, then located a pen and paper while she waited. His friends watched, too.

"Roger? You paged me?" she said.

Roger. Was that the cretin who'd come charging into her house the other day?

Danni's voice was suddenly tense. "Yes, she is. How high is it?"

"Epigastric pain?... Visual disturbances?... Did you run a chem sixteen?...Okay. I guess we need a mag-sulfate drip... Sure. You okay with this?... Okay. Then I'll talk to you later."

She listened for a moment and her demeanor shifted again. She looked...embarrassed. She glanced at Matt, then took a few steps away from the group. "Oh, I don't think I could do that, really.... No, not even dinner. I'm—I'm out on the river, with a—a friend. I don't know when I'll be back."

A wisp of jealousy curled in Matt's gut. *Cool it, man,* he told himself. *It's her job.*

Gil rolled his eyes at Matt as Danni rejoined the group, but Matt ignored him. "Everything okay at the hospital?" he asked her.

Danni sighed. "Sometimes I'd like to fling this pager into the river, you know?" The others nodded sympathetically. "But for now, everything's fine."

"Then let's eat!" Ty said with exaggerated gusto.

The foods Matt had selected for her were yummy, but spinach quiche and cream-cheese brownies were not exactly on Danni's diet. She decided to make do by limiting her portions and chewing slowly.

Everybody else gobbled fried chicken like starving truckers while the men recounted droll firehouse anecdotes. Danni enjoyed the stories and laughed with the other women, but the whole time she felt as if she were being put through some kind of subtle initiation.

When the others had gone down to the riverbank to wade, Matt leaned casually on one elbow and quietly asked, "Are you having a good time?"

"Yes. The river is lovely," Danni said and looked out over the water.

"I'm glad you're enjoying the river. What about the company?"

"Miss Verbena makes excellent conversation—" she started to gather up the picnic items "—and you're...*okay,*" she teased.

But instead of a retort or a chuckle, there was a moment of strangely uneasy silence, accentuated by the sound of the others at the river. Finally Matt said, "I wasn't talking about me and Miss Verbena."

Danni stopped folding the napkins in her hands and turned to him with a puzzled look. "What *are* you talking about?"

Matt shrugged. "I get the feeling you don't care for my friends."

"Why would you say that?" Danni protested, even though, truth be told, she *was* uncomfortable with these people. She'd even caught herself wondering what Dr. Stone would think of Matt and his buddies. Did it show?

"Gil's crude—" Matt nodded toward the group down by the river "—but he's saved my ass more than once. He's really not a bad guy. And Ty is one upstanding dude." He stretched out on his side, stroking Miss Verbena as if considering his next words carefully. Then he narrowed his eyes at Danni and his voice had a definite note of challenge in it. "You know, Doctor, you're hanging out with the kind of guy who likes to sit with a hot dog and a beer and watch sports on cable TV night after night."

"I don't have anything against people eating hot dogs, *or* drinking beer, *or* watching sports on cable TV," Danni said defensively.

"What I mean is, is that kind of guy good enough for a lady like you?"

She was completely unprepared for this conversation. "I don't know what you mean," she said, playing for time to gather her wits.

"I don't know what you mean," he echoed. "That's just the kind of answer chicks like you give during a confrontation."

Chicks like me? Danni thought. *Where on earth did that come from?* But she passed over it. "Are we having a confrontation?" she asked.

"Maybe *confrontation* is the wrong word. Getting the cards out on the table—call it what you like. Don't act like you don't know what I'm talking about."

"What *are* you talking about?"

"Look. I like you. And I think you like me. But we're different. I'm talking about my life. This is it." He spread an arm in a wide circle. "And crude friends and beer on a blanket are the *good* parts.

What about when I come home with soot and slob-
ber all over me? What about if I *don't* come home?
What about some night when a chief or a chaplain
shows up at the house in my place? Being hooked
up with a fireman isn't as easy as you might think.''

"You have no idea *what* I think,'' Danni countered, feeling sudden irritation rise. "I'm a *doctor,*
for crying out loud. The very one who stitched you
up.'' What was he getting at? Talking about a chaplain and a chief and coming home or not coming
home. *Whose* home?

"Exactly. You're a doctor. Used to fine things
and fine people. Where would I fit in?'' But before
she could form an answer, Matt abruptly stood.
"Forget it,'' he said as he started to jam things back
into the picnic basket. "I shouldn't have gotten into
this. I'm probably overreacting.''

Danni was speechless. Overreacting to what? The
fact that she'd turned down a beer?

He scooped up Miss Verbena. "I think she's
thirsty,'' he said, then strode down toward the river,
carrying the dog.

And for the remainder of the afternoon, Miss
Verbena became like an unfortunate child caught
between feuding parents. Matt and Danni talked,
each in turn, to the little dog, but said precious few
words to one another.

In the long silences as they floated on down the
river, Danni kept wondering exactly what he'd
meant by the phrase "hooked up.''

And Matt kept thinking that he'd done it again:
gone and turned another classy woman off.

CHAPTER TWELVE

"SOMEONE HERE TO SEE YOU," Carol mumbled in Danni's ear.

"Who?" Danni looked up from her charts with irritation, but Carol had already zipped back around the corner of the dictation booth. *What's Carol acting so weird about?* Danni wondered.

She rolled the desk chair away from the doctors' counter and craned her neck to look down the hall.

Leaning against the nurses' counter, and drawing a lot of appreciative glances, was Matthew Creed. Decked out in cowboy hat, boots, snug jeans, a crisp plaid shirt and that one-of-a-kind leather jacket.

"Hi," he greeted brightly as Danni approached, then said, "Excuse me," to a flirty little nurse who pressed up within inches of him as she squeezed her way into the nurses' station.

"Matt. What are you doing here?" Danni reached up to pull her paper cap off, then thought better of it because her grown-out hair probably looked like a fright wig.

"I went by your office and they said you were over here delivering a baby. Is this a bad time?"

"The delivery's over." Danni glanced around

her. The nurses, lab techs, and ward clerks all seemed intently absorbed in their paperwork. One usually couldn't hear oneself think in this place and suddenly it was as quiet as a morgue.

"Could we talk a minute?" Matt asked.

"Uh, sure. Let's go get a cup of coffee. Carol, I'm on my pager."

The benevolent smile Carol flashed her looked like something straight off the faces of Walt Disney's Flora, Fauna and Merriweather.

Pu-leez, Danni thought. *Is there no such thing as privacy in this joint?*

Apparently not. On their way to the elevator, Danni glanced back down the hall. The whole crew was staring at Matt like rock-star groupies.

They stopped at the snack shop and got a coffee for Matt and skim-milk hot chocolate for Danni. Then she led the way outside to the center courtyard of the hospital, away from prying eyes. They found a concrete bench, out of the November wind, under a low water oak.

"I hate to bug you at work—" Matt aimed his coffee cup at her paper cap "—but I'm getting ready to pull a three-day stretch at the station, and I didn't want to wait to apologize."

"'Apologize'?" Danni pulled her lab coat tighter and sipped her hot chocolate.

"It's a little chilly out here, isn't it?" He moved close against her on the bench, to block the wind. "That better?" he asked.

Danni nodded. Boy, was it better. How could you

get turned on just sitting next to someone? Just breathing the aroma of his aftershave?

"Yeah. Apologize," Matt continued. "For the way I acted on Saturday. I thought about it all the next day—"

"I'm sorry I didn't answer your pages," Danni interrupted. "Sunday was terrible. Three deliveries. One difficult. There really wasn't time." She sipped her hot chocolate.

"I understand. I know I have to be flexible about your job. That's why I'm here. Look. Let me be straight with you. I'm very attracted to you. But I... I guess I've got some old hang-ups. You see, I swore I'd never get involved with another woman who didn't accept me exactly as I am—"

"Danni! There you are!" Roger Bryant was standing with his arms spread wide and his lab coat flapping like some clown who'd jumped out from behind a tree trunk. "I've been looking for you everywhere."

"Is something wrong with Mrs. Reese?" Danni jumped up, threw the side of her lab coat back and checked her pager.

Bryant held up his palms. "No, no. Nothing's wrong. Everything upstairs is fine. Hi. Dr. Roger Bryant." He abruptly thrust out his hand at Matt, who slowly stood beside Danni.

"Matthew Creed." Matt took Bryant's hand in a firm handshake. "We met before—at Danni's house."

"Oh, yeah. The handyman." He turned back to Danni. "Stone was looking for you, and guess what? He agreed to arrange his calendar so we can go to the Caribbean *together*. How's *that* sound? A whole week in paradise?''

For one flashing instant, Matt looked as if he'd been gut-punched. Then he smiled and backed up a space. "Well, listen. I've taken enough of your time at work." He touched the brim of his hat and turned away.

"Matt, wait—" Danni started after him, but Bryant grabbed her elbow. "Come on. Let's go get this trip nailed down before the old man changes his mind."

Danni wrenched free of Bryant's grasp. "Matt!" she cried out again just as he reached the door to the courtyard. "Call me!"

He turned. "You never answer my pages," he called back. "You know my number." Then he was gone.

"NOW YOU'RE COOKIN'" Carol gushed enthusiastically when she caught Danni alone in her office that afternoon.

"Huh?" Danni said distractedly, because her mind was on the pile of lab results in front of her.

"The fireman! You've got him coming to the hospital to find you! Way to go, girl. Whatever you're doing, keep it up."

"Oh, for crying out loud!" Danni tossed the papers aside and pushed back in her desk chair. "Would you pull your rose-colored glasses down long enough to see reality? I've hardly got him chasing after me. He's still insisting that I call *him*."

"He is?" Carol seemed disappointed.

"Well, after…" Danni shrugged. "The whole thing was weird."

"*What* whole thing?" Carol pressed.

"The scene with me and Matt and Bryant."

"*Bryant?*"

"Well, Matt and I were sitting on a bench out in the courtyard, and then Bryant came up and—"

"Bryant showed up?"

"Yeah. To tell me he arranged to attend the ACOG convention with me on St. Martin."

"He's going to St. Martin with you?"

"Yeah."

"He said that in front of the fireman?"

"Yeah."

"Damn!"

"What do you mean, 'damn'?"

"Well, how'd the fireman act when Bryant started talking about going to the Caribbean with you?"

Danni frowned, chewed the end of her pen. "Well, he looked funny for a second…and then he left."

"Don't you see? You can't let men get territorial over you in front of each other. One of them always backs off, and it's usually the decent one."

"Territorial? Oh, Carol. You are so full of it. Roger Bryant isn't interested in me romantically. This is a professional convention."

"You are deaf, dumb and blind. Why do you

think Bryant's arranging this cozy little trip to the Caribbean? Think. You said yourself he commented on your—what'd you call it?''

"Hinder.'' Danni rolled her eyes. "A medical term.''

Carol pointed at her. "This is not a joke. You watch that man. Before you came on board at Holy Cross, he had an affair with a nurse and broke her heart, nearly killed her. He's making moves on you, all right, and in the process he's apparently chasing away your decent prospects.''

"Prospects? For crying out loud. You make it sound like I'm digging for gold. Matt and I have just barely begun dating. And besides, I wonder about him. He had some kind of bad divorce—''

"There's such a thing as a good one? And Bryant's not even divorced, he's only separated—for the millionth time.''

"I know that. He told me about it. From what I hear, it sounds like it's her fault.''

"A separation is never all one party's fault.''

"Why not? My mother always said it takes two people to build a marriage, but only one to wreck it. And besides, Bryant's marriage isn't even an issue. This trip to St. Martin is professional.'' Danni waved a palm at Carol. "Listen. I've got to call these patients. Don't worry. Roger Bryant and I are just colleagues—''

"Colleagues, schmalleagues. Mark my words. Bryant is up to something. And it's probably X-rated.''

Carol started to leave, then stopped with her hand

poised on the doorknob. "You'd better watch your p's and q's in the Caribbean."

SOMETHING—VANITY? masochism?—drove Danni back to the Tres salon the day before she left for St. Martin. She didn't want to get too specific about *why* she submitted to not only a manicure and a pedicure, but also a leg wax, bikini wax and total body exfoliation. She wasn't trying to be attractive for Roger Bryant, that was for sure, but she didn't want to go to the Caribbean looking *unattractive,* either.

This time she opted for a quieter, more conservative hairstylist named Patty, who squinted at Danni's hair, snapped her fingers and went to work. After adding some soft highlights, she gathered all the layers in front into a poofy upsweep topped by a small chignon, then round-brushed the rest of the hair to tumble over Danni's shoulders in a sleek pageboy.

The style was dignified, but also dramatic and feminine.

"I love it!" Danni exclaimed. "It's professional, but also…"

"Alluring?" Patty suggested.

"Right," Danni said. *And just plain sexy.*

AT LAST DANNI WAS ON the beach—a glorious beach—and for the first time in her entire life she didn't mind being seen in her bathing suit.

She slathered on plenty of sunscreen, plunked on a straw hat and sunglasses, settled down on her beach towel, and opened the thick romance novel she'd been saving for this trip.

Ah! Bliss! No waiting room full of pregnant ladies. No irritable Dr. Stone. No full-moon madness this month. For once, she intended to relax and enjoy herself. She adjusted her foam headrest, then made a conscious effort to let her shoulders, her hips, her calves and her heels settle into her beach towel on the hot sand.

It seemed as if she'd been relaxing for all of two seconds when a familiar male voice from above her said, "Hey, lady, wanna see my scar?"

Danni lowered her book, tipped her hat brim up, then placed a palm over her breastbone like a heroine in a Victorian melodrama. "Matt? Wh-what are you doing here?" she stammered as she squinted up at his silhouette.

He was shirtless, wearing loud, baggy swim trunks, and she could see her image in his Gargoyles—the wraparound mirrored sunglasses favored by firemen and cops.

He squatted down and took off the glasses. Even with the tropical sun behind him, she could see that he felt self-conscious; his smile was a little lopsided. "Hi," he said. "I just came down here..." His goofy smile dissolved. He sighed and turned his head, squinted out at the ocean. "This is stupid, isn't it?" he mumbled. "Acting like I'm bumping into you on the other side of the world?" He shrugged and looked down at her. "To tell you the truth, I'm not real sure why I came down here."

Danni dropped the book on her chest. "You didn't come down here to find *me,* did you?"

Matt's face grew solemn. He shrugged again, then nodded.

Danni was stunned. "You mean you flew all the way down to St. Martin because you knew *I* was going to be here?"

He nodded again.

"But how did you know when I was coming?"

Even though he was backlit by the bright sun, Danni could see that his face was turning red.

"Don't be mad at Jackie. She said you'd have some time on your hands while you were here. Is that not true? At first I thought you were coming down here to be with that Bryant guy, but Jackie told me—"

"Jackie!"

"Yeah. She was having a burger with Ty and me, and she started talking about this trip—how she was going to get the week off while you were gone and all—and I...well, I guess I got the wrong idea the other day at the hospital. Jackie said this Bryant guy's nothing to you, and—"

"Since when have you and my housekeeper gotten so chummy?"

"Since I fixed her up with Ty."

"Oh, for crying out loud!" Danni was furious now, at all of them. So, she fumed, Carol must have gone to Jackie and told her about the misunderstanding in front of Matt and then the two of them cooked up this deal and manipulated Matt into following her down here. Danni supposed on some level she should be flattered. In truth, she was embarrassed.

"Please don't be mad at Jackie." He leaned toward her. "It was my idea to fly down here. I thought we could, you know, do some stuff together, have fun."

Danni stared at him. "This is a *medical* meeting! I have a seminar to attend."

Matt looked down at her in her modest bathing suit. "Always so serious. But I saw you having drinks last night."

Now Danni felt herself blush. When she'd consented to drinks with Bryant she'd been merely socializing with a colleague. That was beside the point. What Matt had done—followed her to the Caribbean—was the issue here.

She propped herself up on her elbows. "You *watched* me having drinks last night?"

"Don't make it sound like I'm some kind of stalker, or something," Matt protested. "I was just waiting for my chance to talk to you without Dr. Blondie around."

"You followed me to the Caribbean and you've been *watching* me?" Danni accused. "I have half a mind to call the police."

"And tell them what? I'm just a guy on vacation. This is a tiny island, and it's plausible that we'd run into each other if we're both on it. I have the right to come down for a vacation, don't I? Isn't that guy married?" he asked abruptly.

"*What?*" But Danni's cheeks flamed.

"Jackie said he's still married. Listen, a guy like

that's no good for you. Even if he is a high-and-mighty doctor. If he were a big boy, he'd get a divorce before he started messing with you." He rose on his knees, swayed and placed his hand on his chest as his voice got louder. "You deserve somebody decent and honest...like me."

Danni sat up and started throwing her suntan lotion, romance novel and sunglasses case into her tote.

"Wait," Matt implored with an outstretched hand. "I was kidding— I mean, this is getting all screwed up. Now you're mad at me, when the whole reason I came down here was to be with you."

Danni looked around. Nearby sunbathers were peering over their sunglasses at them. "Come on," Matt continued, heedless. "I'm sick of playin' games. You know, all that 'Give-me-a-call-sometime' business. The truth is, I'm crazy about you!"

He was practically shouting now. What had happened to the calm, cool firefighter with the controlled monotone?

"I used all my vacation time, not to mention all my money, to fly all the way down here, just to be with *you!* That's all I care about—being with you." He threw himself forward on his palms so that his face was only inches from hers.

The smell of beer on his breath convinced her. He was tipsy. Danni jumped to her feet, snatched up her beach blanket, flipping sand on Matt. She whirled away, then swung back toward him. "I'm

not on vacation, here,'' she said. ''This is a professional conference and I have work to do. So you
stay away from me.'' As an afterthought she added,
''I hope you enjoy your holiday.''

Then she turned and marched up the beach as
fast as her legs could pump her flip-flops against
the sliding sand.

SHE HAD BEEN BACK IN HER room long enough to
shower when two batches of flowers arrived—one
from Roger, one from Matt.

Roger's card read: ''To my gorgeous colleague.
Dinner again?''

Matt's said: ''Sorry I acted like a jerk. Let me
make it up to you tonight.''

Danni sank down on the bed, staring in disbelief
at the card in each hand, marveling at how much
her life had changed. Amazing. Three months ago
she'd thought she couldn't get a man to even *look*
at her, and now *two* very good-looking men were
sending her flowers. In the Caribbean, no less.
Amazing.

The trouble was, Roger made her…ill at ease,
and she was mad at Matt.

What are you going to do about Matthew Creed?
she challenged herself. *Isn't it a little pushy to pump
your housekeeper for information and then follow
you to St. Martin?* But then she thought about what
he'd said, tipsy or not. *I'm crazy about you.* No
man had ever said words like that to Danni Goodlove.

In the end, she decided to get dressed and go out

to dinner—alone. After that, she'd take a mind-clearing, soul-searching stroll on the beach in front of the hotel. Alone.

Then she noticed that the message light on her phone was blinking. She dialed for voice mail. There were two messages. The first one, Bryant's voice, said: "I know a perfect place to eat. Be ready at seven."

Well, heck. Nothing to think about there. Merely obey the doctor's orders. Danni supposed some women would enjoy this setup. She did not.

The second message was Matt's voice, sounding sober now. "Danni... I want to show you something beautiful, if you'll let me. We have time for dinner first. How about it? I'm in room 334. Call me. Please."

Call me. Call me. With Matt it was always "Call me," even when he'd already made a fool of himself—and her—on the beach. She decided to stick with her solitary plans. She threw on a bright yellow-flowered sundress and strappy sandals, twisted the front half of her hair up the way the hairdresser had, then fluffed the rest into wild waves. She brushed on minimal makeup—she'd gotten too much sun anyway—splashed on her high-dollar perfume, grabbed her purse and was out the door, feeling fine, just before seven o'clock.

When the elevator at the end of her hallway dinged and the door slid open, there stood Matt—in one of his fire-department T-shirts, baggy orange tropical-print swim trunks, flip-flops, a straw hat, and the reflective sunglasses. Wearing a pile of leis around his neck and holding two tumblers of bright yellow liquid with little umbrellas stuck in them.

"Whoa! Lookit here," he said as he stepped off the elevator and gave Danni the once-over. "Aren't you gorgeous!"

Danni eyed his hideous getup and said dryly, "Is *this* the 'something beautiful' you wanted to show me?"

Matt threw his head back and laughed. "I hope that means you're not still mad at me for the way I acted on the beach," he replied.

"Depends." Danni couldn't help but grin.

He shoved one of the drinks at her. "Here. Peace offering. But sip it slowly. The free drinks in this place'll kill ya. Take my word for it. I enjoyed a few too many this afternoon." He looked contrite. "So will you go with me tonight?"

"Will I be taking my life in my hands?"

"I promise you won't be taking your life in your hands." He turned and punched the elevator button. "Not as long as you can swim faster than a shark." He turned back to her and winked. "And let me take care of the flames—" He stepped back and frowned down at her feet. "But, ooh… Those sandals will never do on the bed of hot coals. Never mind. I'll carry you." He smiled. "Seriously, I'm not driving. I've got a *lovely* cab waiting out front."

She took a sip of the drink, which was so strong it opened her sinuses. "Okay. Where to, Hula Boy?"

"Isn't it obvious? We're on an island with thirty-seven white-sand beaches."

MATT HAD CHOSEN A DESERTED shore on the north-west side of the island. Here the sand was coarser, the vegetation denser, the hotels farther away. In the trunk of the cab, he had stashed food, a large beach blanket, and more of those yellow drinks in a stoppered carafe.

He took her hand and pulled her from the cab. "Look at that sunset." He swept an arm out toward the sea, then turned to her profile. In her peripheral vision she could see his dazzling smile. "I lied about the sharks." When she turned to face him he took off one of the leis and slipped it gently around her neck, letting the backs of his fingers graze her collarbones. He swallowed.

Danni didn't know if it was the tropical drink she'd sipped in the cab on the way over, or the breathtaking amber-tinted beauty surrounding her, or maybe it was simply this man, but she was suddenly overcome with the strangest sensation—as if the two of them were all alone on the planet, as if no one else in the world mattered or even existed. The light seemed surreal.

Neither of them looked at the sunset now; they looked steadily at each other. And for a moment, she thought he was going to kiss her. "I'd better pay the cabbie," he said without taking his gaze from her mouth.

"Yes," she whispered.

He stepped away and as she stared out at the coral sunset, she overheard him giving instructions to the cabdriver to come back in two hours, and then the cabbie's effusive thanks for what must have been a generous tip.

Everything seemed to slow down to match the timing of the gently sinking sun as Matt spread the blanket, laid out the food, and the two of them talked and joked while they ate the meal and drank till the carafe was emptied to the last drop.

After the sun had disappeared into a hazy line on the rim of the ocean, the moon rose, full and milky, and they fell silent, as if spellbound by its magic. The only sound was of waves washing the beach in a steady rhythm.

They were sitting side by side on the blanket, and Matt turned toward her, leaning on one arm, with one knee hitched up and the other arm draped casually over it. His other knee grazed her thigh. "That moon," he said quietly, "sort of makes a person...feel things."

He leaned closer and instantly, Danni felt the heat of response in her cheeks, in her breasts.

She raised her legs and folded her skirt around her ankles, hugging her knees to her chest. "Actually, I have a somewhat adversarial relationship with the moon," she answered.

"Oh yeah?" Matt moved even closer—so close she could feel his warm breath on her bare shoulder.

"Yeah. Some people think the full moon stimulates pregnant women to go into labor." She braved a look into his shadowed eyes. "So you see, the full moon makes me jittery."

He raised his hand and caressed Danni's cheek with the backs of his fingers. "Just 'jittery'?

Doesn't it also make you want to…kiss somebody sometimes?''

He slid his fingers down to caress her shoulder softly, waiting for her reply. But Danni couldn't answer; she could hardly breathe.

He leaned forward, tilted her chin up and looked into her eyes for a heartbeat, then brought his mouth down on hers.

When he did, it was as if a storm suddenly gripped the quiet beach. Just as on the other occasions when their mouths had met, something beyond mere chemistry seemed to take place—something so wild and electric and compelling that Danni was fearful of its power.

But only one of them fully understood how truly rare and potent that response was. In that first instant of contact, it was Matt who again realized— as clearly as if the words were emblazoned on the night sky—*Here is my match, my mate.* He pressed his mouth to hers in a devouring motion, wanting only to consume and consume; to be joined with her forever.

Danni released her knees and slid her arms around his neck and he crushed her against his chest with sudden fierceness. A charge ran the entire length of her body, as she felt herself becoming fused to him by something far deeper than lust.

Matt eased her backward, as he explored her soft and sensuous mouth with his. The things he wanted to do with her… The things he wanted to do *to* her…

In his massive arms, she seemed as fragile as a

ballerina. Her body felt like the ideal blend of delicate slenderness and aching fullness. He stretched out over her, as close as he could get, and he marveled at their perfect fit.

She responded to him with her whole body, in a motion that felt to him strangely paradoxical: soft and submissive, yet at the same time as savage and urgent as his own reaction.

"Danni," he said hoarsely. "I swear, I've never felt like this with any other woman." Then he kissed her again—fiercely, consumingly—as he moved his hands up and down the length of her.

In Danni's mind she could almost see them, as if she were the moon, watching from above. His dark head against hers. His tanned body against her lighter one. Like lovers in a romantic movie on a deserted moonlit beach. And everything was perfect, perfect. Except—

Danni wrenched her mouth from his. "I can't do this!" she cried, pushing at his binding arms, his exploring hands.

"Why not?" He loosened his hold.

She turned her face away from him, and her head swam for a moment. *Your timing is great, Danielle. Wait until you're alone on a moonlit beach and your brain is about half-pickled,* then *decide to explain your moral tenets to the man.* "I...I promised myself long ago. I...I wouldn't do this with a man until we're...committed to each other."

Matt rolled away from her, propped his elbows on raised knees, ran his hands through his thick hair. In the moonlight, she could plainly see the front of his neon swim trunks, poled into a tent. The sight made her both fearful and guilty. What had she done?

"I'm sorry." She laid a placating palm on his massive shoulder.

"Don't apologize," he said, staring out at the waves. "I admire a woman with high standards. But if you're talking about marriage…" He looked away before continuing. "It's just that I promised myself after Carla that I'd *never* get married again."

"Carla?"

"My ex-wife." He gave Danni a penetrating look. "But I don't think I ever really loved her." His eyes narrowed as he studied her face. "I don't think I knew what real love felt like."

Danni looked down. "And you think you know what it feels like now?"

"I *know* I do."

Danni put her trembling fingers to her lips, felt herself wanting to give in to him, felt herself wanting to say "I love you," too. But did she love him? She knew so little about love, about men.

He threw his arms up, let them flop back down to his sides on the blanket and heaved a theatrical sigh. "Well, so much for stupid promises. Let's go." He jumped up and pulled Danni to her feet.

"Go where?"

"Back downisland." He grabbed the blanket, gave it one powerful shake, and rolled it into a ball. "Wait." He stopped, bent his head and checked his sports watch by the moonlight. The cabbie won't be back for...thirty minutes. Well—'' he smiled broadly, his white teeth flashing in the moonlight ''—I guess that gives us plenty of time for a *courtship*.'' He shook the blanket back out, letting it float to the sand like a parachute.

''Courtship? And go where?'' Danni repeated.

''To get married.'' He dropped to his knees on the blanket and offered his fingertips to her.

''Married?''

''Yeah.'' He lowered his hand, swayed slightly, sank back on his heels. ''If that's what you want, I'm game. It's what you want, isn't it?''

''I have no earthly idea what I want.'' She shook her head, trying to clear it of the effects of the powerful drink.

He took her by the waist and guided her down to her knees in front of him, then pulled her tightly against him and claimed her mouth with a mind-numbing kiss.

When he lifted his head he said, ''I'll tell you one thing, sweetheart. Your *body* knows what it wants.''

CHAPTER THIRTEEN

MATT'S IDEA OF "courtship" was a hands-on experience, laced with comments like, "I love you. I can say that now, can't I? Now that we're getting married?" and, "How many kids do you want? Six or eight?"

Somewhere in her tipsy mind, Danni decided this was all a wacky game—a wild, fabulous, Caribbean game—until she heard Matt actually asking the cabbie where they could get a quick marriage performed. A strange mixed thrill—part fear, part abandon—darted through her.

"Oh, you want de Marriage Man," the cabbie called over the seat cheerfully. "We wake him up. He do this all de time. All de time."

The place was small—cracked adobe, a real hole. Matt kept using words like, "quaint," and "humble," as the cab came to a bumpy halt on the dirt road. Marriages was scrawled in black charcoal on a cardboard sign propped in a hibiscus bush.

"The ring!" Matt swayed when he got out of the cab and slapped his forehead.

"He got 'em! He got 'em!" the cabbie said and waved Matt and Danni toward the cottage.

Matt threw some money at the grinning cabbie,

telling him to wait, and Danni realized this definitely wasn't going to be an opulent—or lengthy—ceremony.

The marriage man had rings, all right. A huge selection. Danni could tell they weren't exactly Tiffany quality but to her slightly unfocused eyes, they seemed cute. As did the plastic flowers and the recorded music.

Matt picked a ring—a Florentine thing with a heart at the center—and slipped some cash to the Marriage Man.

The "ceremony" began. The Marriage Man spoke quickly and without much expression. But somewhere in the middle of it, the whole thing turned strangely solemn.

Danni only had time for a fleeting thought that one shouldn't make vows under the influence of alcohol, before Matt—suddenly appearing sober—began saying his.

"I, Matt—" he looked deep into her eyes "—take thee, Danni, as my lawful wedded wife—" he continued in a quiet, solemn voice "—to have and to hold, for richer or poorer, in sickness and in health, until death do us part."

He slipped the ring on her finger, and Danni realized his hands were shaking.

When they left the Marriage Man, Matt told the cabbie to stop so he could buy another carafe of yellow drinks, then he kept her so "busy" in the back seat that Danni didn't even realize where they'd ended up until she felt the sand slipping under her sandals as Matt helped her out of the cab. The same beach.

She heard Matt telling the cabbie not to come back until he called on the cell phone. *What cell phone?* Danni wondered fleetingly, but by now she was far beyond thinking clearly. *I'm in my husband's capable hands,* she thought, giggling at her own double entendre. Then she sobered briefly as she studied his back. *Husband.* Was this any way to get one?

The moon had risen higher now, nearing its midnight zenith, and it looked firmer, more permanent, in the ink-black sky.

Matt took her hand and led her to the exact spot where they had been before. The trees seemed taller, more sheltering, with the moon shining like a spotlight directly over the dark cove.

Somehow they were both on the blanket and as he started to kiss her neck and slip the straps of her dress off her shoulders, it dawned on Danni that this time Matt meant business. She was going to give herself to him—right here, right now.

"This will be so beautiful, Mrs. Creed," he murmured. He'd been calling her that—Mrs. Creed—ever since they'd left the Marriage Man's house. To her it sounded foreign, exotic, but at the same time wondrous and real.

He trailed his fingertips, then his lips, over her bare shoulders and upper breasts, and chills broke out all over Danni.

"Oh, Matt," she whispered. "No man has ever affected me like this." She stretched her body against his, tense with passion. "Is this how it always feels?"

Matt's answer was throaty, passionate: "Only if you're lucky." And right through her sundress he fastened his mouth over her nipple.

Danni's reaction was so fierce it made her ears ring. As if driven by a force outside herself, her body arched up to him, and he, in turn, took everything she offered.

After he'd worked the sundress down completely he tilted his shoulder back so that the moon illuminated her. He looked her up and down from eyes to breasts to hips and then back again, and gently stroked her hair away from her forehead.

"Oh, Danni, every inch of you is so incredibly beautiful," he whispered.

For Danni, the attention he lavished on her body with his eyes, his hands, his mouth, was beyond anything she had ever imagined. This was what lovemaking was supposed to be like. So...completely euphoric.

Every look, every kiss, every firm, bold touch made her more ready, more his. And each time he raised her body to a new level of pleasure, he would bring his mouth back to hers briefly, and kiss her in silent communication.

Danni felt as if she had been waiting for this all of her life.

Finally, he broke off an excruciatingly deep kiss and as their breaths mingled, he seemed to be asking an urgent question with his eyes.

She met his gaze, with total passion and invitation.

"Matt...make love to me...please," she managed to whisper.

"Oh, Danni." He swallowed and drew her to him, kissed her temple softly and briefly, with a tremor of restrained desire.

"Yes," Danni murmured, wanting him more than she had ever wanted anything in her life.

He rolled on top of her and within seconds, he realized something was wrong.

"Danni—" He pulled back, touched her gently where he had tried to enter. "This isn't— It isn't your first time, is it?"

Danni closed her eyes. She was so overcome by so many things at once—desire, shame, the way he was caressing her—that she couldn't speak. She tried to pull away from him, her thoughts swimming against an intoxicating, confusing tide of emotions.

But he held her tightly. "Look at me," he said.

Why hadn't she found a way to tell him before this? Rationally. She could have made a simple announcement: "When we finally do it, Matthew, I want you to be aware that I have had only one other relationship, and not a very satisfactory one. As for the psychology behind being thirty-three years old and so inexperienced, please don't ask."

She closed her eyes, let the words out in a rush. "I'm just a little tense. I'm not very experienced."

She opened her eyes and in the moonlight, she all too clearly saw the stunned disbelief on his face and turned her head away from it. "I'm not a virgin, if that's what you're thinking." She said this to the moon over his shoulder. "I had a relationship in college. But I—"

He took her chin and guided her face back toward his, then placed a light kiss on her mouth. By the guarded feel of his lips, she could tell that her unhappy revelation had unsettled him.

"Maybe it was the guy," he offered hopefully.

That would be so easy. To lay it all on poor Wesley. "I don't know," she said truthfully.

He inched a little apart from her, propped himself above her on one elbow, and held her waist tenderly with his other hand. "How do you feel now?" he asked gently, then rubbed a thumb just below her navel, reassuringly, while he waited for her answer.

Danni was afraid to tell him the truth—how terrified she had been all these years; how terrified she suddenly felt now.

He reached down for her dress, tucked it around her naked breasts and hips, then laid his palm on her lower abdomen protectively. "Sometimes talking helps. It's all right, you know. I'd just like to know why you seem so upset—if you can tell me."

"It's—" she began, then faltered. "It's nothing to do with men. But after that relationship, I promised myself that I would never have sex again until I was married to the right man."

He ran a palm over his face, absorbing this: *the right man.* "I see." He thought back to how she'd reacted the first time he'd kissed her in her bedroom. Now here she was on a beach with a drunk fireman. *Was that the right man?*

"Let me get this straight." He sighed. "You wanted to be married first because—"

"I just *did.* Okay?" Danni threw an arm over her eyes.

He drew the arm down, kissed her fingertips. Did she have any idea how beautiful she was?

"Okay," he said gently. "And I think, under the circumstances, we ought to go a little slower—a lot slower." He stroked her cheek, her neck, and then, ever so lightly, the mounds of her breasts. "Intimacy takes time, especially when it's new to you." Through the fabric, he gently caressed her. "Especially if you're afraid."

Danni had closed her eyes again, and now tears seeped out—tears that told him how afraid she really was.

Matt was troubled, and suddenly sober, as he realized there was much he didn't know about this woman he had just married. "Hey," he said softly and slid his hand away, to her waist—a less threatening place. "It's okay. We don't even have to do anything." Then he smiled, wanting nothing except to alleviate her distress. "After all, now we have our whole lives ahead of us."

"Oh, God. Don't—" Danni choked off her words.

"Don't what?" His voice was incredibly sincere, incredibly tender.

"Don't humor me with that marriage talk. I know I seem...weird to you."

"No, you don't. You are what you are. And right now, I wouldn't change a thing. You're a warm person, a good person. And everything will be okay."

She looked at him, but couldn't make out his expression clearly; the moon was behind him. "Are you always so understanding about everything?"

"I've had to accept some pretty hard realities in my time. It doesn't do any good to pretend, does it?"

Something about the simple way he said that undid Danni, undid the last of her defenses. The tears came bubbling up with force now, like a torrent of hot lava. She covered her face with her palms and sobbed. Here she was, on a moonlit beach about to have sex with a gorgeous male and she was crying—crying as she had not let herself cry since the day Lisa had died. Bitter, bitter tears. *He must think I'm crazy,* she thought.

He drew her hands away and kissed her palms. "Why don't you just tell me about it?" he said, and pulled up a corner of her dress to dry her cheeks.

"Can you understand losing someone—someone you're really close to—and feeling like you'll never get over it?" she asked.

He nodded. "Is that the problem? Did you get hurt once?"

But as much as Danni wanted to tell him, she found she couldn't bring herself to say more. Suddenly there was only one thing she wanted from him. Only one thing that she thought might heal

her, free her. "Matt," she whispered, swiping at
tears, "please just make love to me, okay?"

"Is that what you really want?"

Danni nodded.

"Okay. We'll go slow."

His voice sounded thick and shaky. As he started
caressing her again, she herself couldn't seem to
focus on anything besides the overwhelming feel of
the man, the smell of him, the warmth of him as
he covered her body with his.

He gently kissed her lips while he pressed his
warm palm over her breast, and she pushed away
the little voice that warned her not to succumb.
Couldn't she just allow this? her body seemed to
implore her. Didn't she deserve one night like this
in her lonely life? After all, she was thirty-three
years old. Wasn't it about time?

And so, that night, Danni Goodlove decided to
forget her lifetime of pain and loneliness and allow
Matthew Creed to sweep her away with his passion.

Matt felt her mouth soften under his, loosening,
imploring. God help him, he knew now that he
loved this woman. And he could no more stop his
own urgent responses than he could stop the tides
from responding to the pull of the moon.

CHAPTER FOURTEEN

THE NEXT DAY, DANNI KNEW she'd made a horrible mistake. She almost screamed when she woke up and found herself pinned to her hotel-room bed by Matt's massive arm. He was snoring softly, right next to her ear.

She tickled his nose and when he grunted and raised his hand to rub at it, she slipped out from under him. He flopped over and snored on.

She dashed to the shower and stood under the spray of the hottest water she could bear. What had she done? Oh, God, *what had she done?*

All the muscles of her body—muscles she didn't know she'd used last night—were sore. What had they done? Her head felt large and fragile and her throat was as dry as sandpaper. She put her mouth under the hot torrent and rinsed. Oh, what had she done?

When she turned off the water, she thought she heard someone pounding at the suite door. She quickly wrapped herself in a towel and peeked out of the bathroom.

In the outer room she saw Matt, wearing nothing but her beach towel around his waist, heading toward the suite door. Before she could yell "No!" he'd jerked it open.

Framed in the doorway stood Roger Bryant, wearing a crisp nautical-crested navy blue blazer and white slacks—and a look of undisguised revulsion on his face.

"What're *you* doing here?" Bryant demanded.

"I was just about to ask you the same thing," Matt said, and straightened to his full height.

"I came to escort Dr. Goodlove down to breakfast and then to this morning's seminar." Bryant gave Matt an acid look.

"She's busy right now." Matt reached to close the door.

Danni inched the bathroom door shut, cowered behind it, and bit her knuckles. Damn! Now everyone at the hospital—even Stone?—would know what *she'd* been up to at the conference. Oh, what had she done?

"I'd like to speak to Dr. Goodlove personally," she heard Bryant saying.

She peeked out again and saw that Bryant had his hand on the door, preventing Matt from closing it.

"Well, she can't talk to you right now. But I'll tell her you came by." Matt gave the door a shove.

Bryant pushed back. "Listen, I saw you last night with your stupid getup and your jug of hooch—" He gave Matt's appearance a disdainful assessment, but Matt only returned the favor, giving Bryant's blazer a frowning once-over as if it were a pink tutu.

"I demand to see Dr. Goodlove." Bryant tried to shove his way around Matt, but Matt shoved back, sending Bryant out into the hallway.

"No, *you* listen," Matt said, while Bryant smoothed his fine hair back in place. "It just so happens, Dr. Goodlove and I are—"

"Matt!" Danni shrieked and flew out of the bathroom, towel and all. "I... We... I don't owe anyone an explanation of my private life." She walked forward with as much dignity as she could muster in a towel, hid her torso behind the door and said, "Roger, I'm sorry. I can't come down to the seminar right now. Please excuse us." She closed the door in Bryant's stunned face.

She whirled on Matt immediately. "Do *not* go around telling people we're married!"

"Why not? We sure as hell *are* married."

Danni threw her hands up, feeling as if she might burst into tears. This was absolutely *not* how she'd ever imagined her married life would begin. "Because...because I work with these people, and I have to maintain the image of a competent physician. I can't have everybody thinking I'm some idiot broad who'd run off to the Caribbean and get married on a drunken whim!" She turned away from him and covered her face and actually did burst into tears, which infuriated her. Why was she always crying around this man?

Matt came up behind her and gently grasped her shaking shoulders. "Danni, sweetheart." He squeezed. "You are anything but an idiot broad.

And hey—'' he turned her to him ''—we did not get married on a drunken whim.''

''Of course we did,'' she sobbed, and wiped at her cheeks with trembling fingers.

''Okay, maybe we were a little stewed, but I, for one, meant it when I said those vows.''

''I was drunk!'' she whined, wiping at more tears.

''Okay. Maybe you were. But you're not drunk now. How do you feel now? Can you honestly tell me you're sorry about everything that happened last night? Huh?''

He bent his head and tried to look into her face. Danni sniffed. Then he straightened and pulled her tightly to him. ''Can you honestly tell me you don't want that to happen again?'' He felt her body sink into his.

''That's what I thought. Come on. Don't cry.'' He leaned back and reached to her cleavage, pulled out the corner of her towel and raised it to dab at her cheeks. The towel came loose and slipped away.

Grinning, he said, ''Oops,'' and tossed it aside, wrapping his arms back around her again and cupping her bare bottom in his hands. ''Listen to me. We did *not* get married on a whim. The truth is, I've wanted you since the first time we kissed.'' He looked into her eyes innocently as he unfastened his own towel. Then, as if they weren't standing there stark naked and he wasn't pressing against her, he kept talking. ''Do you remember that tiny little kiss in your bedroom?''

Danni sniffed again and nodded. Then she giggled, because so far, there hadn't been such a thing as a "tiny little kiss" between them. But he gave her one now. "Just one tiny little kiss," he murmured as he ran his mouth over her jaw and started nibbling her ear. "And I knew I wanted you to be all mine." He pulled her pelvis up to his in one sharp thrust.

Danni gasped at the impact.

"Don't you want to be married to me—" he whispered while he nibbled down her neck " —so we can do this all the time?"

She nodded—not actually at the question, but more at the nibbling, at the rhythm of his hips. Her tears were now completely dry, her skin felt hot, and her breathing was getting rapid for another reason.

"Well, there you go, little lady. And *I* wanted to do this from the very minute I saw you." He was talking in an exaggerated Okie accent. He leaned back and stared openly at her breasts. "And that was before I'd even gotten ay-quainted with yore considerable charms."

"Stop it!" She slapped his biceps without thinking.

"Ouch! Ooh!" He moaned and grabbed his shoulder, then doubled over dramatically. "She hit me directly on my injury!" He stumbled backward toward the bed. "Help! I need a doctor!" He flopped spread-eagle on the bed as if dead.

"You *are* crazy." She stood over him, smiling.

And so wonderfully made, she thought, admiring him.

He sat up and grabbed her wrist and pulled her closer. "I really do need a doctor," he said, his blue eyes glittering with desire.

She went limp and let him pull her down.

"Oh, yeah." He settled her on top of him on the bed, and forced her legs apart with his knee. Now his eyes were smoldering. "I need a doctor in the worst way."

OVER AN ELEGANT room-service breakfast two hours later, Matt finally mentioned it.

"You know, birth control?" he repeated.

At the words, Danni nearly choked on her bagel. What the hell kind of obstetrician was she? A really stupid one, obviously.

"Well," Matt continued, "I guess I should have asked last night. This *is* my business now. We're *married,* Mrs. Creed." He joked, then raised her trembling hand, kissed her fingers. "Hey—" he seemed to notice then that something was wrong "—you're shaking. What is it?"

Danni tried not to look into his eyes. Why was it so hard to conceal anything from this man? Was a person always this vulnerable when they made love to somebody, or was it just with him? She certainly couldn't remember feeling anything like this with Wesley Fuerborne. All she could think about during *that* incident had been, *What if I get pregnant?* But with Matt, for heaven's sake, she hadn't given it a thought—or at least, not a conscious one.

"Nothing," she lied, and felt her cheeks turning red, for last night she had made a terrible, terrible mistake—a mistake that was, for Dannielle Goodlove, the worst. And there was nothing she could do about it now. As she'd always gently chided her patients in this predicament, the horse was out of the barn.

She dared a glance at his face and for an instant saw shocked realization there. Then he raised her fingers and kissed them again. Hard. "Danni," he whispered against her flesh, "don't think I'm nuts for saying this, okay? But I swear, getting you pregnant would be the high point of my life."

She jumped up from the little table on the balcony and ran into the bedroom, threw herself across the king-size expanse and buried her face in a pillow.

Matt followed her, put one knee on the bed and wrapped his hands around her hips, turning her onto her back.

"What have I done?" she asked as he slowly lowered his muscular frame over her upper body.

"Don't you mean, 'What have *we* done?' I should have been prepared. I'm so sorry." He smoothed her hair back. "Hey. It'll be okay. And as for the rest of what you've done, I hope—" he kissed her chin "—you've married—" he kissed her nose "—the man—" he kissed her cheek "—you'll always—" he ended at her mouth "—love."

Then, without another single word, while Danni
watched in awe, as if she were a witness outside
her own body, he used an exquisite combination of
drive and tenderness to make love to her yet again.

TIME FLASHED BY LIKE some sort of brilliant dream
for Danni. She felt as if she were in one of those
gaudy travel brochures where carefree couples in
skimpy swimsuits were holding hands on white
sandy beaches.

Thanks to Matt, she missed several of Dr. Donnar's lectures. And thanks to Bryant, she felt hor-
ribly guilty about it.

Every day, Bryant left voice mail upon voice
mail, trying to drag her back into the sane life she
was supposed to lead—the life before Matthew
Creed.

But every night Matt won her over anew. Matt,
who tempted her with his carafe of yellow drinks.
Matt, who ended up staying in her room, in her bed.
Matt, who led her deeper and deeper into the cham-
bers of passion.

And though he fed her gourmet meals, exotic del-
icacies, and even another of his famous long picnics
on the beach, she could tell she was still losing
weight. All this "activity," she supposed, burned
up lots of calories. She smiled to herself as she
adjusted the straps of the bikini he'd bought her—
"Can't a man buy his old lady a little present?"
he'd said—then she slipped the yellow-flowered
sundress over it.

And all the time, everywhere they went, his

hands were constantly on her—her waist, her hips, her thighs—all those places that seemed to be coming more and more alive, hungering more and more for his touch.

Matt, she discovered, was a shoulder kisser, a finger kisser, a knee kisser. He called her things— "Mrs. Creed," "Honey," and when they made love, "baby"—that no man had ever called her before.

Tonight he was taking her back to "their beach" to celebrate "their third anniversary."

The sun had already set when they got there, and they waded out into the warm Caribbean waters and stared off at the twinkling lights of the quaint village nestled against the mountains in the distance.

"Look, honey. Over there's where we got married," Matt said and pointed.

She studied his profile instead of the village, trying to read him, but the rising moon did not illuminate his expression clearly. Again she wondered, what he really thought about their marriage.

"What happened to your first marriage?" she asked quietly.

He turned to her, his eyes guarded, assessing her. "Old story. Selfishness. Immaturity."

"Hers or yours?"

He smirked. "You have to ask?"

Danni turned her back and walked out of the water, onto the sand. "Come here." She held her hand back toward him. "We need to talk."

He stood in the waves for a brief moment, hesitating, then slogged slowly onto the beach and took her hand.

She led him to the blanket, pulled him down beside her.

"I know so little about you," she explained. "What I do know I like, but I need to know more."

"I'll tell you anything you want to know," Matt said sincerely.

"What went wrong with your first marriage? Really."

Matt sighed and looked out at the ocean, at the mountains beyond the bay. "Okay, if it's that important to you. It's actually pretty simple. When the bombing happened, after the rescue work was done, we just fell apart."

Danni waited, but he didn't offer more.

"Why?" She felt the same tension from him that she'd had on the night she'd asked him about the bandanna, but she felt she had a right to ask now. She could help him, maybe. After all, they'd slept together. They'd *married* each other—even if the whole thing had been a little crazy. "What happened?" she repeated.

"Real life. Real pain. Stuff Carla couldn't understand. Everything was one big trip to her. A trip to the mall. A trip to the .mountains. A trip to a friend's party." He picked up a handful of sand and let it flow through his fingers. "With Carla it was just *go...do...buy*. She never stopped to *feel* anything, except physical pleasure, or maybe to feel sorry for herself. She was good at that.

"Instead of trying to figure out what the bombing

meant, or at least grieving about it properly, or even letting me grieve about it properly, Carla just wanted it to go away, because it was ugly, because it was messy.''

He pitched the handful of sand toward the sea in frustration. ''I know I wasn't the easiest guy to live with after the bombing, but Carla wouldn't even try to understand. She only wanted comfort, pleasure, escape. She announced one day that she wanted a divorce. At first I was upset, but then I realized I didn't want to be married to someone who was that selfish. To me, that's like living half a life.'' He dusted the last of the sand from his palms, then turned his head to look into Danni's eyes. ''I guess that's what first attracted me to you. The first time I saw you, you were right in the middle of it—life. You were so *real*.''

Danni didn't know about that. She certainly had her own demons, her own self-pity, her self-indulgences, even if to him her preoccupations seemed loftier than Carla's. But her mind and heart were focused on Matt now, trying to understand him. ''Tell me—'' she touched his forearm, running her fingers softly across the springy hairs ''—what happened to you in the bombing?''

He inhaled and exhaled slowly. ''The same thing that happened to everybody else. Horror. Grief. Helplessness.''

Danni closed her eyes. Hearing those words spoken aloud in his deep, reverberating voice was almost more than she could bear.

''But I also learned that even though my heart

was breaking, I still had it in me to be strong for
someone else. I learned to give to the limit, that
there's no point in holding back. I learned to do
whatever had to be done, say whatever had to be
said, to go on with dignity. I learned all that by
watching the families and the victims.''

''Oh, Matt,'' Danni whispered, tears shimmering
in her eyes.

He wrapped her in his arms and they clung to
each other tightly for some moments, while Danni
felt his strong heart beating against her breast and
was grateful that this man had become her lover—
even if, because of their differences, the relationship didn't last, she knew she would always have
this moment.

''I'm so glad I had this time with you,'' she told
him honestly.

He studied her face, as if trying to read her meaning. After several moments he quietly asked,
''Could I make love to you?''

On that isolated beach far from the world—far,
far away from horror and sadness and helplessness—he took possession of her again.

And just like every time she climaxed in Matt's
arms, Danni was newly surprised, as if she couldn't
believe that this vital, sensuous creature was really
herself, responding in this way.

But Matt seemed to expect her response, to relish
it. And when it was over, when she was limp, her
insides quivering with the echoes of passion, he'd
tell her how feminine she was, how wonderful.

It was as if he'd possessed her and freed her—

all in a matter of days. *Hedonism,* Danni would think every time Matt worked his magic. *I've lost my inhibitions—and my good sense—to pure hedonism.*

No. I've lost my mind—*my* self—*to hedonism,* she would think every morning when she woke up with Matt's strong arms and legs tangled around her. And though she planned to break off this foolish liaison with a man she hardly knew, she didn't. She couldn't.

Instead she waded in deeper. Literally. Matt took her snorkeling. He took her deep-sea fishing. He took her out on a Hobie Cat. *My,* she thought, watching his broad shoulders flex as he mastered the sail of the catamaran, *Matthew Creed is such a vigorous man.* It seemed he wasn't afraid to try anything.

But what Danni couldn't see was that deep down, a part of Matthew Creed *was* afraid. He was afraid the woman he was holding night after night would wake up one morning, come to her senses, and leave him. He was afraid she'd finally answer the perpetual voice mail from Dr. Dashing. He was afraid to think about what would happen when she got back to her medical career, her fancy house, her prominent social position.

He would wake up in the middle of the night, wanting her. While the moonlight poured in through the sheer drapes, he'd prop himself on his elbow and watch her sleep. He would vow to go slow, to be gentle in their lovemaking, but it was no good. He wanted to ravish her every time he looked at her. Didn't she know how utterly beautiful she was?

Whenever he was free to adore her body—not just during sex, but when he scooped her up in his arms and carried her through the surf or admired her silhouetted in the morning sun on the balcony—he found himself thinking of their future. Daydreaming about bringing her back here when they were old. Or better yet, bringing their kids back here with them someday.

Kids.

Somehow he'd never been able to imagine actual offspring with Carla, though he'd asked her to consider starting a family often enough.

But with Danni, even though they'd only been together a few days, he wanted, fiercely, to get her pregnant every time he entered her. Which was just plain crazy.

So he took the responsibility for birth control upon himself. But despite that, he caught himself saying things to her like, "Someday we'll have lots of kids—" he'd kiss her irresistible forehead "—beautiful ones that look exactly like you."

And he meant it.

What Matt didn't know was that Danni, with her obstetrical knowledge, with every woman's secret cognizance of her own rhythms, comprehended certain things he didn't. What he didn't know was that when he said things about having kids someday, Danni had to bite her tongue to keep from blurting, "I hope someday isn't sooner than you think."

But she never said it. Why spoil things by harping on a calamity that might never happen? Statistically, the chances were very remote.

WHEN THE DAY CAME TO catch their respective planes home—Danni's tour flight left in the morning, Matt's later in the afternoon—Matt woke Danni up early. He'd ordered a room-service breakfast and had it set up on the balcony.

"I don't want this to end," Danni sighed as Matt poured her coffee and she looked out over the ocean calm, beneath a castle of clouds, pink and golden in the sunrise.

Matt kissed the top of her head, and went around the table to his chair. Then he proceeded to consume the eggs and bacon he'd ordered, frowning out at the sea and the sky.

An uneasiness settled on Danni as she sipped her coffee and watched Matt, because suddenly she was worried about what she would do if this had really been nothing but a big romantic adventure to him. She'd been so preoccupied with her own mixed-up feelings, about his taking it too seriously, that she hadn't considered how she'd react if he didn't. How would she handle that? Some unnamed fear churned deep within in her.

They took the fifteen-minute cab ride from Divi Little Bay to the small airport together, and Matt noticed Danni growing more quiet on the way.

"I wish we were flying home together," he said, breaking the silence.

Danni only smiled.

He worried. Was it settling in on her now? What

they'd done? She was not an impulsive woman. What would she do when she got back to Tulsa?

Her plane was already being boarded out on the tarmac and the attendant at the intake desk rushed them along. Danni had brought only a carry-on bag to St. Martin and Matt hoisted it over his shoulder and took her elbow as they jogged across the blacktop. She would have been on time had she ridden the tour shuttle from the hotel, but the truth was, she had wanted to savor every last minute with Matt. And now that it *was* their last minute, what would she say to him?

It seemed as if he wanted to be with her for as long as possible, too. And their mutual reluctance to part seemed to give the inevitable goodbye more weight—as if it were permanent. Was that because this *was* goodbye and neither one of them wanted the fairy tale to end?

When they got to the boarding ramp, she turned and looked up into his face. She couldn't read him at all, she realized, because the sun was reflecting off his Gargoyles.

The flight attendant standing at the top of the steps motioned for Danni to hurry.

"Listen, Matt," Danni started, "I want you to know there are no obligations, here. I mean, just because this happened, that doesn't mean you have to—" When he didn't say anything, her fears won out. "Maybe this was all a huge mistake.... We can see about getting the marriage annulled back in Tulsa."

Over the roar of the jet engines, Matt wasn't sure he'd heard her right. *"Annulled?"*

And suddenly, as if in a waking nightmare, Matt was recalling the breakup with Carla. It had been like this—sudden, without rhyme or reason. A flat, cruel announcement: "I want a divorce." Just like that. Just like *this*. Never again. He wasn't going to throw himself at the feet of some woman who'd jerk him around, trying to change him, acting as if she were doing him a big favor by letting him participate in her wonderful life.

The flight attendant called out, "Ma'am!" and motioned with her hand toward the open door of the plane. Danni looked over her shoulder nervously, then back up at Matt.

Matt found his voice. "Whatever you want," he said quietly.

Danni made a gesture, as if she couldn't hear him above the noise.

"I said—" he raised his voice "—an annulment's fine with me if that's what you want."

Danni nodded, grabbed her carry-on and ran up the steps before she had time to think about what they were saying to each other. She didn't want to think about it.

But on the long flight back to Dallas-Fort Worth, she did think. She thought of Matt's long, muscular body; of his hands, so warm, strong and comforting; of his eyes so blue and sincere.

But then, as she closed her eyes and leaned back against the headrest, she thought of his words about annulment. Had he really considered this whole thing a mere fling? Was Danni going back to resume her lonely life?

Matt also did some thinking during his trip home. He thought of Danni's scent, her laugh, her breath coming faster when he made love to her.

He thought of the way he'd become involved with this woman in the first place. How he'd tried so hard to be careful this time. And how he'd chased her halfway around the world—and for what? So he could scare her off with a premature marriage and she could end up rejecting him the same way Carla had?

The one thing Matt hadn't thought about was the possibility that Danni might actually be pregnant.

CHAPTER FIFTEEN

AS SHE TURNED OFF Terwilliger Boulevard into her mother's winding driveway, Danni asked herself why she felt so apprehensive. Was it because she was worried about hurting her mother? Her mother certainly had experienced enough pain for one lifetime.

The gardener hadn't cleared last night's heavy snow from the drive so she slowed the car to a crawl as she entered the wrought-iron gates and steered up the steep slope toward the huge house she had once called home.

In recent years, since her father had died, her feelings toward her mother had become an uncomfortable mixture. Danni loved her mother, and her mother gloried in Danni's demanding career as a physician, yet she expected Danni to come trotting over to the stately old house for every little social do-dah, which made Danni feel tethered somehow.

Danni parked her car way up beside the delivery entrance, stomped the snow off her boots, and let herself in the back door that opened into the narrow hallway flanked by pantries on both sides. She went directly to the kitchen because she wanted to avoid having this conversation in her mother's formal parlor, if at all possible.

Monika, the daytime helper and cook, was there, laboring over the stove, stirring a huge pot of something that smelled delicious.

"Hi, Monika!" Danni called out and crossed the room to give and receive their customary hug.

"Danni!" Monika smiled. "You look a little pale," the older woman added in her faint German accent. "Are you sure you're not overdoing this diet? Look here. You are just in time to try my new batch of seven-bean soup." She turned back to the counter and raised the lid of a Japanese rice cooker and started to ladle beans over a bowl of freshly steamed rice.

"Monika, not now, thanks." Danni touched the cook's shoulder to stop her. She wasn't sure, in her current state, if she could keep the spicy seven-bean dish down, especially not while she told her mother the news. "I need to see Mom. Is she around?"

"Olivia? Last time I saw her she was in her office, on the phone, making arrangements for the Taste of Tulsa."

"The Taste of Tulsa," Danni mumbled. "I forgot she has to start getting ready for that thing in January."

"Ja." Monika smiled and nodded. "She works so hard at her volunteer projects. It's amazing how she gets so much done."

Getting so much done—the Goodlove credo, Danni thought as she made her way through the enormous house toward the office tucked in the northeast corner.

She stopped in the living room to stare up at a glowing portrait of herself and Lisa as children, wearing frilly pure white dresses and sweet smiles. Too bad they couldn't have stayed that innocent forever. Her expression grew solemn as she thought how ironic it was that she'd made the same mistake Lisa had. Only she was older than Lisa had been, and should have been wiser. Was it something in the blood?

"I'm sorry, sissy," she whispered to the portrait. "I guess I screwed up." She turned on her heel and marched to the office.

She knocked politely, and a well-modulated matron's voice said, "Yes?" from behind the oak door.

"Mom, it's me," Danni said.

"Sweetheart! Come in!" the voice called. Danni heard her mother's footfalls on the rug, then heels clicking across the parquet flooring. She was greeted with a hug as soon as the door swung open.

"Darling! How wonderful of you to take time to visit me in the middle of the day!" Her mother squeezed her so tightly Danni almost lost her breath. Olivia was fully dressed, coiffed, and made-up, though she was probably spending the entire day right here in this office. She would probably even have Monika serve lunch here.

Danni's mother was wearing Clinique's Aromatics, the only fragrance she ever wore, and Danni breathed it in, finding comfort in its familiarity. Her mother loved her. Surely she would not judge Danni for one moment of foolishness.

"Come," her mother said. "I'll have Monika bring us a little coffee and Danish in the parlor."

Danni looked around the room, at all of her mother's books lining the walls, at her orderly work station, her enormous desk framed by sunny, paned windows overlooking the sloping, snowy yard. A small fire warmed the space between two wing chairs.

"No, Mom. I don't want coffee. And I'd rather talk in here. I… I don't have that much time. I came to tell you something." Danni pointed at the stack of invitations—for a preliminary organizational luncheon, no doubt. One of her mother's endless distractions. "I'm sorry to disturb your work."

Her mother, always intuitive, frowned. "My work can wait." She studied her daughter. "Would you like to sit down? Here. Let me take your wrap."

Danni allowed Olivia to remove her coat and they both sat facing each other at right angles to the fire. Her mother slipped a silk shawl from the back of her chair and fitted it neatly around her shoulders. "Now. Tell me," she said simply.

Danni smiled a sad little smile. Her mother's world was so perfectly orderly, so serene. She looked at Olivia's slender legs, the way they crossed gracefully, the toe of one sensible chic pump pointed just so. How could a daughter do this to her mother? Yet Danni knew the longer she delayed, the worse it would be.

"Mom," she started, then focused her attention on the fire as she said the words: "I'm pregnant."

She refused to look at her mother's face, but she heard the gasp, and then, in a voice quickly reined under control, "Are you certain?"

Danni smiled again, this time ruefully. "Mom, I'm an obstetrician. Of course I'm certain."

"But... But, how did this happen?"

"The usual way, Mother. Intercourse." Danni regretted her sarcasm as soon as she said it. It was not her mother's fault that she'd messed up her life.

"Danielle!" her mother chastised. "This is a shock to me. I wasn't even aware that you were seeing anyone."

"I'm not—not really." Danni wanted to keep this simple, to force Olivia's acceptance, to quash her mother's chronic impulse to make things right and proper, to fix things.

There was no fixing this. The only way out of this mess was straight through it. Danni was going to be a single mother, she was convinced of that now. She'd done her first pregnancy test a few weeks after she'd returned from St. Martin—long weeks in which she hadn't heard one word from Matthew Creed—and when the results were positive she'd sat in her darkening office for an hour deciding whether to pick up the phone.

In the end, her decision had been to wait, and wait, and wait. All through the Christmas season she'd waited, alone in her big, beautifully decorated house.

If Matthew Creed wanted her, this time he would

have to be the one to call. And she'd be damned if she'd keep him in the relationship because she'd gone and gotten herself pregnant. It wasn't as if she didn't have the resources to take care of this baby by herself.

But it was going to be complicated, she didn't kid herself about that.

After several long moments, Danni looked into her mother's eyes, and saw there total confusion and pain. And disbelief. For this was the last thing Olivia would have expected from Danni—getting herself knocked up outside a serious relationship. "It was a…a brief fling, Mom. In the Caribbean."

Her mother sank back in her chair, her perfectly made-up face beautiful even when her mouth was slack from shock. "At the obstetrical conference in November?"

Danni nodded.

"This man. Who is he? Not… *Wesley?*"

"Mom." Danni shook her head.

"Who, then? Another doctor? Where is he from?"

"It doesn't matter who he is. He's totally inappropriate for me, and he so much as told me he has no interest in marriage. In fact, the last time I saw him was when we said goodbye at the airport on St. Martin."

"But…but do you love him?"

"What?" Danni didn't want the conversation to turn in this direction. This discussion was about the baby. This discussion was meant to prepare her mother to be a grandmother.

"I said, do you love him?"

"I hardly *know* him," Danni said evasively.

"So it was just a sexual encounter?" her mother questioned.

Danni almost smiled at her mother's choice of words, then she closed her eyes. "I suppose you could call it that." She thought again of herself and Matt on that beach; of how this baby had been made.

Their lovemaking had seemed like the furthest thing from mere sex. To Danni it had seemed like an awakening, a resurrection. But that sounded so crazy, so hideously idealistic. Danni supposed she was not the only thirty-something woman to impulsively take a lover and then exaggerate the significance of the encounter, but she was determined to keep her silly feelings forever her secret. "It certainly wasn't true love, whatever in the world that is."

"What do you mean, 'whatever that is'? You know what love is. You were raised in a very loving family."

"Mom. Dad was always gone on business, and you were always..." She looked at the stack of invitations. But Danni knew she was being unfair. Her mother had always loved her, even when Olivia's challenges and pursuits distracted her. Danni sighed. "Sometimes I think there was only one person in this family who had time for love. It doesn't matter."

"Yes, it does matter," her mother countered.

"Love is the most important thing in a person's life—"

"Look. Can we not talk about love right now?" Danni pleaded, thinking how it had been her desperation to find love that had gotten her into this mess in the first place.

Her mother studied Danni apprehensively. "Aren't you even a little happy about this?" she finally asked. "I mean, this *is* wonderful news— that we're going to have a baby in the family." Suddenly her mother seemed animated. She sat forward in her chair. "Oh, Danni! Think of it that way! A baby!"

Her mother reached out and clutched Danni's shoulders, shook her gently as if to waken her. "Darling, this is wonderful! You'll see! Everything will be all right. I'll help you with the baby, so you can maintain your practice. And so will Aunt Hetra and Aunt Dottie. Don't you see?" She gave Danni another little shake.

Tears stung Danni's eyes. Her mother really was remarkable. She always knew the right thing to do—not only the proper thing, but the *right* thing. So overcome she could hardly speak, Danni looked down into her lap, fought her tears, and whispered, "You're amazing, Mom."

"Ah—" her mother reached up and stroked Danni's hair "—I love you, sweetheart. Having a baby isn't a tragedy, no matter what the circumstances...." Her mother's hand suddenly stilled.

After a heartbeat she tilted Danni's face up. "I know it hurts to think of Lisa. It hurts me, too. But

I still believe her decision to have her baby was the right choice. I truly believe that. Her death was not anybody's fault. I've told you that before.''

The moment her mother said Lisa's name, Danni's tears started to flow, and now she choked back a wrenching sob.

Her mother clutched Danni tightly, her perfectly manicured nails digging into Danni's arms. "Danni! You're not thinking of doing something...something rash about this pregnancy, are you?''

Danni couldn't speak, she was so overcome with emotion. She didn't know what she'd expected from her mother—disappointment, recriminations, maybe. But not this generous understanding. She really *hadn't* trusted her mother, had she?

"Oh, Mom,'' she blurted. "You know how I feel about that! Of course I'm having this baby. I just— I guess I can't believe I'm putting you through this. I didn't mean what I said a minute ago. You and Dad were good parents, loving parents. Really. It's me. I'm sorry I'm doing this to you.''

"You aren't doing anything except giving me a grandchild,'' her mother said firmly, then wrapped her arms around Danni's shoulders. Leaning forward, Danni rested her cheek on the cool silk of her mother's scarf and breathed in the fragrance of Aromatics as if it were a calming drug.

For some moments Olivia simply rocked her daughter. Finally she said, "No, my precious Danni, you aren't doing anything except exactly what you've always done. You are making me very proud of you."

That was exactly the kind of talk that had fortified Danni Goodlove all of her life.

CHAPTER SIXTEEN

MATT FIDGETED. THE CHAIR was too damn small. You'd think they'd have extra-large chairs for pregnant women. He glanced around at the half-dozen-or-so rotund ladies sharing the waiting room with him.

A freckle-faced teenager peeked up from her magazine and beamed indulgently at him. *What's she smiling about?* Matt wondered irritably. That kid was way too young to be having a baby. Her nail polish was *turquoise,* for Pete's sake. But looking at her beat-up Nikes and faded denim maternity dress, he suddenly felt sorry for her and gave her a big-brotherly smile back.

Relax, he told himself. *These ladies probably think you're a father waiting for his wife. Just tough it out. You're here to see Danni. That's all that matters.*

He resettled his broad shoulders and tried to concentrate on the big-screen TV, but it was featuring a tape about breast-feeding. He felt his face go hot and riveted his attention on the fake flower arrangement on the table beside him. Finally, he resorted to hiding behind a parenting magazine.

In the weeks following that trip to the Caribbean,

Matt had made up his mind: He wouldn't bother her if she didn't want him.

But it hadn't worked.

At odd moments—when he was filling his truck with gas, or shaving, or wolfing down another burger alone—he'd find himself staring off into space, while images of Danni played before his eyes like an endless-loop video. And even worse, sometimes he'd hear her laugh, and hear her voice saying, as plainly as if she were standing next to him, "Maybe this was all a huge mistake."

A huge mistake. *Fine,* he'd eventually convinced himself.

But when he hadn't heard from her, seen her, touched her in several weeks and he still couldn't get her out of his mind, he realized it wasn't any kind of mistake. It was exactly what he had thought it was in the Caribbean: true love. And if she was too stupid to see that—

And then he had started to get mad, really mad. Not simply because of her rejection; this was something to do with *rightness.* No, it was more like something to do with *wrongness*…with waste. Cliché or not, he'd learned the hard way that life was too precious—and too short—to waste a single moment. But how could he convince Danni?

And then one evening when Jackie and Ty had been trying to distract him with beer and videos, Jackie had let a little something slip that had blown the lid off his anger, off his whole world.

Interrupting his thoughts, a middle-aged nurse,

who looked vaguely familiar, stepped through a swing door. "Matthew Creed?"

He got up and followed her to an examination room.

There was no sign of Danni on the way down the hall. Like everything else about her, this place was first-class. Immaculate. Softly decorated in pretty pastels. Some kind of tranquil, classical music floating everywhere. He imagined pregnant women thrived on this stuff.

In the exam room, the nurse closed the door, indicated he should sit on the examining table, and then frowned at the paperwork he had filled out. She poked at her salt-and-pepper curls with a pen and anchored it behind one ear. Her name tag read Carol Hollis, but Matt couldn't remember where he'd seen her before. "What exactly can we do for you, Mr, Creed?"

"Well, uh, like I wrote there—" he pointed at the clipboard "—Dr. Goodlove stitched up my arm a few months ago. An accident in a fire—I'm a firefighter—and all of a sudden it's bothering me." He reached across his chest and massaged his upper arm. "She must have left some glass in it or something. I figured she'd want to look at it herself and all."

The nurse frowned. "Hmm," she said. "It would be highly unusual for Dr. Goodlove to miss anything, but she'll want to take a good look at you anyway. Take your shirt off, please."

"Excuse me?"

"So we can examine your arm."

"Oh."

While he unbuttoned his flannel shirt the nurse stuck a thermometer in his ear that beeped, then she took his pulse and blood pressure. "Well," she said brightly, "you don't have a fever and everything else looks normal."

She massaged the biceps area of his injured arm, which was absolutely healthy, and didn't even have much of a scar, just as that nurse in the emergency room had promised— Oh, sh—! He suddenly remembered where he'd seen this nurse before. Well, what was she going to do? Kick him out because he'd flirted with Danni in the E.R.? He was a paying customer.

She was looking at him strangely. Did she know he and Danni had dated? Did she know...everything?

"Dr. Goodlove will be in shortly," she said and left.

He waited in agony. He couldn't sit still on the table so he went to stand by the window. He was staring down at the street, with his arms crossed over his bare chest, when the door flew open and Danni swooped in. A petite redheaded nurse was right on her heels.

"Mr. Creed," Danni said tersely while she looked at his paperwork, not at him. She didn't smile, didn't call him "Matt." Her hair had grown out enough to be cinched up in one of those fancy braids, and she had gained back some of her weight, but that was to be expected, if Jackie was to be believed. Underneath her lab coat, she had on one of those long, baggy, little-girl dresses with tiny flowers all over it. To him, she looked as beautiful as he'd remembered. More so, now.

"Let's see. You have a problem?" She frowned, flipping the pages futilely, as if unable to find anything significant there.

He planted his hands on his hips. Okay. So she was going to be hostile. He couldn't fathom *why*, but he could handle it. "Yeah," he said. "I have…an ache."

He'd said the last word huskily, on purpose, to get her to look up. When she did, he met her eyes with challenge. "We don't need the nurse," he said quietly.

Danni's jaw tightened and her eyes narrowed a fraction, but she turned to the nurse and said, "Becky, please go get Lindsey Webber ready for her ultrasound."

Becky skittered out like a scared rabbit.

"What kind of stunt is this?" Danni demanded as soon as the door closed.

He shrugged. "I've tried every other way to see you. You won't return my calls, and we need to talk."

"Look. There is nothing to talk about. We had a fling. It's over. That's all."

"That's all? What about our child?"

Danni's eyes grew wide and her face ashen as she grabbed the counter and sank onto the rolling stool beside it.

For a split second, concern and pity softened Matt's attitude, but then he let his righteous anger have its way. "Even if it was just a fling to you, even if you think you're too damn good for me, apparently you're carrying my child, so you're going to have to get off your high horse and discuss this."

"How did you find out?" Danni whispered with her eyes riveted on the exam table.

"So. You *weren't* planning to tell me."

Her head snapped up. "There's no law that says I have to—"

"There by God oughtta be!" Matt was suddenly shouting. "And just in case you blocked it out, we're married, lady!"

"You can't be serious. You know as well as I do that we're about as married as—"

"What about love? What about what we *had,* Danni? I can't believe you'd just turn on me like this. You have to tell me why, to my face. You owe me that much."

Danni crossed her arms over her chest defensively. "I don't owe you anything. It's bad enough that I find myself pregnant by a man I hardly know—"

"That's the point, here. You *are* pregnant. That's my child. I've half a mind to drag you into court or something!"

Danni jumped up and got in his face. "And I've half a mind to hoist you up in those stirrups! How *dare* you come into this busy medical office, upsetting me and demanding to discuss this on *your* terms, when there are patients sitting out there—"

she pointed in the direction of the waiting room "—needing my attention!"

Matt jabbed a finger into his bare chest. "*I* need your attention, woman! And our child needs *both* our attentions—attention—*whatever!*" He threw his hands up in the air. Where the hell had that vulnerable, soft, sexy woman in the Caribbean disappeared to?

The door banged open and the little redheaded nurse, bug-eyed and breathless, shouted, "Dr. Danni, we need you in the waiting room! Lindsey's seizing!"

Danni flew out the door and down the hall, her lab coat flapping like wings behind her. Matt, still shirtless, was right on her heels.

A pregnant teenager—the freckle-faced one who'd smiled at Matt—writhed in unconscious agony on the carpet. Her face was puffy and beet red, her jaw was clamped, her eyes rolled back in her head. A ring of distressed females hovered over her, but the nurses were already herding them away, clearing the way for Danni. Carol Hollis was on her knees beside the patient, protecting her abdomen from her own thrashing limbs.

Danni dropped to her knees opposite Carol, supported the young woman's head, checked her eyes and quietly ordered a syringe, Valium, a tourniquet. The request having apparently been anticipated, the items appeared instantly. While Carol steadied the patient's arm, Danni found a vein and asked in a low voice if transport had been called.

"Yes, ma'am," came the answer.

"Shannon—" Danni jerked her head at one of her staff "—get security out in that parking lot to raise the gates and clear the traffic."

Matt's first-responder training had prepared him to deal with any emergency and it was all he could do to keep his hands out of the action as Carol and Danni worked.

"Get an IV started," Danni said as soon as she'd shot in the last of the calming Valium. "Kill the lights," she ordered quietly. "Close those drapes, and turn off that phone. Anything could set her off again."

Carol did not let anything distract her work on the other arm as she quickly inserted an IV. Danni put her stethoscope in her ears and listened to the girl's chest. Then she raised the girl's shirt over her belly and pulled down her maternity pants. She palpated the patient's abdomen, put her other hand up and, with no other orders needed, a Doppler was slapped into her palm while another nurse applied blue gel to the spot Danni indicated.

"Let's be quiet," Matt softly urged the group of murmuring, upset women around him.

Then, through the eye-widening silence came the sound: a steady, fast, whoosh-whoosh-whoosh from the innocent passenger curled inside the endangered young woman.

"Baby sounds okay," Danni said.

A patient standing next to Matt let out a stifled sob, and he helped her lower herself into a chair. The receptionist asked everyone to move to the other side of the waiting room.

"Kelly, reschedule all the routine appointments," Danni called over her shoulder. "Funnel any problem cases over to Stone's office."

"Yes, ma'am." The receptionist and a nurse started to deal with the crowd of patients.

The paramedics arrived then and a fresh upheaval started. Matt watched as Danni gave them orders, too, and then rushed off, without so much as a glance back at him, to ride in the ambulance beside her patient.

When they were gone, he sank down in a chair, still shirtless, and for some reason feeling so badly shaken he wanted to cry.

Was it because his Danni—he thought of her that way, as *his*—was pregnant, too? And because nobody else knew it, nobody in the whole damn room had worried about the stress to *her* system from dealing with such a horrifying emergency. Nobody but him.

FOR THE NEXT THREE DAYS, Danni's every waking thought was of Lindsey Webber. Other events happened mechanically: eating, showering, even office visits and delivering two of the other women in her care. All of life, even sleep, was overshadowed by fear, frustration, torment. Lindsey was going bad. Lindsey was only eighteen.

Danni called in a neurologist, a neuropharmacologist. The ICU team was nothing short of heroic, but in the end, they lost Lindsey...and her baby.

In the end, Danni had to face the girl's parents and the pimply-faced young husband.

In the end, Danni had to go home and taste defeat, like a bitter toxin, rising in her throat, again and again.

OLIVIA ARRIVED AT DANNI'S house bright and early the morning after, just as Jackie was brewing coffee.

"I wanted Danni to get some sleep before we talked," she explained as she pulled off her gloves, then her coat, and handed them to Jackie. "I assume she'll be up soon, to go into the office."

"Yes, ma'am," Jackie replied as she hung Olivia's coat carefully. Danni's mother struck terror into Jackie's heart. Her visits to Danni's home were rare, and always seemed, to Jackie, like surprise inspections. Especially at six a.m.; especially since Olivia stood there in cashmere and wool and full makeup, facing Jackie who was clad in Mickey Mouse sweats and big fuzzy slippers.

"Dr. Danni's in the shower. She's got two inductions starting at seven. She wants to get them delivered before the weather gets worse. Shall I hang up your scarf?" Jackie never said words like "shall"—except when she pulled them out for Olivia's benefit.

Olivia shook her head and drew her silk shawl tighter around her. "I'll keep this. It's freezing out there. And I'm afraid it's already sleeting. Poor Danni. I was hoping she could rest a bit this morning after…after what happened."

"Yes, ma'am."

"Go make her a breakfast tray—something hot

and nutritious—and fix me some coffee, with cream, please, and bring it into the bedroom. I'm going in to talk to her.''

"Yes, ma'am."

OLIVIA HEARD THE SHOWER running and tapped on the bathroom door. "Danni, it's Mother. I came to have breakfast with you.''

Minutes later, Danni emerged from the shower in her old pink robe and with a towel around her hair. "Mom, what are you doing here?" she asked.

Olivia, who was bent over the tray Jackie had brought, straightened and winced as she looked at her daughter. "Oh, sweetheart, you look so tired,'' she said softly.

"Now, Mom. Don't start worrying. Pregnant women are always tired.'' Danni crossed the room and gave Olivia a reassuring hug. "What are you doing here?'' she repeated, looking at the tray of food as if she might retch.

"Carol Hollis phoned me late last night. I guess she figured you'd be needing your mother, after a thing like that.'' Olivia still held a bagel in one hand, a knife laden with cream cheese suspended in the other. She dropped the items back on the tray and extended her arms. "At least, I was *hoping* you'd need your mother.''

Danni threw herself into Olivia's arms. "Oh, Mom!'' she cried and buried her face in the familiar silk scarf on her mother's shoulder. For a moment they stood like that, Danni unable to say anything, and Olivia waiting patiently.

Finally Danni straightened and looked into her mother's eyes. "Carol doesn't even realize how bad this is for me." She turned her face away. "She doesn't even know about Lisa. I've never told anyone."

Olivia stroked her daughter's hair. "I know it's been a nightmare for you," she soothed. "It has been for me, too, imagining what you've been going through these last three days."

Danni released a shuddering, exhausted breath. "She was so sweet! Her name even sounds like Lisa's. L-Lindsey."

Olivia grasped Danni's shoulders. "Sweetheart, listen to me. I was afraid you'd be thinking like this. We can never change what happened to Lisa, but we can't let it torture us, either. Just like this girl, there was nothing anyone could have done for Lisa. You've got to believe that."

Danni shook her head. "You're *wrong,* Mom. I knew what Lisa was doing with Jake. I could have told you and Daddy. But I didn't want her to think I was a baby!"

"Do you honestly think that you, a mere fourteen-year-old, could have made any difference in the outcome?"

"Maybe not with Lisa, but I became a doctor so I *could* make a difference in cases like this!" Danni sighed. "At least, I thought that's why I did it. Now, I'm not so sure of myself."

Her mother gave Danni's shoulders another shake. "Danni, stop it. All doctors, even obstetricians, lose patients. Try to think of all the patients you've helped over the years. Think of the good you've done!''

Danni shook her head in protest. ''I keep thinking—what if I missed something crucial with Lindsey?'' Danni paced a few feet away from her mother, then turned. ''I've been so distracted by my own troubles lately. She was out in my waiting room—a closely monitored patient with pregnancy-induced hypertension—needing to see me, while I was back in an exam room having an argument with Matt!''

''Matt?''

Danni looked at her mother in horror, realizing she'd let his name slip.

Olivia took a step in Danni's direction, hesitated before speaking quietly. ''That's the baby's father, isn't it? Matt.'' She waited, but Danni didn't answer. Finally, Olivia cleared her throat and added gently, ''Don't you think you could at least tell me his name, Danni? He is, after all, the father of my grandchild.''

Danni was too spent to resist her mother. Let her do what she wanted with the information. ''Creed,'' she whispered and hung her head. ''The man's name is Matthew Creed.''

CHAPTER SEVENTEEN

THAT AFTERNOON THE SNOW began to melt, only to be refrozen into a worse mess by another bitter storm at nightfall. Like most Southwestern cities, Tulsa did not keep enough road equipment to deal adequately with massive winter storms, and early the next morning, when Olivia Goodlove summoned Matthew Creed to her home on Terwilleger Boulevard, the roads were solid, rutted ice.

Matt had pulled two extra shifts, filling in to make up for his time in the Caribbean—punishing twenty-four-hour marathons of battling fire and ice. He was dead tired as he came out of the shower at the fire station at seven-thirty that morning.

"The woman's *mama* wants you to drive over to Terwilleger?" Ty's voice was high-pitched with dismay. "In this friggin' weather?"

"Maybe this is a way to reach Danni," Matt reasoned as he yanked his jeans on. "She's not returning my calls or my pages. I figure, what have I got to lose?"

"Your neck! You haven't had any sleep and the streets are coated with ice!"

"I promise I'll take a nice long nappy as soon

as I see what Mrs. Olivia Goodlove has to say,'' he said as he buttoned his shirt.

''Look. If you're gonna go, at least take my Jeep instead of that hunk-o-junk pickup.'' Ty tossed the keys onto Matt's bunk.

Matt arrived at the Goodlove mansion, with its high hedges and low stone balusters separating it from the street, and he understood why the old girl had felt free to summon him, bad weather or not. Mrs. Goodlove's sidewalks and winding brick-paved driveway were completely dry and clear. *Hired help to shovel the snow. Another of those amenities the rich take for granted*, Matt thought as he wound around ancient trees and up the steep slope to the massive brick-and-stone house.

He could imagine any number of reasons *why* this woman had called him: to demand that he take responsibility for his actions? Well, hell, he'd tried. To pay him off? Don't need your money, lady. To see what kind of stock her future grandchild would issue from? Matt looked down at his barn jacket, well-worn jeans, and scuffed cowboy boots. *A simple fireman, ma'am.*

But the real question was, why had *he* agreed to come here? This matter was between him and Danni. This child was *their* child. Mrs. Goodlove had better remember that, or he'd be more than happy to remind her of it.

He jerked on the parking brake, got out, slammed the Jeep's door and stood assessing the place for a minute. Three stories of porticoes, balconies, turrets. Jeez.

So this is where she'd grown up—in the bosom of luxury, as they say. Why had a woman like Danni Goodlove ever dated a guy like *him* in the first place?

He noticed a shadowy movement behind one of the high leaded-glass windows. He tugged on the brim of his well-worn cowboy hat and rolled his shoulder muscles uncomfortably, as if his jacket were suddenly too tight.

The reason she'd dated him had been obvious since the trip to the Caribbean, hadn't it? Okay, she'd gotten what she wanted, plus a little bonus. Trouble was, he couldn't stop thinking about that "little bonus." And he adored its mother.

He sauntered up the broad, scraped-clean stone steps and pushed the intercom button. A female voice answered. "Yes?"

"Matthew Creed to see Mrs. Goodlove," he informed the speaker.

Two seconds later, a slender woman with a blond bun opened the frosted-glass door. "Mrs. Goodlove?" he said.

"No. I am Monika, Mrs. Goodlove's day helper."

Matt felt himself turn red. Of course, a maid. With an accent, no less.

"Come in, please." She escorted him into a long entry hall that was probably bigger than his apartment, took his hat and jacket, then asked him to have a seat on a bench as if he were some door-to-door salesman.

Matt sat listening to a grandfather clock tick off

the seconds, willing himself to be calm. He rubbed at the crease on his forehead left by his hatband and raked his hand through his hair a couple of times, but refused to check his appearance in the massive mirror behind him.

"Mr. Creed?" An amazingly elegant and beautiful woman appeared at the end of the long foyer and extended a slender bejeweled hand as she walked toward him. She was petite, slender, almost birdlike, with faded blond hair, pale skin, an aristocratic mouth. Only the high cheekbones and clear green eyes were the same as Danni's. She was dressed for the occasion—whatever that was going to be—head to toe in expensive wool and fine leather accessories.

"I am Olivia Goodlove," she said in a sonorous, modulated voice—why did society women always have those Lauren Bacall voices? "Thank you so much for coming." And why did they always know exactly what to say?

She took his hand lightly. He thought he should say something, but what?

"Nice to meet you," he muttered, although, truth be told, it wasn't at all.

"Won't you come into the library? Monika has been kind enough to lay out some coffee and pastries for us."

"Sure." He nodded.

She led the way.

There was a moment of extreme discomfort, at least for Matt, while she poured the coffee from an ornate silver coffeepot and he looked around the room. A fire blazed in the huge stone fireplace. He wondered fleetingly if the old girl had all the chimneys in this joint cleaned as often as she should. Usually people didn't.

He sipped the coffee and studied her over the rim of the fancy china cup. She didn't look particularly hostile.

"Well!" She smiled, then sipped her coffee. "I suppose you're wondering why I called you."

Matt nodded, giving her a slight, assessing frown.

"The simple truth is, Danielle has told me that you are the father of her baby, and I thought we should meet, clear the air, come to some kind of cooperative arrangement."

"Cooperative arrangement"? What the hell does that mean? But he kept silent. Matt was good at letting people talk themselves out.

"First of all—please forgive me if I seem to be prying, but we have to start somewhere, don't we?—what do you do for a living?"

"I'm a fireman."

"Oh! How exciting!"

Matt thought she said that a little too quickly, and wondered what she really thought of his profession.

"And how did you meet my daughter?"

"She stitched up my arm in the emergency room. Did a bang-up job."

Her smile brightened, genuinely this time. He supposed she was proud of her daughter, the doctor.

"And then?"

"And then she called me for a date."

Olivia Goodlove's smile dimmed for a second—he supposed calling a man was against the rules for ladies like her—then she smiled bravely again. "Oh, my, I forget how times have changed. And then, once your relationship grew, you accompanied her to the Caribbean for the obstetricians' conference?" she prompted.

"No." Matt leaned forward and set his cup and saucer on the marble-topped table. "I followed her there and seduced her. Listen," he continued quickly before she could react to that. "Let's cut to the chase, here. Danni and I are going to be parents. But she hasn't let me in on that deal. Anything you could do to help her come to her senses would be appreciated."

He heard the china rattle as her hand shook. She set the cup and saucer down carefully, frowned, stood, smoothed her high-dollar skirt, and walked to the lofty windows.

"You've got to realize, Mr. Creed," she said without turning from the snowy view, "that my daughter is one stubborn young woman. She has accomplished every single thing she has ever set out to do in life, no matter what the cost, no matter what the obstacles. If she is determined to have this baby alone, I'm afraid there is very little I can do about it." She laid a hand on the window sash as if for support. "In fact, she is going to be terribly upset with me for contacting you." Her shoulders slumped and her elegant appearance dissolved in a posture of defeat. "I just didn't know what else to do. You see, the truth is, my daughter is hurting terribly.''

Matt watched the blinding winter sun glint off her diamond-clad fingers as the older woman raised a shaky hand to her brow, and he felt a sudden wave of compassion for her. ''Danni doesn't know you called me?'' he asked.

''No.''

''I see.'' He thought about that while he studied her. She stared out at the snow as if seeing something far away, and around her eyes there was a look of long-borne pain. ''So why *did* you call me?''

Straightening her shoulders, she turned to him. ''Truthfully? I wanted to see what you were like. I must say, I can understand Danni's attraction to you. But I had a deeper motive. May I show you something?''

She led him to a smaller room that looked like an office. She reached across the desk and handed Matt a silver-framed photograph of an older gentleman in a suit. Though smiling pleasantly, something about him looked formidable and—this startled Matt—a little like an older version of himself. Despite his glasses and receding hairline, the older man's resemblance to Danni was also obvious.

''This is Danni's father,'' she said simply.

Matt stared at the picture. ''Where is he?'' he asked quietly.

''Long dead,'' Olivia answered just as quietly. She took the picture, touched the glass gently and placed it back on the desk, facing them. "But his name lives on. And so does his influence."

Matt rubbed his eyes with thumb and forefinger as if wiping a sudden realization away. "Conrad Goodlove." He sighed. "Goodlove Oil." He stared up at the ceiling, impatient with his own thickheadedness.

"You hadn't made the connection?" she asked kindly.

He looked at the woman. "No. I just thought of Danni as Danni. I never gave her last name—her family—much thought. Sorry."

"I hope you'll give us some thought now, Mr. Creed. Because we are all inextricably linked by this baby. In many more ways than you realize."

"If you're talking about the Goodlove fortune, don't. *I'm* going to support my child." He jabbed his chest. "*I'm* taking part in this kid's life. *My* way. I don't want—*or need*—any part of the Goodlove money."

"Please—" Olivia raised an imploring palm "—I was speaking of our emotional connection, of our mutual interest in this baby's welfare. And there are other things you don't understand. Things that make this baby no ordinary baby. Will you permit me to show you something else?"

Once again he allowed himself to be led to another huge room. This one looked like something from the cover of *Southern Living*. A grand piano. Live floral arrangements in the dead of winter. A blazing fire at eight o'clock in the morning.

She showed him to a spot in front of the fireplace, and pointed to a huge painting above it. Matt recognized a childhood Danni at once. An older child, who resembled the delicate Olivia, hugged her. Their radiant, innocent smiles brought a lump to his throat. He imagined—hoped—that he and Danni would have a child that beautiful. "Danni?" he asked.

Olivia nodded. "And her older sister, Lisa."

"Danni has a big sister?"

"Had. Lisa died when she was seventeen."

Matt glanced sideways at the woman, not sure he had heard her correctly. But he had. He could see the sheen of tears in her eyes as she gazed steadily at the portrait. All he could think to say was, "I'm so sorry." Then he added softly, "How?"

"Eclampsia. She was only two weeks away from childbirth."

In that instant, Matt was hit by a slew of sudden realizations. Was *this* why Danni was still afraid of sex at the age of thirty-four? Other questions swarmed in his head. *How old was Danni when her sister died? What happened to the baby? To the father of the baby? What happened to this family after that? How did you ever survive?* After what he'd seen in Oklahoma City, he'd thought that nothing could pierce him anymore. But this did. This was Danni.

"I don't know what to say. That must have been so horrible for you—for all of you, for Danni...." His voice trailed off and he looked up at the portrait, trying to imagine Danni, still an innocent girl, losing a sister that way. "Oh, God," he murmured. "That's who she was talking about."

"What?" Olivia asked as if she didn't understand.

"Danni...that first night...she talked about losing someone and feeling like she'd never get over it. I thought it was some guy in her past—you know, a boyfriend."

Olivia started to speak again, then hesitated for a moment and fixed her gaze steadily on the portrait before continuing. "Danni and Lisa were so close. Called each other 'sissy' all the time as a joke. Lisa was quite a case. Very bright. Very witty. Rebellious. Danni adored her. Danni was only fourteen when it happened and she's felt a loneliness ever...." Her voice faltered, then she cleared her throat, squared her shoulders. "I admit that at times I haven't known how to help my own daughter."

Matt towered over Olivia, but looking down at this tiny woman he realized he was in the presence of a special person. Her unselfish concern for Danni when her own pain must have been enormous touched him. "I'm really so sorry," he repeated.

She looked up at him, directly into his eyes for a second, then turned her gaze back to the portrait. "Lisa's baby died with her, so with Conrad gone, Danni is all I have now. She is my entire concern. I wonder if you know that a few days ago she had a patient go bad."

"I was there when it happened."

She turned her aristocratic head, studied him.

"Yes. She mentioned that. You went to her office?"

"Yeah. But she didn't like it. I made an appointment as a patient and we had a big fight in an exam room."

She smiled, assessed him with obvious admiration in her eyes. "You might prevail in this, after all, Mr. Creed."

"We'll see. She hasn't returned my calls since that showdown. But I was hoping—or guessing, I should say—it's because she's preoccupied with her patient."

Olivia's face clouded with sorrow. "I'm afraid the poor girl died...and so did her baby."

"No." Matt took two steps back and sank to the couch. "Poor Danni," he mumbled.

Olivia sighed, lowered herself to the couch next to him. "Yes. That has always been my worst fear for Danni, that she would lose a patient the same way Lisa died. She became a doctor in reaction to Lisa's death. Danni is taking this loss badly, as though it were some kind of personal failure."

Matt nodded. If there was anything he understood, it was the need to be a hero, to believe you had the means to rescue someone from tragedy, and the pain of failing at that.

Olivia went on calmly. "Conrad and Danni both changed after Lisa died. Conrad had been outgoing—a risk taker—and overnight he became quieter, repressed, controlling. Mostly he controlled Danni. And she let him. It was her way of easing his pain, I suppose. I'm afraid Danni's been trying to make up for Lisa's death all of her life."

Matt swallowed, looked up at the portrait of Danni and her lost sister. "Do you think she's feeling scared now—now that she's pregnant herself?"

A softness came over Olivia's expression, and for a moment she pressed her lips together as if holding back an immense flood of emotion.

"Mr. Creed—" she began in a whisper then strengthened her voice "—the fact that you would even consider such a possibility tells me a great deal about you." She managed a brave smile. "And without knowing another thing, I am already glad my grandchild will have you for a father."

Matt didn't know what to say. "Fathers are important," he said simply. "And I think my baby deserves a good one."

Olivia's smile softened. "I agree, Mr. Creed. But I'm afraid with my daughter there is little either of us can do to change her mind."

Matt leaned forward on the couch, braced his elbows on his widespread knees and folded his hands, then glanced up at the portrait again. "Oh, there's plenty *I* can do," he said, and his deep voice had a sudden edge to it. "I can take her to court and sue her for joint custody."

Olivia answered quickly, in a voice that had an edge of its own. "Nasty legal proceedings will solve nothing. Besides, you have no claim to the baby. She would have to name you as the father for you to have any legal standing."

There was silence for a few seconds while Matt

let her words sink in, then he spoke. "Your daughter didn't tell you?"

Olivia looked confused. Poised, but utterly confused.

"Mrs. Goodlove, your daughter and I are already married."

Olivia Goodlove blinked politely, as if weighing her words carefully before responding. Matt had to hand it to this woman—she seemed as intelligent and unflappable as her beautiful daughter.

"Married?" she said at last, quietly.

"I'm afraid so."

"Afraid so?" She shook her head, as if his words confused her. "But I don't understand. How? When?"

"In the Caribbean." Matt felt his shoulders tense. How the hell was he going to explain this? "You can get married down there, on short notice."

Olivia frowned, looked at him suspiciously. "Was this before or after you...seduced her?"

Matt frowned. "Before."

"Danni allowed this...this marriage?"

"Danni wanted it. At least she seemed to until it was time to come back to her real life."

"I see." Olivia bit her lip, and suddenly Matt could see a stronger resemblance between Danni and her mother. They looked similar—absolutely awful—when they were about to cry.

She bent her head. "I'm sorry. It's just—" She bit her lip again, struggling for control.

"You wanted something better for your daughter," he finished for her.

She nodded, and a tear escaped and rolled down the side of her patrician nose. She made a delicate dab at it. "Please don't take offense," she rushed to add. "This isn't about social position. It's just that we are a Christian family. I'd always hoped Danni would marry in the Church, have a proper wedding, a festive one."

"Yeah, I can imagine that," Matt said, looking around the elegant house, picturing the kind of enormous society wedding this woman would consider "proper" and "festive."

As for the Christian part, well, he thought of himself as one, too—although very, very privately. You needed God in his business. You needed those prayers. But the truth was, he hadn't thought about God or prayer when he'd married Danni. All he'd thought about was Danni—having her; holding her; pleasing her.

"I married her to make her happy," he explained, then realized how lame that sounded, and continued, "At the time, I really thought it was what she wanted."

Olivia rose and plucked two tissues out of a box on a nearby table. "Oh, I'm not accusing you of anything untoward. Danni is an adult. So, now what do you propose to do?"

"She doesn't have to stay married to me. For all I know, she's already getting a divorce or an annulment or whatever. But I do want the baby. The baby is my child, too. Whatever happened or didn't happen between me and your daughter, that doesn't change. The baby is mine."

"Yes. And the baby is Danni's. I'm counting on that to... I don't know. Things change when babies arrive. Have you ever noticed that, Mr. Creed?"

Matt nodded.

"Then I guess this is between you and Danni. It seems you and I don't have anything more to discuss."

"You're right. This is between Danni and me." Finally he'd said what he'd planned to say in the beginning, but it hadn't happened with rancor and animosity, the way he'd imagined it would. Instead he felt a genuine sympathy for this woman, who had no one in her life now—no one but her stubborn, workaholic daughter. Then something dawned on him. He stood and faced Olivia. "The baby is yours, too," he said kindly. "A grandchild. Someone else to love."

Olivia stopped her dabbing and examined him over her tissue. She lowered it and smiled. "Mr. Creed—"

"My friends call me Matt."

"Matt. Despite all that's gone wrong between you and Danni, I must repeat that I'm glad you're my grandchild's father. You seem like a decent man, a kind man."

Matt looked down, pulled back one corner of his mouth in embarrassment. "Decent" and "kind." Too bad Danni didn't see him that way. But you couldn't win them all. At least there was still the baby. He could hold on to the baby.

"Mrs. Goodlove, I promise to take good care of your grandchild. Fair enough?"

She smiled and reached up and squeezed his forearm. Through his flannel shirtsleeve, her palm felt warm, like Danni's always were. "Fair enough," she said. "But please don't give up on Danni, not just yet. She's going through a very bad time and she needs our help. And please call me Olivia. After all, for now at least, I *am* your mother-in-law."

At last Matt smiled. She really was a cool old gal. "I guess, for the time being, you're stuck with me." He grew solemn again, thinking. "I'll promise you one other thing, Olivia. I'm going to do my best to keep it that way."

CHAPTER EIGHTEEN

LATER THAT DAY, THE WEATHER grew worse. A second blizzard blew down off the plains of Kansas and coated the trees and streets with so much ice that life in Tulsa froze to a standstill. Power lines collapsed all over town, and without electricity, homeowners used candles and fireplaces in desperate attempts to generate light and heat. It was every firefighter's nightmare. Icy roads hampered emergency vehicles. Every fire call was going to feel twice as long and twice as hard.

Matt, like all the other firefighters, tried to set aside his personal problems and focus on the situation. With every shift certain to be an endurance test, getting enough sleep and calories in the off-hours became each man's priority.

But after Matt had left Olivia's, grabbed some fast food, and returned Ty's Jeep, he suffered through an afternoon of fitful, inadequate sleep.

He'd drift off, thinking of Danni, of her sad past, and wake up entangled in the covers and bad dreams.

He'd get up, go to the bathroom, gulp down a glass of water, peek around the tinfoil he'd put over his windows to cut the snowy glare, then throw himself back on the bed and try again.

Finally, when he awoke from a different kind of dream, sprawled on his belly, hard as a rock, he gave up on sleep. He let Miss Verbena out to sprinkle the snow, then filled her food and water dishes.

He showered, dressed and walked the five icy blocks back to Ty's to ask if he could use the Jeep again—this time to go find Danni.

Ty tried to talk him out of it—stalled him with a beer, fed him some chili. "Matt, buddy," he implored, "don't get into this with her now. It's—" he glanced at the clock on his CD player "—it's almost nine o'clock at night. And you look like you could use some more sleep. The green shift already has three guys out with injuries. What if they have to call you in early?"

Matt was already pulling on his heavy parka and damp hiking boots. "I've got to try to talk to her. You don't know her state of mind. She's pregnant. Did I tell you that?"

"Jackie did."

"Figures. She's also depressed about the loss of a patient. I keep picturing her sitting in that big house with no lights and no heat. I have to check on her and don't want to wait until after I pull another twenty-four-hour shift." He stood and held up a palm.

Ty shrugged and tossed the keys. Matt caught them. "Thanks, pal," he said and disappeared into the frozen night.

AT DANNI'S HOUSE JACKIE answered the darkened door in sweats, loud striped leg warmers, a man's ski vest, a pair of red wool gloves and an old cobalt-blue University of Tulsa stocking cap.

"You guys without heat?" Matt asked and muscled past her into the dark foyer without being invited.

Jackie slammed the door against the wind. "Can you believe it? Since this morning. *Nothing* works without electricity. Can't cook. Can't iron. Even the gas central heater doesn't work." She huffed. "At least it's so cold the food won't rot."

Matt took in the situation with one glance. Every surface had a candle burning on it, and the fire in the fireplace blazed hot enough to smelt iron. Even so, with its banks of naked glass and ten-foot ceilings, the house was as cold as a meat locker.

"Danni shouldn't be here in her condition." He turned on Jackie accusingly. "Take her to a damned shelter!" Matt charged back toward the kitchen, then the master suite, looking for Danni. "Or take her to her mom's!" he called as he turned into the central hallway. "That part of town still has power. Danni!" he bellowed into the darkness at the back of the house.

"She ain't here!" Jackie hollered back at him.

He stopped and walked into the living room. "Where the hell is she?"

"At the hospital. Everybody that was there when the second storm hit stayed on. Iced in. She'll be sleeping in the doctors' lounge." Jackie folded her arms over her billowy bosom smugly. "All cozy.

She doesn't even know our power's out. I figure, why worry her? Her plate is full over there. They'll get the power back on soon."

"Maybe. I'll call her later anyway." Matt marched back toward the front door, then turned. "Meanwhile you put all this stuff out—" he swept a hand at the candles and the fire "—and go somewhere warm. There are shelters open all over the place. Right over at First Methodist." He pointed in the general direction of the church. "You understand?"

He didn't even see when Jackie dismissed him with the wave of her palm, because he'd already jogged halfway down the sidewalk to Ty's Jeep.

Jackie decided maybe she should call Dr. Danni and tell her about the power outage. She picked up the phone, which was dead. Well, terrific. Okay. Maybe she should do what Matt had said and go over to First Methodist—just for the night. There was no chance that her little Toyota would make it all the way across town to her own mama's house.

She went to the utility room to check on Pearl and Smoky and finally found them on Danni's bed. The dogs raised their eyebrows, but not their heads, at the sight of Jackie's flashlight. She smiled at them.

"Sorry, guys, I expect doggies aren't gonna be welcome at First Methodist." Still, she felt guilty leaving them alone, so she spread Danni's three-hundred-dollar Ralph Lauren wool coverlet over their sleek bodies. She carried their water dish in from the spot by the fireplace where she'd kept it throughout the cold evening, and hoped it wouldn't freeze up before the power was restored.

Then she went into the cavernous kitchen, intending to get water to douse the living-room fireplace, but when she turned on the tap, nothing came out. "Oh, my Lord," she breathed. "The pipes must be frozen."

She went into the living room and heaped ashes up over the fire until the flames went out, then butted the brass screen up as close to the marble mantel as she could fit it. "That'll have to do," she said nervously, for she didn't like leaving the coals like this. But then, she rationalized, what could happen?

There was a full three-foot width of hearth between the carpet and the fireplace. She spent some seconds debating about closing the flue, thinking that if she did the house might stay warmer; but then she worried that the coals would smoke the living room. Dr. Danni would sure be pissed about that. She left it open.

Already the house seemed colder. Jackie shuddered and went to fetch her coat, pillow, and car keys. Then she hurried around the place, carefully extinguishing every single candle.

No sooner had she closed the door behind her, than an ember popped.

CHAPTER NINETEEN

DANNI RUBBED HER SORE neck muscles as she walked through the dressing room to the doctors' lounge area. The anteroom with the recliner was normally all the doctors ever used, except in extreme situations like this. The small inner room felt sterile, untouched, with only two narrow bunks that were tightly made up, a bedside table with a box of tissues on top, a microwave that had never even been turned on—the digital clock on it read 9:43 p.m.—and a dorm refrigerator that was as empty as the row of lockers along one wall.

Danni went in and closed the door, shutting out the noise and light from the labor-and-delivery unit. The blinds were open, and the three large windows revealed a nightscape frozen in painful whiteness. With only emergency generator power, the hospital had no parking-lot lights and beyond that, most of the surrounding area was dark. At least the clouds had cleared enough for the moon to come out. As far as the eye could see, white rooftops and trees reflected moonlight like a peaceful Christmas scene, aglow with an eerie calmness.

Danni shuffled to the nearest bunk and flopped onto it. She didn't even have the energy to close the blinds or strip back the covers; she tugged the hospital-issue corded spread around herself like a cocoon. She'd really chew out a patient if they tried to work this hard in their first trimester.

As soon as she lay still, she thought of Matt. It had probably been foolish to take his call a while ago. She supposed she'd have to see him sooner or later, but not at the hospital, for crying out loud. There was no privacy here. Someone back in Labor and Delivery had even picked up the line and listened in just as she'd said, "Matt, please. I don't want to see you right now." She cut the call short.

She was so weary. Would there ever be time, in her schedule, to sort out a decent personal life?

It seemed as if she'd been asleep only seconds when she sensed a presence—someone standing over her in the dark. She opened her eyes, saw the tall silhouette of a male, and jumped.

"Isn't the moonlight beautiful?" he asked.

"Roger." She fought to orient herself—how long had she slept? "Is something wrong?" What was he doing back here when it was her turn to sleep?

"No. Nothing's wrong. I just wanted to check on you. I must say—" his voice took on a huskiness that made Danni uncomfortable "—you look beautiful lying there like that."

Danni felt an inner alarm rising. What the hell was he *doing* in here?

She rubbed her eyes and struggled to sit up, intending to tell him once and for all to stop commenting on her looks, but before she could, he sat down on the bunk, forcing her hips over against the wall, pinning her.

"Roger, I'm trying to get some sleep." She managed to push herself up.

He twisted around and reached out to massage the muscles on either side of her neck. "We've both been working too hard. How does that feel?" he murmured. His face was so close beside hers that she could feel his breath—hot, and foul with the smell of coffee.

She couldn't see his eyes because his hair had flopped forward, shadowing them, but in the moonlight she could clearly see his lips. They were glistening. Wet. Parted in lust.

Danni felt a sudden panic. Her heart thudded against her chest. She moved around Bryant and stood up.

"What are you doing?" she demanded accusingly, trying to keep her voice steady.

"I've been waiting for the chance to be alone with you for a long time," he answered smoothly.

Danni stood there, for a moment too shocked to respond.

"We're both adults," Bryant continued. "There's no one around on the night shift, especially with the bad weather. No one will bother us."

Danni had to fight against all her preconceived notions, the part of her that would never believe a colleague capable of such base behavior. But it was happening, whether she wanted to believe it or not.

"Just relax," Bryant continued. "Like you did in the Caribbean with your hired man."

Danni's whole body screamed with a surge of sheer revulsion, then she heard a noise in the outer room. Bryant seemed oblivious as he moved close, and grabbed her arm.

"Danni?" Matt's voice called out just as the door swung open and Matt stood silhouetted in the light from the outer room.

Bryant froze.

Danni wrenched herself free of his grip.

"How'd you get in here?" Bryant turned on Matt. "These quarters are off-limits to everyone but physicians."

"Danni?" Matt repeated, his voice indicating that he sensed something was wrong. "Is everything all right?"

"N—"

"I said, this area is private," Bryant interrupted and stepped in front of Danni. "Now get out before I call security."

Matt squinted at Danni. She didn't look right. She looked shaken, pale. "I don't think so. I came to see Dr. Goodlove."

"I think she saw all of you she wanted to in the Caribbean." Bryant shoved at Matt—a mistake. Matt jerked him off his feet and body-slammed him face-first against the lockers.

"Matt!" Danni yelled.

"Let go before I charge you with assault!" Bryant said as he tried to twist around.

Matt was already regretting his loss of control but still he gave Bryant a shake that caused the lockers to rattle as if they might fall off the wall before he turned Bryant loose. Matt took a deep breath. "Did he hurt you?" he asked Danni.

Danni shook her head. "No, but I think he had every intention—"

"She's crazy!" Bryant sputtered, then dabbed at his bleeding nose and looked at the blood on his fingertips as if he couldn't believe it. "I was giving her a shoulder rub and *she* started coming on to *me*."

Matt ignored him and asked Danni, "Do you want me to call the police?"

Danni looked up at Matt with horror. "You mean press some sort of charges?"

"For what?" Bryant demanded. "If anybody's going to press any charges, it's me."

Matt stayed focused on Danni's face, reading her. "I'll call the police if you want me to," he offered again.

Danni turned away and rubbed her forehead. Even though she knew it wasn't rational, she felt vaguely responsible for Bryant's actions. As if she should have done something to discourage him sooner. And in reality, nothing of any consequence had happened.

Bryant stumbled over to the box of hospital tissues on the bedside table, tore out a wad and pressed them to his bloody nose.

Matt took a threatening step forward. "Get the hell out of here," he said through clenched teeth.

Bryant started toward the door. "You'd better watch your step—" he pointed the wad of bloody tissues at Matt and his hand shook "—assaulting a doctor on duty."

Matt bounded across the room, grabbed the front of Bryant's lab coat and hauled him up to within an inch of his nose. "I'm her husband, *Doctor*. And from now on, you stay away from her or I'll break your neck."

"Matt," Danni interjected. "Let him go."

Matt gave Bryant a shove as he released his lapels.

Bryant straightened his lab coat, looked at Danni and muttered, "Husband? You've got to be kidding! Serves you right for going slumming," as he backed out of the room.

He didn't bother to close the door behind him, and as the light from the outer room slanted in on Danni's face, Matt was shocked by her appearance. Her cheeks were hollow and she had dark circles under her eyes. All this extra work and losing a patient in her first few weeks of pregnancy. Now this. He wanted to take her away from here. To hold her. To protect her forever.

When the outer lounge door had swung shut Danni let out a huge exhalation and dragged her hands tight against her scalp. "Oh, God," she breathed and sank down on the bunk, then buried her face in her hands.

Matt didn't know what to do. He closed the door against the harsh light, then silently stood above her, looking down at the moonlight reflecting off her beautiful hair. "Danni," he said, then hesitated. "Can I get you some water or something?"

She shook her head.

"Then would you let me hold you?"

She let out one sob, cut it short. "It's been such a terrible week," she said into her palms.

"I know." Matt lowered himself down beside her, placing his hands lightly on her shoulders. When he felt her lean toward him, he wrapped his arms around her and hugged her to him. Her hair smelled like Danni, exactly as he remembered it— clean, pure.

"Even though I asked you not to come tonight, I'm so glad you arrived when you did," she said into his chest.

"I decided to stop by and tell you your power is out at home. But the truth is I just wanted to see you. The nurses told me you'd gone to the doctors' lounge. I knocked on the outside door twice."

"This room is soundproof. They designed it that way so we could sleep at all hours."

"I imagine Bryant was counting on that."

She nodded.

Matt stroked her hair. "Danni, just because he's a doctor, and even though you're one too, doesn't mean you shouldn't press charges."

She shook her head. "I don't want the stress. Not now. And nothing happened really. Besides, the charge would never stick. Too many people have seen us together. We even flew to the Caribbean together."

"Somebody should nail that creep," Matt said calmly.

"You think I don't know that? But he's got

plenty of women who hang on his every word. They'd all come into court and testify that Roger Bryant certainly didn't need to harass anybody to get what he wanted. It's not that I'm afraid of the ordeal—it's just that I know when to cut my losses. It would be his word against mine. I'm an unmarried woman who's pregnant. Who would believe me?'' She covered her face with her palms again. ''Oh, God. I've made a mess of my life,'' she said.

He held her tightly, thrilled to be doing so at last, even under these circumstances. ''No, you haven't. For one thing, you may be pregnant, but you're not unmarried.''

She lowered her hands and pulled back so that she could see his expression. He looked calm, sincere.

He gazed into her eyes and said quietly, ''We *are* still married, aren't we?''

Danni turned her face away. ''You're only saying these things to make me feel better. You only started calling me last week.''

''I didn't know about the baby until last week!''

Danni shook her head. ''You would never have contacted me after St. Martin, except to—well—to have a good time again, if Jackie hadn't told you I was pregnant.''

His brow furrowed and he relaxed his hold on her. ''Now wait just a minute. *You're* the one who refused to see me.'' She twisted away from him and folded her arms across her breasts. He leaned around to confront her. ''You weren't even planning to tell me about my own child. Maybe you're the one who thinks she's too good to get involved with a firefighter—except for a roll on the beach—''

Danni bolted up off the bed.

''I didn't mean that. I'm sorry.'' Matt grabbed for her wrist but she pulled away. ''Danni, listen. Can't you see how it is? How I felt about you in the Caribbean? What that week meant to me?''

Danni kept her back to him, but he saw her shoulders relax, saw that she was listening. ''Danni. I think I know how hard this situation, an unwanted pregnancy, is for you. I...I know all about your sister.''

Danni turned and stared at him. ''You know about Lisa?''

He nodded.

''How?''

''Your mom told me.''

She sank back down on the bed. ''My mother?''

He took her hands. ''Yes. But it really doesn't matter how I found out.''

She turned her face away from him and in the moonlight he could see her jaw tightening. Was she crying? His heart twisted, but he continued. ''Danni, this isn't just about you and me. It's about our baby. I know you've got to be scared, after what happened to your sister and all. I had no idea. I guess that's...that's the reason why you were afraid to get involved with me.''

She said nothing, wouldn't even turn her face and look at him. ''But, Danni, however this happened, it *has* happened. You're pregnant. And the baby is—'' Matt suddenly felt as if he couldn't breathe. He had to make her understand that the past was the past, that he loved her no matter what, that there wasn't anything they couldn't work out, as long as they had each other—and the baby.

"Don't shut me out," he went on urgently, "just because we did something stupid on a stupid little island—"

She looked at him then. He could see the remnants of tears in her eyes, but the rest of her face looked hard with anger. "It *was* stupid, wasn't it?" she said. "Just plain stupid."

"I know you look at it that way. But I don't. I think what happened between us on that island was beautiful. What I'm trying to say is, at least give me a chance. At least get to know me."

She jerked her fingers from his grasp.

"At least let me help you through the pregnancy. Don't—" He grabbed her hand again and squeezed her fingers so tightly that she squirmed. "Don't do anything…reckless."

Danni's eyes flashed with comprehension. "If you are talking about terminating this pregnancy, I wasn't even considering it." Her jaw grew rigid. "And even if I was, you have no right—"

"No *right!*" Suddenly Matt's temper flared. "What about my rights as a father? What about this kid's rights? For as long as I can remember, all I've wanted is a kid, and I'm not gonna let your stubbornness destroy my chance. If you don't want this baby, then give it to me!"

Danni's jaw dropped, then her expression reset,

even harder. "You think *you* could raise a baby alone?"

"As well as you could. If I can handle Miss Verbena—"

Danni let out a sputter of incredulity. "Miss *Verbena!*"

"Listen, I took care of Sparky like he was a child."

Danni dropped her jaw again and rolled her eyes.

"Well? At least I didn't turn him over to some trainer. And *I* don't have to have a maid to clean up after me night and day. My family's decent and kind, even if they are just teachers and cops."

Danni's eyes narrowed. "*Now* what are you implying? That I look down on your family? I've never even *met* your family, much less judged them inferior. I can't help it that my father made a ton of money. I work hard for my money, and if I want to pay a maid with it, that is my business. And for your information, I have a *great* mother and I will be a great mother just like her!"

Matt's anger seemed to suddenly drain from him. His shoulders slumped and he let out a long sigh. "Yeah. I gotta admit I like your mother." He looked straight ahead, then glanced at Danni out of the corner of his eye. "We have a lot to learn about each other, don't we?" He propped his elbows on his knees and dropped his folded hands between them.

Danni studied his broad shoulders, the back of his dark head, the place where his hair was trimmed in a neat, blunt line at his neck. The very place she'd learned to love so much in the Caribbean. The place she wanted to touch while his hot mouth worked its thrilling magic. She stood, before she could give in and touch him.

"Yes. We have a lot to learn about each other. And right now, we're arguing about a moot point, because I am not having an abortion and I am not *giving* this baby to you or anyone else."

"I guess I knew that." His voice was soft and sad, and he examined his loosely folded palms as if the truth were written there. "But with what happened to your sister and all," he went on quietly, "I needed to be sure. I guess I got scared." He did not look up at her.

After a moment he sighed. "You know, it sounds really trite because so many people have said it, but it's true. I learned so much about myself while I was working at the bombing. It took me a long, long time to accept all those deaths. Especially the children. It took me a long time to accept the hard fact that, even when you do your best, sometimes you lose the battle. But life is too short to keep on being angry or bitter over something you can't change."

He looked at her then and she flinched at the intensity, the conviction, in those blue eyes. "Don't be bitter, Danni. Try to see life with a new heart every day." He put his palm on his chest. "Try to look at me—at *us,* at what's happened to us—with a new heart."

When she turned away without saying anything, he sighed again, then stood in front of her. He put his finger under her chin and lifted her face to look up into his. "You know what I'm talking about—your old pain about your sister."

He wouldn't let her turn her face away this time. He kept it tilted toward his own with his strong fingers, looked into her eyes and, without another word, brought his mouth down on hers and kissed her, as if his body might say for him what words could not.

For a moment, standing there in his arms in the profound moonlit stillness, Danni could hear only her own heart pounding in her ears, only Matt's breathing as he moved his mouth over hers. But in the next instant, as his kiss grew more intense, her mind cried out for something: mercy, clarity, relief—something.

Because when Matt kissed her, it was as if she could feel nothing but his warmth, his urgency, pulling her to him. Danni was torn, as she felt herself melting into him. Her mind formed a plea, a supplication. *Yes.*

No!

She pushed against him and he immediately broke away.

"Matt, I'm sorry," she said, and placed her shaky palms on his chest, lowered her head. "I'm sorry.... I'm so confused."

"I didn't do that to confuse you," he whispered into her hair, then put his palms to her cheeks and tilted her face up to his again. "But we only have so much time. Our child is coming. And even if our time together turns out to be a hundred years, it's still only so much. Think about it, Danni. Please.''

She closed her eyes, trying to press back the hated tears, thinking how well she knew that life was short, thinking how Lisa had had only seventeen brief, sweet years.

"I know this is a difficult time for you," Matt was saying, as he rubbed his thumbs over her lips, then her jaw. "And all I want to do is help. We can keep this simple if you want."

Danni opened her eyes. *Simple?*

He stopped his stroking and examined her mouth briefly, then raised his eyes slowly to hers. He winced with some emotion Danni could not read. "At least," he started, "at least, let me be your friend."

She swiped at an escaping tear. "Everything is always so simple for you," she said.

"No. No, it's not," he argued gently. "I know relationships aren't easy. And I don't want to be married to a woman who doesn't want me, heart and soul. But Danni, ever since I talked to your mom I've wondered if what's keeping us apart has more to do with the problems in your past than with our differences."

He waited for her response, but Danni was so confused she couldn't say anything.

She wished for simplicity, all right—the simplicity of her life before she had started on this whole foolish pursuit of love. *Love.* For some people there was no such thing. Maybe she was one of those people. She felt tears building again.

He brushed her hair back off her shoulder, tucked a stray stand behind her ear, like a father grooming a child. "We don't have to talk about this anymore for now. You need to get some rest."

She managed to nod.

"Then I guess I'll go so you can sleep."

Danni nodded again and he turned to leave.

"You know, Danni—" he looked back at her "—maybe you're trying to keep your life simple the wrong way. By not giving yourself."

When she opened her mouth to defend herself, he interrupted, "Giving yourself to your work, to your patients, is not the same as giving your heart to one special person."

Then he waited for her to do something, to say something. But Danni only lowered herself to the bunk and stared at the floor, sitting in the pool of cold moonlight, as frozen in place as the landscape outside the windows.

"I can wait," he said at last, very softly. "I can wait for the rest of my life for you, Danni." He turned and left the room.

CHAPTER TWENTY

DANNI SAT ON THE EDGE of the bunk, dry-eyed and alone, in the cold dark, with the thin pale light of the moon seeping over her.

She bowed her head, curled her shoulders, and locked her palms together between her knees: the pose of a penitent in prayer. But in her heart there was no prayer. In her heart there was only sorrow…and fear.

Hadn't she been denying this sorrow—a great, buried sorrow that wouldn't go away—for most of her life? And the fear that came from never wanting to experience that sorrow again. Fear that would not let her love and be loved.

Now the pregnancy had resurrected her old pain. Was she afraid of it, too?

Everything felt so confusing as she sat alone, trying to sort it out, and it occurred to her, not for the first time, that maybe she should seek help.

All her life she'd pushed past her pain, tried to outsmart it, outwork it—only to have it finally catch up with her now, in the midst of a pregnancy by a man who drove her wild with passion. What had she imagined? Hoped? That she'd be swept away, and never feel this pain again? Had she thought that the person of Matthew Creed would be her salvation from the fear of loss that after all this time, no matter how hard she worked, no matter how busy she stayed, still threatened to swallow her up?

It was the thought of Matt that caused tears, finally, to come. Rolling down her cheeks like the opening notes of some melancholy piece, then endlessly flowing, chord upon chord. And with those bitter tears, those tears that she'd fought for so long, she felt the last of her fierce will to suppress the old pain seep out of her.

She let the pain come.

And with it came the images of Lisa. Lisa singing a crazy song. Lisa dancing around the kitchen while they did the dishes. Lisa playing cards with eleven-year-old Danni after Danni's best friend had dumped her. Lisa, always there to make life fun and good and right. Smiling, softhearted Lisa. Sweet Lisa.

Danni clutched her folded hands under her chin and squeezed her eyes shut.

"Oh, sissy," she whispered aloud to the moonlit air. "I'm so confused. I've hurt him. I'm afraid...that somehow I'll even hurt this baby. I'm not strong like you. Why..." Danni raised her flowing eyes to the dark ceiling. "Why did you have to die?"

She lowered herself to her side on the bunk and lay there without pulling the thin blanket around her, surrendering to it at last. Sorrow.

She lay there for a long time until she'd cried herself out, then pulled some tissues out of the box on the table, dried her eyes, and sighed. She couldn't think when she was exhausted and emotionally drained like this.

In the dark, she reached mechanically for the phone, buzzed the labor-and-delivery desk. She steadied her voice and asked for Carol, the only person she trusted to handle the message.

"Carol, it's me.... No. I'm okay, just exhausted.... Yeah, probably." She sighed. "Listen. Tell Bryant I'm ill and I'm going home... He slipped out on the ice? Then call Stone in. Tell him it's an emergency... No, you don't need to come check on me. I'm fine. Don't worry... No. I can make it home fine."

Danni fumbled to replace the receiver, then stood on shaky legs. She'd never left work like this before. But there was no point in staying at the hospital when she was no good to anybody. Exactly as she had always predicted, giving in to her grief over Lisa accomplished nothing except to impair her ability to help her patients. Nothing would ever change. Lisa would always be gone. And she, Danni, would never feel any better about that. This sorrow, this fear, would always overshadow her.

Right now, all she wanted to do was go home, curl up on her bed, and shut out the world.

WHEN DANNI ARRIVED AT HER dark house, the garage-door opener didn't work. Of course. No power. She peered through the fogged windows of the BMW. Not a single light anywhere. Apparently the whole neighborhood was without electricity.

She fumbled for a flashlight in the glove box, then followed its beam up the sidewalk and into the house.

She turned and called up the stairs: "Jackie!" But apparently, Jackie was gone—probably to someplace warm. Danni pulled her sub-zero sleeping bag from the shelf in the hall closet and hauled it back to the master suite.

Pearl and Smoky were wrapped around each other in the middle of the king-size bed, huddled against the pile of pillows.

"Thanks for warming the nest, guys," she said, and shoved their compact bodies aside enough to pull the heavy bedclothes back. Without even removing her coat, running shoes, or stocking cap, she crawled inside the sleeping bag and zipped herself in, reaching an arm back to flip the heavy comforter over the top of the entire mound.

The spot where the dogs had lain felt warm, and they nuzzled up beside her to try to regain their place. Danni managed a wan smile and muttered, "Spoiled brats," before her eyelids grew heavy. She could sleep a couple of hours like this, she thought dully, and if the power wasn't restored then, she'd head to her mom's or maybe she'd get up and build a fire. That was her last coherent thought before the dark clouds of sleep obscured her consciousness: *Build a fire.*

Out in the living room, the ember, no bigger than a dime, burrowed deeper into the carpet, just beyond the invincibility of the marble hearth. There it lay, emitting no smoke, no flame, no warning...

Smoldering steadily in the silent, frozen house while the grandfather clock ticked evenly, while frost crept up the windowpanes, while the dead alarm system sensed nothing.

But still the fire didn't start. It waited. Brooded. Festered.

CHAPTER TWENTY-ONE

WITH FIREMEN, FOOD WAS always important when they returned from a call. The firehouse kitchen was thick with the aroma of overbaked ham—Tom Clark's extra one, left over from Christmas—and with the jokes that served as a way to relax after a bad fire scene.

That last alarm had taken it out of them. As Ty had predicted, Matt had been called back in to finish out the green shift, to fill in for a captain who had fallen on the ice and injured his back.

Now, at two in the morning, the neglected ham had been baked and rebaked while the teams had answered back-to-back alarms. The men of the green shift were tired and hungry, but spirits were high. No civilian injuries in either fire.

"Is that thing smoked?" somebody quipped, and they all laughed.

The men kept up the banter, urging Clark to hurry up with his carving before the next alarm came in or before the spring thaw—whichever came first. The "drop" always seemed to happen when they sat down to eat. They all stood around the waist-high butcher-block island in the center of the room, sneaking stray pieces of ham to nibble, snorting and guffawing at their insider put-downs.

All but Matt.

He sat off in the captain's office by himself, behind the beat-up metal desk, shuffling paperwork—and his thoughts.

She hadn't reached out to him. He'd blown it. *You can't make somebody love you,* he reminded himself. But, for the hundredth time, he thought of them together on that beach; remembered the impact when her warm skin had pressed fully against him for the first time.

The silver pen in his hand stilled and he stared at the glare of the desk lamp, first hearing her laugh, then other sounds she made—the ones that made him want more, made him want to give her more.

And the baby. God, what about the baby? Was he going to have to be one of those daddies who *entertained* his own kid a couple of weekends a month? That wasn't what he wanted. He wanted little league, cooking his special spaghetti, yard work, dog training, kite flying, morals-teaching, character-building family life. Every single, blessed day.

Why was Danni making this all so damned hard? Why had he ever started up with a woman who wouldn't, couldn't, share his dreams? And now a child. Dear God. His child.

"Ah, man! No Cool Whip?" a guy peering into the giant steel refrigerator shouted. "You can't have pumpkin pie without Cool Whip. Dolby! Run over to the twenty-four-hour store and get some Cool Whip!''

"No deal," Matt, now acting captain, hollered through the open office door. "We're down to twelve men on three engines."

"Ah, man!" came the chorus from the butcher-block crowd.

"What're you, Creed? Some kind o' badass?" the veteran leaning against the door of Matt's office mumbled.

"Okay, okay—" Matt raised his voice above the chatter "—but send Smith. And make it snappy."

Smith already had his coat on, was heading for the door. He was the probie, the new kid, which was why he was assigned to the pumper, and why Matt figured they could do without him for a few minutes. Matt and Ty and Gil had handled many a fire as a three-man team on the pumper without trouble. It was doable. Nothing was happening right now. No apparatus was out. Let the guys have their Cool Whip.

But the ham still wasn't completely carved and the Cool Whip still hadn't arrived when the next alarm came.

OUTSIDE DANNI'S HOUSE, the weight of the ice brought a limb of the giant old red oak crashing to the ground. When it did, a huge icicle broke from the eave of the garden shed and pierced the snow below like a crystal sword.

But inside, Danni was unaware, warm and toasty

within her bulky cocoon, her mind and body buried under the weight of fatigue.

The ember had succeeded in carving a dark hole the size of a quarter in the lush living-room carpet. A thin trail of smoke rose at last—the first sign that the fire was ready to break free of its suppressed state into critical mass. Now, the accumulating gases needed only the merest push of oxygen in order to reach ignition temperature and burst into flame.

A little gust of wind—no more than a puff, not even enough to disturb the ashes—whispered down the flue.

ACROSS THE STREET, DANNI'S neighbor, Mrs. Forde, was irritated to find that once again she couldn't sleep. The joys of menopause. Of course, even with her hot flashes, it was too damn cold for anyone to sleep comfortably tonight. When would they get the power restored? The kerosene space heaters her husband had set up were running low. She was making her way down the stairs with a flashlight when she saw a glow through the beveled glass of her front door. The orange incandescence on the snow stood out like a beacon in the blacked-out neighborhood.

Strange, Mrs. Forde thought, as she moved to her picture window. *Where is that light coming from? Seems awfully bright for a fireplace.*

Ever nosy—Mrs. Forde liked to think of herself as "vigilant"—the stocky matron pulled on her

wool-lined boots and goose-down parka and scur-
ried out onto her icy, snow-packed front lawn to
investigate. The smell of smoke in the air didn't
immediately alarm her—the entire neighborhood
had been burning firewood around the clock.

She planted her feet wide with each step as she
made her way down the icy slope, across to the far
corner of her lawn so that she could see into her
young neighbor's wall of southern windows—the
light was coming from there.

As soon as the massive Colonial-style windows
on the side of the house across the street came into
view, Mrs. Forde's eyes went wide and her throat
went dry.

The drapes were being devoured by a wall of
flame!

Mrs. Forde sucked in a freezing gasp, then finally
managed to scream her husband's name.

She kept on screaming his name while she
clawed her way back up the icy slope of her lawn.
At the same time she prayed to God that no one
was in that house—didn't Dr. Goodlove have a
maid and some dogs? And dear, dear Lord—Mrs.
Forde glanced frantically over her shoulder—
wasn't that the young woman's BMW in the driveway? Should she run and see if anyone was in
there? But she feared she'd never make it up the
doctor's steep-sloped yard. She had to get the cell
phone! That poor woman's house was on fire!

IN THAT SAME INSTANT, Pearl, and then Smoky,
whined. Sat up. Sniffed the air. Then Pearl barked

a panicked retort to the screams of the woman outside.

Beside them, Danni's mind fought for awareness. First came irritation at the dogs' barking. Then she heard some kind of commotion outside—somebody screaming?—then saw, through still-closed eyelids, a glow coming from down the hall. Had she gotten up and built a fire?

A boom and sudden brilliance caused her eyes to fly open. She sucked in a smoke-filled breath and it hit her: Her house was on fire!

A rush of adrenaline shot through every cell of her body and she screamed, "God!" as Pearl and Smoky, now barking furiously, bounded off the bed toward the door.

She heard her own whimper as she kicked at the sleeping bag in a split second of mad claustrophobia, unable to find the zipper with her clawing fingers. Finally she calmed herself enough to flip the tab inside and frantically zipped it down. *The baby,* she thought. *Think. Stay calm. Get out.*

She remembered enough to roll off the bed onto the floor. Despite the fire, the air in the bedroom was freezing and she was instantly gripped by vicious chills. She forced her shivering muscles to work and stayed low, crawling along the edge of the bed in the direction of the door. She could see no flames in the bedroom, only blackness, but already the smoke made her eyes and throat sting. She didn't want to breathe, tried holding her breath, failed in a fit of coughing. *What was this doing to the baby?*

She crawled forward, toward the door, then, realizing she should be climbing out a window, not heading toward the fire, she crawled in the direction of the tall windows. But the heavy panes were invulnerable, the transoms above them impossibly high. Her own coughing and the barking dogs seemed to interfere with her ability to think.

Fifteen precious seconds had already elapsed since the dogs had roused her.

WHEN THE DROP HIT, EVERY light in the firehouse went on automatically. At the same instant the piercing *beep-beep-beep* of the alarm jarred Matt and his team into action. The heavy doors in front of the engines started to rise as the men grabbed fortifying bites of ham, ran to their bunkers, pulled on fire pants, and shoved feet into rubber boots. In his office, Matt listened to the radio call while he bunkered up.

"Utica Square assignment," the unmistakably clear, monotone female voice was saying. "First alarm: engine five, engine seven, ladder fourteen. Level-three housefire at Twenty-one twenty-five East Twenty-second Place. Repeat. That's *Two-one-two-five East Two-Two Place*. Map page: *one-zero-seven-five*.

For a split second Matt froze, hoping that, just this once, he'd heard the call wrong. But the printer spat out the location almost before the dispatcher had finished calling it. *Danni's house.* He tore off the printout and raced to the pumper. Mason and Hernandez were already aboard, hooking on their pass devices. The other men were still piling onto engine seven.

"Go!" Matt screamed. "Dammit!" For the first crucial minute there would only be engine five—only the three of them. "Don't let her be home!" Through his clenched teeth it sounded more like a threat than a prayer.

Now Danni fought to breathe, to stay conscious. Had she closed the bedroom door? Where were Pearl and Smoky? She opened her eyes again to try to see, but all was black, except for the occasional flare of flames, massive flames, filling the hallway. The roaring in her ears was pierced by the sound of distant sirens. If she could only hold on...

In the dark she groped for the bed, but her hand found only smoke. She opened her eyes again to blackness and stinging pain. She clamped them shut and began to feel weak. She needed something—a wall, a glimmer of light at the window—to orient her, but there was nothing. She hugged the floor, barely able to crawl forward now.

She dragged herself until she finally felt the cool tile of the bathroom floor under her palms. She inched herself into the room and collapsed. Her cheek felt as if it were being pressed into the cold tile by the weight of the world. The floor seemed to be spinning, spinning. Though her body felt leaden, she managed to bring her knees up and fold her arms tightly around her lower belly, curling herself into a ball around the tiny baby inside her. And suddenly, as she clutched her middle, the child became very real to her. More real than anyone or anything. Did this child know that she loved him?

She thought she heard, from somewhere far, far away, the faint blast of an airhorn.

She began to feel disembodied as her thoughts seemed to float, to move away. Blue and soft and sweet.

Some part of her was surprised when her life did flash before her, but not in the way people always said it did. This was a flashforward—ahead—to her future. To a future she might lose now, if she didn't survive. To a future she had almost cheated herself of because of fear. To a future with Matt. To a baby with Matt's blue eyes, a shock of his dark hair, and perfect, tiny muscles.

In her mind she saw Matt, wrapped around them both. Felt him. So strong. So full of the life that was ebbing from her now. *Matthew. I need you. Here is our baby. Please. Come and get him, Matthew. Save him. Matthew.*

Then Dr. Danni Goodlove had her last thought. One word. One feeling. *Love.*

As soon as the engine roared up in front of Danni's house, Matt jumped off the pumper and looked around for Danni. She wasn't among the huddled neighbors.

Right behind him the other two men in this company—guys he hardly knew, green-shift guys—jumped off the truck and stared up at the house where flames already licked through the roof. Then they stared at the white BMW parked in the driveway.

"Think there's a victim in there?" Mason yelled at Matt's back as Matt started spooling hose off the pumper—they'd connect to the hydrant after the rescue.

"There's a glass-block wall at the back of the house!" Matt yelled at Mason as he hoisted three folds of hose over one shoulder. "Bust it out. I'll take the attack hose—"

Mason shook his head, yelled, "Creed! This is too big for a one-man rescue. We'll just end up pulling *you* out."

Matt mowed past Mason. He wouldn't have had to argue with Ty and Gil, dammit. "When rescue gets here," he shouted over his shoulder, "send them in through that glass-block area." Mason trotted after Matt, straining to hear his instructions. "There's a big bathroom. I'll be headed there with the victim."

Mason nodded.

Matt knew attempting a rescue when the crew was one man short was suicide, but one man had to ventilate the structure immediately and somebody else had to hold fireground command until backup arrived. That meant one of them had to go in alone. There was no decision to be made. This was Danni.

The other man—Hernandez—was talking to their backup on his two-way shoulder radio. "Engine seven's less than a block away!" he yelled as Matt ran headlong toward the front door.

The other sirens screamed through the night air. "No time!" Matt yelled as he lugged the hose forward. "It's at flashover!"

Hernandez ran ahead of him and axed the front door open, wedged a chock in it. They crouched as a heavy wave of black smoke rolled over them.

"Gimme some water!" were the last words Matt said before he plunged into darkness and smoke.

The inside of the house was murky black, except for the vague red glow of fire shrouded in smoke. Superheated, poisonous. Matt crouched and took a right search pattern—the long, straight wall of the entry hall would lead him to her the fastest. *Let her be in the bedroom. Let her be exactly where I think she is,* he thought as he crawled along.

At these extreme temperatures Matt figured his effective work time was less than five minutes. In a nighttime fire such as this, victims usually died in their beds, overcome by smoke.

Matt wanted to save his good air for Danni, but he was forced to shove the mask on and hook up the tank hose. He'd never reach her breathing smoke at this rate. Inside the Darth Vader-style mask his own breathing sounded villainous, enraged. Fire was an enemy he could fight—if it was not too late. He would not *let* it be too late.

He cursed into the mask as he battled the hose forward. Handling the hose was difficult, even with another man humping it, even before the line was charged. He quickly pulled as many folds forward as he could and braced himself for the hose to harden. Just before the spray started, he heard the dogs. Barking.

They'd be with Danni!

The nozzle reaction on the inch-and-a-half line kicked in like a bronco. He shot the water above the fire, rebounding it off the ceiling, creating a hard rain that bounced back at him like BB's. He didn't wait for the flames to back down. Aiming the hose with both hands, he duck-walked forward on his haunches toward the sound of the barking, each frantic woof giving him a surge of hope in the black heat.

Twice he stood upright and plowed through a wall of flame, roaring at the fire. She was there. He could feel her. He could sense her.

And in those seconds, with each move, he prayed. An insentient, unformed prayer. A prayer of desperation that propelled him like an angry lion through the roiling flames. He could see nothing as he made his way around the maze of doorways and corners that was Danni's architecturally ingenious hallway. One doorjamb. Two. Her bedroom.

"Danni!" he screamed into the mask. More barking answered his call, in the direction of the bathroom. He fell to his knees, crawled under the bank of smoke toward the barking, wrestling the hose as if it were a living thing, subduing it against his side, under one arm.

As he crabbed forward, his gloved hand rolled down hard off something firm yet soft and one of the dogs yelped, running out of his reach. He threw the hose behind him into the bedroom, where it sprayed away wildly. The pumper would be dry soon anyway.

He yelled, "Here boy!" through the mask and was rewarded by Pearl's flailing, muscular body against his chest. He grabbed a handful of hide and allowed himself to be hauled forward and suddenly his free hand was on Danni's familiar form, lying completely inert. He felt for her head, ripped his mask off and fitted it over her face.

In the same instant the sound of crashing glass caused him to throw himself over her body. He felt a rush of cold air and scooped her off the floor, clutched her to his chest with mad determination. Only a few feet. He charged toward the opening he imagined being chopped into the glass blocks by the rescue team, heard them yelling above the roar of the fire and the hiss of the hose behind him.

He hoisted Danni over the side of the tub, his boots crunching chunks of glass.

But as he began to raise her to his shoulders to pass her through, he realized something was wrong. Glass was still crashing down. The rescue guys were having trouble getting through the thick blocks.

He sucked in one breath, turned, and charged back through the black smoke in the other direction, toward the window seat on the wall by Danni's bed. He'd finished every inch of this floor himself, knew the exact distance.

When his knees hit the edge of the window seat, he wrapped himself around Danni's body and hurled himself through the thick panes like a bolder.

He fell tumbling onto the snow and ice, trying not to crush Danni. He got to his knees, sucked in the blessed air and felt someone pulling him up by the back of his coat as he took great gulps, coughing at the bitter cold. A second later, Pearl and Smoky came flying out, barking and yelping, right on top of him.

"Is she breathing?" Matt screamed at the same time that two of the rescue-crew guys were yelling, "We got her! We got her!" while they pulled the mask free and hauled Danni up.

They were already carrying Danni away as he slipped and slid on the snow and ice behind them while Ty seemed to be holding him back and holding him up at the same time. "Matt, I came as soon as I heard," Ty was shouting.

Matt strained against Ty and screamed, "Danni!"

He was losing it, and he didn't care. Let the house, the neighborhood, the whole town burn to the ground. He managed to fight Ty off and stumbled around the corner of the crumbling, burning house. They had her by the ambulance.

Paramedics snapped an oxygen mask over her face, wrapped her up on a stretcher. He stumbled forward, his boots feeling like blocks of concrete, his chest as stiff as a tree trunk. He forced out breath, his voice. "Load her, dammit!" He shoved at a black female paramedic.

The young woman said, "Calm down, buddy. We've got her."

"I'm going with her!" Matt yelled. He heaved himself up into the ambulance after they slid Danni's stretcher in. "Go! Go! Go!" he screamed. Ty and a fireman he didn't recognize slammed the doors shut, and the sirens wailed.

Then he got a good look at Danni. She was unconscious, sooty, frighteningly black around the mouth and nostrils. How much smoke had she eaten? But, miraculously, she didn't look burned. He grasped her hand while the paramedics worked.

"She's pregnant," he informed the paramedic.

The guy nodded, glanced at Danni's still-flat abdomen, then said, "You know her, man?"

Matt didn't take his eyes off Danni's face. "She's my wife."

The young paramedic's busy hands stilled. "Holy sh—! That was *your* house? Man!"

"How about getting some fluids into my wife?" was Matt's answer.

"Right." The guy reached for IV supplies.

Matt pressed Danni's limp fingers to his forehead, then to his lips. "Please live," he whispered against her knuckles, and felt his eyes sting with tears.

"She's holding her own," the female paramedic said. "Heart rate's good." They started the IV.

Danni coughed into the mask, her eyes tried to flutter open, and Matt's heart rose in his chest like a sun. "Danni," he croaked. "I'm here, baby."

The female paramedic took a four-by-four gauze and wiped mucus from Danni's nose and mouth, then repositioned the oxygen mask.

Danni's face relaxed behind the mask, and Matt was relieved to see her smile weakly. Then she looked at him through puffy, bloodshot eyes. "Matt. You came." She closed her eyes and swallowed, her brow furrowed with pain. "Oh, Matt, I've been an idiot. I'm so sorry…" she started.

But he shushed her. "Don't talk now, baby. Just breathe your oxygen. Keep breathing." He stroked her brow. "Atta girl."

She nodded and her eyes slid closed.

After she'd breathed awhile, her eyes came slowly open again, and Matt, who had never taken his watchful gaze from her face, leaned forward.

"This is how we started, isn't it?" she whispered hoarsely, then smiled, and Matt's heart beat a rhythm of pure gratitude. "Only—" she coughed "—you were the one wearing the mask."

Matt squeezed her hand. "Rest, baby, and breathe that oxygen for me. We'll be at the hospital soon."

Danni tried to obey, closed her eyes, breathed calmly. Then her eyes popped open again. He was still looking at her. "What did you think of me?" she mumbled behind the mask.

"Huh?" A crease formed between his brows.

"That night. When we met."

Matt smiled, more with relief than remembering. Relief that she was talking to him—even if it was drivel. "I thought—" he brushed the hair back from her brow with the tips of his fingers "—that you were the most beautiful thing I'd ever seen."

Danni squeezed his hand. "Oh, right."

He looked into her eyes, nodded solemnly, and then leaned over and kissed her forehead. "I love you," he said against her sooty skin.

Danni clutched the back of his neck and her eyes filled with sudden, anxious tears. "Do you think the baby's okay?" she asked.

He placed his large hand low on her belly, near the place where he'd loved her so well. "She's all right, Danni. I just know it."

"She?" Danni croaked. "I was envisioning a he."

"She or he." He pressed gently. "Doesn't matter. This is our baby."

Danni squeezed her eyes shut. "Oh, Matt," she whispered. "Don't you ever leave me."

"You know I won't. Not ever."

"If the mama's okay, baby's usually okay," the young EMT, whom Matt had forgotten, announced confidently from his station above Danni's head.

"We'll know for sure, soon," Matt reassured Danni.

"Are we almost there?"

Matt looked out and saw the red letters of the Holy Cross emergency-room sign scroll by. "We're pulling in," he said.

Her fingers gave his another squeeze. Her grip was feeble, but for him, it was enough. His Danni was alive.

CHAPTER TWENTY-TWO

DANNI AND MATT agreed that the next few days felt like a strange emotional roller-coaster ride, full of elation, longing, impatience.

They experienced elation every time they celebrated the miraculous fact that Danni was not seriously injured. She had a few bruises and scraps, and had inhaled enough smoke to cause a mild case of bronchitis, which was easily treated with IV antibiotics. At this stage of her gestation, Dr. Stone was even able to pick up faint fetal heart tones, and when Danni and Matt heard that beautiful sound, they clasped hands and got tears in their eyes.

Their longing—to be alone, to hold each other, to have each other—simply had to be set aside while Danni was confined to the hospital. But Matt managed to be constantly at her bedside, taking care of her, touching her at every opportunity. He'd traded shifts and used up all of his remaining leave in order to stay near her.

On the second day of her hospital stay, Danni awoke to find him asleep, with his head down on his arms at the side of her mattress. She reached out and softly caressed his dark hair as she studied his sleeping face and marveled at how wrong she had been to ever think she could live without this. She realized now that one might choose to live without being loved, but only a fool would choose to live without *giving* love.

The impatience was mostly hers. For Danni, the passive role of patient was particularly irksome, especially in her own hospital, monitored by a hovering Dr. Stone whose primary prescription was, "Rest."

"I can do that at home, you know," she argued on the second day when Stone came by during morning rounds.

"Dr. Goodlove, you forget that I am a physician myself," Stone said drolly without looking up from her chart, "and I don't trust any doctor to rest for long unless it is enforced. Another day of observation won't hurt." He smiled. "Let the nurses spoil you a bit. Perhaps you can go home tomorrow. But even then, I don't want you anywhere near your office for a few more days."

"Who's taking care of my patients?" Danni worried that it might be Bryant. She had decided hell would freeze over before he'd ever touch one of her patients again.

"I am," Stone said. "And everything's fine. Although I must admit I'll be glad when you're back on board." He sighed. "I suppose you know Dr. Bryant has taken leave as well. He slipped on the ice. Apparently broke his nose."

Matt came in the door then, back from breakfast in the hospital cafeteria.

"Hello," Matt said cordially as he set a mug of skim-milk hot chocolate on the bedside table for Danni.

"Matt, this is my obstetrician, Dr. Kenneth Stone. Dr. Stone, this is Matthew Creed, my... fiancé."

Stone extended his hand and shook Matt's. "Ah," he said and smiled broadly after he glanced at the Tulsa County fire department T-shirt, "You're the man who saved our Dr. Goodlove from the fire."

"Yes, sir," Matt looked down at Danni tenderly as he pushed a strand of hair off her shoulder. Danni returned his gaze with an adoring smile.

"Well, we're certainly all grateful to you. Dr. Goodlove is not only one of our top physicians, she is also one of the most beloved."

Danni blushed and Stone cleared his throat. "Well, I'll be going now. Just say the word if you need anything, Dr. Goodlove."

When Stone was gone, Danni reached for the hot chocolate. "Boy! There's a world of difference between having that man for your chief of staff and having him for your doctor."

"So I gather," Matt said and pulled a chair up to the bedside. "What's this fiancé business?"

Danni sipped the cocoa and peeked at him over the rim of the mug. "Well, I thought I'd give everybody at the hospital a chance to get used to the idea that I've got a man in my life. Besides, mother wants to give us a big, official wedding.''

Matt sat at a right angle to the bed with his knees spread wide so he could lean close. He propped his elbows on the mattress and took Danni's free hand in both of his. "And how do you feel about that?"

"How do you feel about it?"

Matt shrugged. "Would that be so bad? To humor your mom and let her throw us a wedding? I mean, wouldn't that be our chance to give a nice lady a little happiness?"

Danni looked into his eyes and smiled. Then she raised his hands to her lips and gave his knuckles a sticky little smooch. "I love you, Matthew Creed."

"And I love you," he dropped his voice to a conspiratorial whisper, "Mrs. Creed." Then he did an expert job of kissing her chocolatey sweet lips.

CHAPTER TWENTY-THREE

Six weeks later

DANNI STOOD VERY STILL with her hands at her sides, studying herself in a full-length mirror. Through the stone walls of the church, she heard the muffled tones of the organist starting the prelude. Soon, Olivia would bustle back in from giving the photographer last-minute instructions, ready to walk her daughter down the aisle.

This wedding wasn't the kind Danni had dreamed of when she was a little girl. No, this wedding was far better than anything she could ever have dreamed of. She studied the woman in the mirror. Was this vision really her?

She turned slightly to view herself in profile. The dress was incredibly full. Olivia had found it, after combing the poshest stores in Dallas and Denver, right here in Tulsa, in Utica Square, only a few blocks from the site of Danni's old house. It was a glowing shade of ivory, draping down from her shoulders, revealing a gentle swell of cleavage, but softly disguising her growing middle, although Danni was actually proud of her pregnancy. Matt's baby. Her baby. Their baby. The fetus kicked and Danni placed her hand on her tummy and smiled.

She turned to try to glimpse her back. So much lace! The softest, softest lace imaginable, woven in a delicate roses-and-ivy pattern, flowing down into a twenty-foot train. The veil, layers of spiderweb-fine tulle, cascaded from a corona of tiny pearls and sequins and floated back like mist over the lacy train. Beneath the veil, she wore her hair long, flowing, simple—the way Matt loved it.

Finally, she looked at the one-karat diamond solitaire on her left hand. It was radiant, flawless, perfectly cut. Somewhere, lost in the ruins of the burned house, was the silly cheap ring Matt had bought her in the Caribbean. Matt had never mentioned it, but she'd secretly grieved over it, wishing that she had never taken it off. Of all her destroyed possessions, that ring was the one thing she would miss forever.

When he gave her this ring he'd kissed her gently first, then reached into the pocket of his jeans, pulled it out slowly—no box—and slipped it on her finger, without a word, while he looked deeply into her eyes. Without a single word.

She looked in the mirror into her own eyes now, then closed them tightly and folded her hands under her chin. "Thank you, God," she whispered.

Someone knocked on the dressing-room door. "Danni?" It was Ty's voice.

"Come in," she called out.

He poked his head around the door. "I've just

escorted Matt's parents to their seats. Where is everybody else?"

Danni looked at his reflection in the mirror. "Jackie's getting me some water. Carol's getting ready to sing her solo. Mother's bossing the photographer around and I'm supposed to stay here and stay clean."

Ty grinned. "You're the prettiest bride I've ever seen. I guess this is as good a time as any for me to do this." He stepped into the room and closed the door.

"Do what?"

"Bring you a present from Matt." He held forth a small, foil-wrapped gift box.

"Oh, no!" Danni framed her cheeks with her palms and looked at the box, then at Ty's face in horror. "I didn't get him anything!"

Ty shook his head. "All he wants is you, hon. You're what he wanted from the very start—" Ty stopped and chuckled to himself, as if having an amusing memory.

"What?"

"I was remembering how I had to practically break his arm to get him to call you and ask you to that bonfire. He was scared to death."

"You're kidding!" Danni couldn't believe *her* Matthew would ever be afraid of *anything*. "What on earth was he scared of?"

"You."

"Me?" Danni pointed at herself.

"Your money. Your education. Your life. He

couldn't believe a successful woman like you would ever want to be involved with an ordinary guy like him.''

"Matthew Creed is *not* ordinary!'' Danni protested.

"No kidding. I'm glad you realize that, because Carla always made him feel like he was barely average. Carla was a bi—'' Ty looked suddenly mortified. "Sorry. I shouldn't have brought her up.''

"He really was afraid to call me?'' she quickly asked in order to cover his embarrassment.

"Yeah. Then, when I finally forced him to dial your number,'' Ty went on, "he kept betting me a woman like you would never say yes to a date at the last minute. Oh, he had all kinds of funny ideas about you.''

Danni could feel her cheeks flame, which added considerably to her radiance in the ivory gown and veil. "Well, I surprised him, didn't I?''

"Again and again,'' Ty said tenderly. "Go on. Open the box.'' He held it forward.

Danni took it and removed the delicate lace tie and fragile foil paper and uncovered a small blue velvet jewelry box.

"Oh, my,'' she whispered. "What has he done now?''

From the chapel the muted strains of Carol's rich alto voice singing "The Rose'' drifted through the dressing-room walls.

Danni lifted the lid slowly. A single key rested

on the cotton nesting inside. She raised her questioning eyes to Ty.

He had to swallow a lump in his throat to reply. "It's..." He swallowed again, and Danni could see a shimmer in his black eyes. "It's the key to your new house."

"My new house?" Danni didn't understand.

Ty nodded. "Yours and Matt's. He found an old house similar to yours. It's smaller and it needs a little fixing up, and he won't sign the contract until you see it, of course, but he wanted to give the key to you as a symbolic wedding gift."

"Oh, my God." Danni's eyes filled with tears.

"He was afraid you'd do that, so he sent this, too."

Ty reached into his pocket, and pulled out a clean-but-faded red gingham square—Sparky's old kerchief. Danni took it with shaking fingers and carefully dabbed her eyes, then tucked it into the bodice of her wedding dress, over her heart.

A new house? What on earth would the rest of her life be like with Matthew Creed? Danni couldn't even imagine.

Jackie bustled in with a paper cup of water.

"Doc! You're crying!" she exclaimed. "What's the matter?" She hurried across the room to Danni.

Danni held the key out to Jackie, but Ty had to explain its meaning, because Danni couldn't get any words out.

"That man! I swear!" Jackie scolded. "He's gone and made you cry and ruined your makeup.

Here." She made Danni sip the water, then grabbed a makeup brush and dusted powder on Danni's cheeks.

"Matthew Creed has always had the ability to make me cry," Danni sniffed.

Jackie gave her a suspicious look, then whirled and shook the brush at Ty. "You've caused enough trouble here! You get yourself back with the men where you belong!"

"Be careful where you point that thing." Ty grinned, brushed at his tux lapels, and left.

Olivia arrived and when Jackie showed her the key, she smiled and said, "I knew that man was a keeper."

Then Carol arrived and they all showed *her* the key.

"Didn't I tell you that the right man would find you someday?" she intoned.

"Oh, he found her, all right—" Jackie winked "—on the island of St. Martin."

Danni figured she and Matt would probably never live down their unorthodox beginnings. Matt said it would all make a great story for their grandchildren. The idea of grandchildren with Matt caused her sentimental tears to well up again.

"Would you stop that!" Jackie came at Danni with the makeup brush again.

"I don't know what's wrong with me," Danni said while Jackie tsked and powdered. "For years I could never really cry no matter what happened, and these days I can't seem to stop!"

Then Olivia stepped in to assist Jackie with the last-minute touch-ups. "It's because of the baby, honey...and happiness," she said and tenderly arranged a long curl over Danni's shoulder.

"Well, that's just about enough happiness for now," Jackie lectured. "You've got to get out there and say your vows in front of two hundred folks."

"And three dogs," Danni reminded.

Olivia rolled her eyes. That had been her one, and so far her only, bone of contention with her son-in-law. Dogs at a wedding. Simply unheard-of. But Matt had said they'd get married down by the river and skip the church if Pearl and Smoky and Miss Verbena were not welcome there. So the dogs were inside, sitting quietly on the stone floor of a side aisle, with a fireman in a full-dress uniform holding their leashes.

"Yes, and that's about the dumbest thing I ever saw," Jackie was saying while she again powdered Danni's brow. "He's even got white satin bows on Pearl and Miss Verbena, and a gray doggy ascot on Smoky."

Danni smiled an indulgent smile and hugged Jackie when she had finished the powdering. Then she turned and hugged Carol, and then Olivia, and when her pregnant-woman tears threatened yet again, the three women calmed her and hurried her into the church to marry—for the second time in her life—the man of her dreams.

EPILOGUE

THE MOON WAS FULL, AND the patient was not co-operating.

"Push!" Carol commanded, but Danni was having none of it. Her face—red, puffy and strained—said it all: utter exhaustion.

Matt put his palms on Danni's cheeks and positioned his face squarely in front of hers. He spoke calmly: "Dr. Creed, you know what you have to do. Now, you aren't gonna embarrass yourself in front of all your staff, are you?"

Carol stepped back up to the bedside with a cool washcloth and placed it on Danni's forehead. "Let me talk to her," she mumbled to Matt.

"Danni, honey, I know you're tired," Carol said in her husky no-nonsense voice. "Eighteen hours of labor would make anybody tired. But we're almost there. You've got to help us. You've got to reach down inside yourself and find the strength to push. The baby, honey. Think of the baby."

The baby.

Danni's square jaw suddenly looked set in stone. She rose up on her elbows. "One's starting." She signaled Matt, her eyes wide, her mouth forming a fierce line of determination.

Matt got behind her and supported her shoulders with a blend of love and will that made his muscles ache. If only he could push this baby out for her.

Danni held a mighty breath and pushed with the ferocity of Atlas lifting the earth. An hour and a half of this kind of pushing and still no result. Matt didn't take his eyes off her face as he counted aloud for her, trying not to let his concern show. What if something was wrong? Where in the *hell* was that doctor? Why wasn't she in here? Surely Danni should have special care, since she was a physician herself. Every damn nurse at Holy Cross Hospital had popped into Danni's labor room during the past few hours to tease her. Matt wanted to chase them out. Danni was hurting. Why didn't somebody *do* something? He'd suggested a C-section hours ago, and Danni had actually laughed breathlessly and patted his hand.

"If the baby's still posterior, do you want to try knee-chest?" he heard Carol ask as she checked the monitor strip. Danni flopped back on her pillow and nodded. He supposed she knew exactly what Carol was talking about. He wished to hell somebody would tell *him* what was going on.

Carol examined Danni, then pressed a call button and another nurse appeared from nowhere. Together, they got Danni up on her knees, positioned her with her head down and her rear in the air. Was this safe? Matt wondered. Was this even sane?

But the three women acted as if this voodoo were as normal as pie. Danni, particularly, seemed filled with fresh resolve. He didn't want to interrupt the proceedings with inane questions, but wasn't this *his* kid, too? "What's going on?" he blurted.

"Baby's facing the wrong way," Carol said as she reached under and spread a monitoring palm on Danni's pendulous abdomen. "Pushing in knee-to-chest turns them around sometimes."

"Don't worry—" Danni's muffled voice came from her pillow "—we do this all the time." Then she cried out as a contraction hit her full force and she again pushed with all her power.

"It worked!" Carol cried triumphantly when she did another quick exam. "Go get Dr. Clemmons," she told the other nurse, who shot out of the room.

A different nurse appeared as if she'd been hiding in the closet somewhere and, as quickly as a pumpkin turning into a carriage, the labor bed became a delivery table. Danni, suddenly energized, started giving orders herself. Dr. Clemmens arrived and they were all laughing and joking and opening instruments and pouring liquids, all being so efficient, so unflustered, even Danni—that Matt presumed everything was now okay.

Matt put on the mask they'd given him earlier, and draped one arm over the back of Danni's bed, which was raised to almost a sitting position. This time when he kissed Danni's forehead she didn't bat him away.

It seemed Dr. Clemmens and Danni were in total

accord. They merely nodded at each other and the whole room fell silent, even Danni, as with one held breath and one controlled push she issued her baby's perfect dark head into the outside world.

Dr. Clemmens busied herself maneuvering the tiny shoulders and Matt and Danni watched in awe as their daughter's body slipped out. Then, as suddenly as if she had materialized from heaven itself, their tiny angel lay on Danni's belly, already squirming and crying.

"She looks like you," they said in unison, and both laughed. Danni's hands were around the baby, and Matt offered the tip of his large index finger for the tiny infant palm to grasp.

The baby reflexively closed her wee fingers and immediately quieted, staring with hazy blue eyes at the man whose finger she gripped. A current ran through Matt's whole six-foot-three-inch frame.

One of the nurses took the newborn to the Ohio unit in the corner to clean and weigh her. Matt followed as if pulled by a tractor beam. "Aren't those lights too bright for a baby's eyes?" he demanded.

"Is he always like that?" the nurse attending Danni asked her.

"Always," Danni replied and lay back on the pillow, for once content to be the one ministered to.

Then she saw it: a full moon, shining into the delivery-room window like a great silent witness.

Thoughts of Lisa came, as they always did on full-moon nights. *I love you, sissy,* she thought, as the familiar film of tears clouded her eyes. *I always will.*

But this time, through her tears, the moon seemed to be smiling down at her, as if giving her a radiant benediction.

She glanced toward the corner where a strong man named Matt crooned over a tiny baby named Lisa, and then for a long, long moment Dr. Danni Goodlove Creed laid her head back, smiling at the moon, and letting pure bliss, and—at long last—true peace fill her heart.